WALLOWING

WITH

WOLVES

A NOVEL BY

J.T. HALVORSEN

This story was *inspired* by my brother, Tim. For years he battled cancer like a steadfast warrior, never once complaining as he suffered in silence. Throughout his life he was uniquely honest, authentically kind and uncommonly compassionate. My brother was a real life, hero.

This story is however *dedicated* to those blessed with health and abundance; yet carry a hollow heart. I write to enlighten these blinded sorts, for these sad souls represent the truest of life's unintended tragedies.

Amidst a small clearing
Lurks a lone black boar
Massive in stature
He's hard to ignore

Within the forest surround
Wolves lay in wait
As the oblivious hog wallows
Unaware of his fate

Alerted to the scent
Of the carnivorous clan
He scans the clearing limits
And hatches a plan

Off, he darts
In steadfast retreat
Into the forest
Nimble on his feet

The wolves quickly follow
At a hastened pace
Howling aloud
Savoring the chase

The boar's soon cornered
As wily wolves abound
He faces his pursuers
And stands his ground

He thrusts his tusks
And with a warning glare
The pack leader advances
Accepting his dare

They collide in tussle
Teeth tear into the boar
Tusks slice the wolf
Now mortally gored

The triumphant boar struts
Face bristled in blood
As the pack turns in retreat
He hobbles toward the mud

PROLOGUE

Sugarloaf Key, Florida

CHRISTMAS DAY, A young family travels south on US1, snarled in bumper-to-bumper holiday traffic. Destination, the Sugar Shack Motel.

"It should be up here on the left," Mom anxiously navigates, map on her lap.

"I see it!" Dad excitedly confirms, with a refreshing sense of relief in his heretofore tired tone, as he quickly cuts across oncoming traffic and pulls into the gravel lot and parks. "Everyone hang tight while I check us in," he apprises, as he exits the car.

Inside the dated motel lobby, he amiably announces, "I'd like to check in please".

"Name?" the disheveled clerk growls, as she wipes residual mayonnaise from the corner of her lip.

"The reservation is probably under my wife's name, Donna DaVita," Joe volunteers.

"Yup. Sorry, but check-in isn't until 4 p.m." the grumpy clerk snaps in a challenging demeanor.

"We've been driving for two days straight, is there anyway

we might be able to check in sooner?" Joe asks, in a nonconfrontational tone.

"*NOPE!* 4 p.m. is the best I can do!" the snarky clerk reiterates, through an unflinching glare and a (*fuck-you*) stare.

Lost for words, Joe's unable to conceal his dismay.

The motel manager (having just finished with another guest) overhears the conversation and intercepts. "Let me take a quick look," he says as he logs onto his computer.

"Thank you," Joe replies with hopeful eyes.

"Well, seems your wife had requested adjoining rooms. If you'd consider separate rooms, I might be able to check you in a little sooner," he suggests with a welcoming smile.

"I'm fine with that," Joe quickly concedes.

After a brief delay. "Looks like we can check you in closer to 2 p.m. if that helps!"

Joe glances at his watch. "That's still three hours from now," he notes in a defeated tone.

The motel manager pauses then proffers, "Tell you what. We'd be happy to stow your luggage behind the front desk and because of the inconvenience, I'd like to offer your family a complimentary kayak excursion, to help kill time," he concludes with a hospitable smile.

"Wow, that sounds great! Thank you," Joe says, before heading outside to collect his family and their luggage.

Beachside. The DaVita family waits in line, anxious to commandeer a couple of colorful kayaks.

Before long, they sign in, vest up and push off. Joe and Joey Jr. take lead, as Donna and Sebrina paddle feverishly to keep pace. They travel south hugging the mangrove limits, as the midday sun braises their wintery white skin.

Well into their aquatic trek, Joe spots something shiny,

bobbing in the brackish shallows. He removes his once active paddle from the water, as their papaya yellow kayak sets adrift. His eyes widen in horror the moment he realizes that it's a child's naked corpse. He turns toward his wife, hand raised, fingers fanned, "Stay back!" he warns in a distressed tone, as he quickly retrieves his cell phone from his waterproof pouch and dials 911.

CHAPTER 1

Norfolk, Virginia

CHRISTMAS DAY, BUCK'S BAR. A thin framed, crusty old sort (impeccably dressed in full military garb) reeking of yester-year cologne, occupies a lone stool in a dark and musty, street corner bar.

Sporadically placed, green and red Christmas lights (intended to provide consolation for those who lack holiday plans) blink intermittently behind the bar.

"Santa been good ta ya this year, Harlan?" Scotty, the amiable bartender inquires, as he refills a near empty ice bucket.

"Well… I'm still breathin… God knows that's a fuckin gift!" Harlan mutters with a self-pitting scowl.

"Any plans for Christmas?" a kind-eyed Scotty, gingerly asks.

"Dinner at my son's place… Same shit, different year," Harlan grumbles into his Scotch Rocks, unable to mask his embittered tone. "Stopped here to fuel up beforehand," he adds, anchored by a big swig. "Hit me again, Scotty!" Harlan directs, index finger softly tapping the brim of his iceless glass.

"Can't be that bad?" Scotty rebuts with a compassionate smile, as he refills Harlan's glass.

"It'll be fine… They just don't like me drinkin around the kid," Harlan whines, followed by another sizable sip.

Suddenly, an unexpected blast of unfiltered sunshine invades the dimly lit bar, as a semi-sloshed, unruly crew, spills inside.

"A rounda drinks on me; and pour another one for the old fucker at the bar," an overtly boisterous (big bellied) fellow, roars.

"Don't want yer fuckin charity!" a disgruntled Harlan barks back, punctuated by a finishing chug, as his righthand sleeves inside his front pocket, searching for cash.

"It's on me, Harlan… Merry Christmas," Scotty intercepts.

"What'd you say, old man?" the chunky chap interjects in hastened approach, with an angered glare and crazy guy eyes.

"You, hard a hearin?" Harlan snarls, no eye contact proffered.

"I just offered to buy you a fuckin Christmas drink you, ungrateful old bastard," the red-faced ruffian growls, now towering over a seated Harlan. "Pour this old prick another drink," the big man commands, gesturing to Scotty with his club-sized paw.

Scotty nervously complies, as he shakily refills Harlan's glass.

"Either you accept that fuckin drink like a gentleman, or I'll throttle your old ass out back," the big guy threatens with a puffed chest and an agitated expression.

Harlan spins in his stool, now facing the mouthy monster. "You know what they call a toothless crack-whore?"

"*WHAT*?" the aggressor begrudgingly replies, with a disinterested smirk.

"Your mama!!" Harlan unloads, as he grabs his cane and shuffles off toward the door.

The antagonist pauses, then pursues Harlan's exit in a huff, soon grabbing hold of Harlan's left epaulet.

Harlan halts and firmly cautions, "It would be in your best interest to remove your hand… *NOW!*"

"Or *WHAT?*" the big guy questions, in a challenging tone.

"Or you'll be spending Christmas in the ER," Harlan confidently fires back.

The big fellow bursts into laugher.

A comparatively smaller, arguably frail Harlan, pivots in place and thrusts his aluminum cane into the unsuspecting man's crotch, followed by an abrupt thumping to the back of his head, dropping his pursuer onto the floor for a lights-out nap.

The big man's entourage instinctively stands, then wisely reclaim their seats, in response to Harlan's game on glare.

Harlan sneers, turns, then exits the darkened bar.

Outside, Harlan's callused hands fail to shield his aged eyes from the blinding midday sun, as he heads off toward his dilapidated, pea green Gremlin.

CHAPTER 2

Naval Amphibious Base, Little Creek, Virginia.

"Dinner's ready!" Helen (Harlan's daughter-in-law) gleefully announces, prompting dinner guests to funnel in queue toward their tiny, pale pink dining room.

Etiquette's ignored as ravenous invitees compete for seats, amongst a collage of mismatched folding chairs that clumsily envelop their oval-top table. All stand behind their chosen chair, respectfully awaiting Helen's protracted arrival.

Helen, festively dressed (wearing a prideful smile and holiday red lipstick) enters the room, carrying her perfectly prepared turkey. The distinctive aroma of crisp skin and seasoned stuffing fills the air, swarms the senses and tantalizes taste buds.

Slater (Harlan's son/Helen's husband), the consummate gentleman, relieves his wife of her heavy platter which he promptly positions in the center of the table, before tendering his bride rightful seat at the helm. With a subtle nod and a welcoming smile, he cues their guests to be seated.

Helen takes restful pause, smiles around, then bows her petite head, hands pressed in prayer. "Dear Lord, we thank you for this bountiful meal and the company of family and friends, to share it… We thank you dear Jesus, for all of your blessings, your wisdom, your guidance, and your divine glory, Amen."

"Amen," all echo, heads, spirits and forks soon lifted. Platters pass clockwise, with hefty helpings had by all, as the unmistakable sound of clanging utensils and competing conversations highlight the grandeur of Christmas.

TJ (aka Tane/Slater's son/Harlan's grandson/Helen's stepson) wears a devilish smirk, having procured a coveted drumstick.

Harlan (grandad), long retired, insists on dressing in full uniform (with medals proudly displayed) at all family functions, forever clinging to his coveted past. Before platters complete a second lap, Harlan's slurring his words and sporting an all too familiar inebriated smirk. Intoxicated, he stands, stumbles, then quickly recovers. He eventually wobbles his way around the table, to retrieve a bottle of wine (purposely placed beyond his convenient grasp), as seated guests, share snide-eyed glances.

"Dad, please sit down," Slater respectfully requests in an indulgent, yet firm fashion.

"One glass a wine never killed anybody!" Harlan justifies.

"Looks like you already had your fill, Dad," Slater delicately rebuts.

Helen's piercing stare prompts an otherwise hesitant Slater to intercede.

Slater reluctantly stands, circles the table then gently attempts to intercept the bottle of wine from Harlan's dogged grasp.

"*HANDS OFF, SON!*" Harlan erupts with wildcat eyes. "I may be old; but I can still thrash you like an obstinate child," he warns.

Hoping to avert a potentially embarrassing situation, a flush faced Slater acquiesces, as he sheepishly retakes his seat.

"Speaking of children, when's that kid a yers (pointing to TJ with a directive lift of his pronounced chin, both hands preoccupied pouring a glass of wine) enrolling in the Naval Academy?"

"You mean your grandson?" Slater pounces with a frustrated shake of his head. "His name is TJ by the way and for your edification, he's *FOUR!*" Slater snaps, hoping to dissuade further debate. "The sooner the better they say… It's in our blood, son!" Harlan proclaims, as he fills, then spills a fresh glass of wine. "Don't make the same mistake we made with your brother," Harlan cautions.

"And what mistake was that, Dad?" Slater fires back.

"What mistake?" Harlan rhetorically responds in an elevated voice, lagged by a sarcastic chuckle. "You're kidding, right? Your brother was soft. Your mother babied him… Instead a playin the goddamn piano he should a been playing football like the other kids his age."

"Maybe if you were around more, you might have had some influence… Respectfully, Dad, Hawk's dead. God rest his soul. I don't think it's appropriate to disparage your deceased son, particularly on Christmas."

The conversation rapidly escalates. "Even in death, your brother was a wimp," Harlan rants. "Suicide's a coward's way out. Worse yet, he overdosed on pills… I'd almost respect him if he shot himself or jumped off a cliff!" Harlan adds, shaking his head in disgust.

"You're a stonehearted bastard, Dad," Slater bluntly berates, followed by a look of contempt.

Helen lowers her head in defeat.

"One day your boy will be a proud cadet just like you, me and your grandad were," Harlan emphatically exclaims, lifting his goblet in tipsy toast. "To the men and women who defend our nation's liberties. The brave few who keep the weak safe," Harlan disparagingly concludes.

"And what do we have to show for our patriotism, Dad? Tell me… please!"

Harlan's thoughts simmer.

Helen gently squeezes Slater's knee, hoping to squelch her husband's tirade.

Undeterred, Slater continues. He sees his father's silence as weakness. "Helen and I are lucky if we have five hundred bucks to our name… Our family lives on base, in a shoebox of a house," he passionately exclaims. "Oh, thank you Uncle Sam," he cynically augments. "Hell, we're having Christmas dinner in a closet-sized dining room," he notes with a self-deprecating laugh. "And what about you Dad? What do you have to show for your fifty plus years of military service? Huh? A limp, one lung and an alcohol problem. Oh yeah, let's not forget the distinct privilege of wearing the same tired uniform to every family event. With all due respect Dad, you're no more than a haggard warmonger." Unable to refrain, Slater unleashes. "You love to preach… That's what you do… For once, step down off your high horse and take a hard look at yourself and your measly life. Better said, the life you wasted. Always preoccupied with chasing bad guys, you forgot to be a husband and a father," he finishes with an emotional gulp. "You sacrificed your life for the Armed Forces. For what? To be a 24/7 solider?"

"It's called a commitment, son!" Harlan defends, through a penetrating stare.

"No *DAD*! It's actually a burden and it saddens me that you don't know the difference," Slater unloads. "You've spent your life being battle ready. Forever the consummate soldier. News flash Dad, the country doesn't need a seventy something warrior. Try enjoying life, what little you have left. Try having fun for a change. Who knows, you might enjoy it," Slater scolds "My son, your grandson, is a kind and gentle soul and fortunately he's not cut from the same cloth," he closes.

Harlan, unwilling to concede, offers a staunch refutation. "That's where you're wrong, son! Your boy's a Jensen and we Jensen's are born warriors. That sword on your wall (Harlan points with a tilt of his head) represents our Viking heritage. It's in our blood. No different than the common farm pig. Deep down they got the same DNA as the feral hogs we used to hunt with your grandad," Harlan concludes with a somber expression. He pauses then retakes his seat. He remains uncharacteristically quiet, flushed face, shadowed with humility. He ponders a bit then makes the unflappable decision to leave. He folds his linen napkin, grabs his walking cane and stands. He circles the dining table, pauses in place, turns toward Slater and with a concessionary smile, adds, "I'm sorry I'm such a disappointment, son... You're right though, I don't enjoy life, never have; but I walk proudly, head held high... Raise your boy as you see fit; but never forget, he's a warrior at heart, like it or not!" Harlan exclaims, as he exits the room and Slater's life.

Later, that evening, Helen relieves Slater of kitchen duty. "Why don't you go put TJ to bed while I finish up here?" she volunteers with a compassionate smile.

"Sounds good to me," Slater replies, as he surrenders his apron and sheds his plastic gloves.

Upstairs, father and son share a plump pillow.

"Daddy, can you read the pig story again?" TJ asks with hopeful eyes.

"You mean *The Three Little Pigs*?" Slater corrects, through a compassionate gaze.

"Yeah." TJ nods excitedly... "And Dad?"

"Yes!" Slater replies, with loving eyes.

"What's a feral hog?" TJ asks, carrying an inquisitive expression.

"A feral hog is a wild pig... And a boy wild pig, is called a boar. Different than farm pigs, feral hogs have thick bristly coats and sharp tusks."

"What's a tusk?"

"Tusks are basically super long teeth, that wild pigs use for foraging and protection."

"Would you rather be a wild pig or a *Brick Pig*?" TJ asks with a cute smirk (likening himself to the industrious *Brick-House Pig*).

"Well, if I had to choose, I'd probably pick wild pig."

"Why?" a perplexed TJ questions.

"Well, it's important to able to protect yourself in case the wolf gets inside," Slater anecdotally rationalizes.

"He can't get inside. The walls are brick," TJ quickly defends.

"What about a *wolf in sheep's clothing?*" Slater fires back.

"Huh?" TJ blurts through a baffled mien.

Slater chuckles, then offers an age-appropriate response. "In the wild, a wolf always looks like a wolf, so there's never a mistake in identity. Chances are, you'll never see a pig *wallowing with wolves.*"

TJ giggles at the mere notion.

"In the real world however, our enemies can disguise themselves as friends. Hence the expression, *wolf in sheep's clothing*," Slater explains as he closes the book and the conversation.

CHAPTER 3

SLATER WAS THE eldest of two sons of Harlan and Elsa Jensen. Elsa passed some years back. Hawken (aka Hawk/Slater's younger brother), took his life after a two-year struggle with Battle Fatigue, commonly referred to as Shell Shock, eventually diagnosed as PTSD (Post Traumatic Stress Disorder) in 1980.

Slater was named after his grandfather, Slater Vaughn Jensen, a renowned Rear Admiral. Slater's father, Harlan Brock Jensen, was a highly respected captain, his career cut short by chronic emphysema, a consequence of incorrigible smoking.

Slater excelled in the Navy SEAL program. He quickly rose to Commander, having completed two, back-to-back tours of duty. The Navy SEAL program bred tough men and Slater Vaughn Jensen was quite literally the toughest of the bunch, having won the coveted hand-to-hand combat tournament for three consecutive years, earning him the distinct privilege and prompt appointment of overseeing the NAS Technical Combat Training Systems Unit. Slater's a man of few words, a gentle smile and an iron fist. *Translation,* he has a hardened reputation as a nice guy, you never want to cross. Slater's a tall, exceedingly handsome chap, with a fit physique, chiseled jaw and hauntingly hazel eyes. His demeanor surprisingly humble, yet tempered by an ever-present, quiet confidence.

Helen's an uncommonly pretty woman. She has a buttery complexion and strawberry blonde hair. She lights up the room with her piercing blue eyes and a welcomingly, winsome persona; but one should be fooled by her unassuming size and demure demeanor. Slater may be tough, but Helen rules their household with pure German grit.

Helen and Slater were high-school sweethearts, separated by college and career. Helen headed off to Boston College while Slater took to the sea.

As a young naval recruit, he was stationed in New Zealand with routine patrols throughout the Cook Islands. His appointment proved fateful. It was in the Cook Islands where he met and fell head over heels in love with a Polynesian beauty named Talia. They soon wed and had a son, Tane (aka TJ).

Tragically, breast cancer took Talia's life before TJ was a toddler.

Two years following Talia's passing, Slater and Helen's paths coincidently crossed at a high-school reunion and the pair soon reconnected.

Today, Helen and Slater enjoy an enviable relationship, rooted in mutual respect. Helen, as a practical matter is the only mother TJ's ever known. She eagerly assumes the role of stepmother, lavishing TJ with love and affection.

A couple of years into their marriage, Helen and Slater have a son of their own. His name is Brandon, an adorable doe-eyed boy nearly five years TJ's junior. With Brandon's birth came change, a change that ultimately reshaped Helen's relationship with TJ. From Helen's unspoken perspective, Brandon was her maternal son and TJ was (for the lack of a more apt description) a byprod-uct of her marriage to Slater.

Baby Brandon just home from the maternity ward. He lays snugly swaddled in a baby blue blanket, safely inside his wood-framed bassinette as base neighbors gather to see the newborn.

An ever-precious TJ stands outside, hair dampened and meticulously combed, dress-shirt buttoned high, clutching a bouquet of wildflowers he hand-picked for his new baby brother. He's surprised to find the screen door locked. "Mommy... can I come in, please," he calls out in a soft (little boy) voice, tiny nose gently pressed against the forgiving screen.

After several unanswered calls, Helen (wearing a frustrated face and irritated eyes) marches toward the side-door, where TJ waits with a hopeful smile. Thoughts of entry indelibly banished by Helen's decision to close and lock the solid core door, stifling further requests for entry.

That was a defining moment in their relationship. Even at the innocent age of five, TJ was ever mindful of where he stood in the maternal pecking order.

Over the years, their relationship (by outward appearances anyway) seemed to steadily improve. Helen marshalled a renewed (debatably disingenuous) effort to reestablish her relationship with TJ at Slater's behest.

CHAPTER 4

LITTLE CREEK IS ground zero for Navy SEAL training. It's strategically positioned on a small inlet, on the south shore of Chesapeake Bay. It's been sanctioned as an amphibious training operation since 1942, ultimately supporting 15,000 naval personnel. The grounds encompass some 2,120 acres of interconnecting lakes, meandering creeks, tranquil coves and forested woodlands, making it a virtual kids' paradise.

Like many Navy families, the Jensen's chose to live on base as an economically viable option, afforded to select enlisted with their children free to roam the vast limits of the base.

TJ and his base buddies relish the natural amenities. They spend the better part of most every weekend exploring the grounds, hiking the vast woodlands and fishing the limitless waterways.

It was a sweltering summer day, as the unforgiving sun shines down upon a lanky TJ, as he lingers creek-side. He's wearing a pair of torn sneakers, a tattered tee and faded cutoff jeans (crudely crafted that morning). He stands knee deep, trying to catch a fish with a makeshift stringline, loosely tied to a rusted hook, from which an uncooked (thumb sized) hotdog, dangles. Futilely, he tries to cast his hand-held line cross-creek, toward a shadowy pool, a half-meter beyond the reach of his precut line. Frustrated yet undeterred, he makes the daunting decision to take the proverbial plunge, as he slowly immerses himself into the oh so soothing waters. He wades yet deeper, soon stopping midway, as he cautiously pivots toward his creek-side pals wearing a fretful face.

"Go for it!" his patronizing pal Pete shouts back, unable to conceal a devilish sneer.

TJ pauses in ponder, then proceeds. Propelled by peer pressure, he pushes yet deeper, struggling against the forceful flow of the cold creek's current, toward a mid-stream boulder. He eventually reaches, then carefully climbs upon the mammoth, moss-covered rock. He soon stands, albeit unbalanced, slowly turning back toward his shore-side pals with a prideful grin. Atop his new vantage, he re-tosses his line and to his surprise snags a bite. "Got one!" he yelps elatedly, as the spirited fish breaks surface with a demonstrative splash. TJ crouches low and tugs hard, anchoring the rusted hook into the gill of the feisty fish. In the process, he loses his footing, slips on the moss and plunges headfirst into the frigid creek waters, as the overpowering current whisks him downstream like an aimless Styrofoam cup.

For a brief, fretful moment, his body is fully submerged as he frantically attempts to resurface, gasping and gulping for precious air. After a few (fear inspired) flailing strokes, TJ inadvertently discovers buoyancy. Head safely above water now, he floats surprisingly relaxed, leaving his intended quarry and fear of drowning, upstream.

CHAPTER 5

Years later

A FULLY FOCUSED TJ combs the creek-side shallows with a make-shift net, in search of the ever-elusive bullfrog.

His oblivious little brother Brandon, shadows his shoreline quest, tasked with carrying a murky mason jar. Distracted by the sighting of a small, unidentifiable animal, Brandon squeals, tiny fingers point excitedly.

TJ halts, turns and spots a baby raccoon, curled into a small ball, under the canopy of a majestic creek-side oak. He rushes ashore, pushes past Brandon and quickly crawls up and under the burdensome branches, to get a better glimpse of the orphaned coon. He draws nearer, then carefully cups the tiny pup in his hands and hustles on home.

By day's end, the baby coon has a warm bed, a full belly and a new name, 'Rigby.' In no time at all, Rigby's an integral part of the family, with full roam of the house.

It was the morning of TJ's twelfth birthday. Helen and Slater wait downstairs in the kitchen, for the birthday boy to awaken. Slater relaxes at their 'U' shaped breakfast nook, shoes off, feet up, savoring a robust cup of French Roast java, as the rising sun brazenly penetrates their bay window, invigorating their faded floral curtains with renewed vibrancy.

Helen's in full Mommy mode, squeezing oranges, flipping hotcakes and burning bacon.

Slater hears TJ rustling about upstairs.

TJ soon emerges. "What's for breakfast?" he beckons in a tired (almost teen) tone, with sleepy time eyes and bed head hair.

"Your favorite!" Helen replies with animated eyes. "Blueberry pancakes." Coupled with a big, arguably inauthentic hug. "Happy birthday, *SON*," she aggrandizes.

TJ's eyes widen when he spots an impeccably wrapped, elongated gift, positioned in the center of their kitchen table. "Wow! A flyrod," he bellows as he starts to unwrap his gift.

"How'd you know it was a flyrod?" Slater teases, lowering his newspaper to delight in his son's reaction.

"You must be kidding! What else could it be?" he excitedly replies, as he carefully removes the classic Orvis flyrod, from its tubular casing. "Can we try it out, Dad?" he eagerly asks, turning toward Slater with an imploring stare.

"Sure. Go get changed," Slater says with a paternal smile, a savoring sip of his fresh brewed coffee, followed by a crisp fold of his unfinished paper.

Within minutes the pair head off, toting their respective rods and gear.

Later, they stand creek-side, knee deep in dense grey clay (the byproduct of a late night, storm).

"I like being in the woods… It relaxes me," a content TJ shares.

"Well, that makes sense." Slater responds, through a soft chuckle.

"What's so funny?" TJ inquires, awaiting his dad's ambled response.

"Tane's Polynesian for *God of the forest,*" Slater reveals.

"*IT IS?*" TJ questions in a surprised tone, trailed by a prideful smile.

"Your mom wanted to name you after her father. Initially we worried that people stateside, might mispronounce it, so we settled upon TJ, as a nickname."

"What's so hard about saying *TANE?*" TJ blurts, through a puzzled gaze.

"It's actually pronounced, *TAA-Ney,*" Slater corrects.

After a brief contemplative delay, "I wish I remembered her more," TJ reveals.

"I know, son. You were just a little boy when she passed… Your mother was a kind soul. You're a lot like her. In many ways, I feel her spirit through you," Slater shares through a somber smile.

TJ's thoughts simmer in self-refection, as Slater transitions back to flyfishing, as he casts his line. "The first thing is to make sure that you're not too close to other fishermen and in this case, shoreline trees. You always want to avoid line entanglement," Slater instructs. "Step two, complete a few practice casts to determine your line's length. This method is called *back casting,* and the route the rod follows through cast completion is called the *casting arc,*" he explains, as he masterfully executes successive casts like a veteran outdoorsman. "Each cast will provide you with an opportunity to make further line adjustments," Slater adds, overtly critical of his rusty casting technique. "Looks like I may need a little more line," he utters as he yanks more line in arm's length increments, illustrated by the distinctive sound of the reel's *click drag* feature. "One of the many advantages of flyfishing, is the ability to present the fly with pinpoint accuracy," he nonchalantly notes.

Conversation suspends the moment Slater detects a slight nibble. His eyes instinctively travel the length of the line. He spots a ripple in the otherwise calm, cross-creek waters. He pinches the taut line between his thumb and index finger and the moment he senses the slightest resistance, he quickly snaps his rod back to set his hook, snaring his quarry.

TJ watches as the fish breaches surface in an airborne tussle for survival.

"Let's switch rods… I want you to experience reeling in a fish," as Slater subtly passes the active pole to TJ.

TJ's face beams with excitement as he reels-in his first speck-led trout. The frisky fish mounts a valiant fight, but ultimately succumbs, finally flapping about in the shoreline shallows.

After several (memorable) father and son hours, the pair have stinging sunburns and three (once wily) trout on a string line, on deck as dinner.

As the late day sun slumps low, the duo decides to pack up and head on home.

They follow the forested footpath, sharing farfetched fishing tales as they laugh aloud. Slater's long arm cups his son close.

Home now, they enter through the open garage door, then tussle to remove their wet waders.

Helen (overhearing the commotion) opens the rear kitchen door. "How was your fishing trip?" she greets in a perky tone, wearing a fresh apron.

TJ proudly hands her their *fishing creel* (small wicker basket).

She opens the lid, surprised to find three sizable trout. She smiles, then heads back inside to pan fry supper.

Later. "Supper time!" Helen yelps as she serves up some scrumptious, sautéed trout, handpicked corn on the cob, balsamic rice and a home-grown, garden salad.

"Wow, trout's my favorite meat!" Brandon innocently proclaims, with a wide-eyed smile.

Slater and TJ share a spontaneous laugh, treasuring his youthful naïveté.

"You're the most *awesomist* fisherman in the whole wide world TJ," Brandon boasts, with puppy-dog eyes and an adoring smile.

TJ playfully muffs his little brother's thick hair.

CHAPTER 6

BEFORE SUNUP. TJ (seemingly comfortable with flyfishing fundamentals) decides to venture out on his own.

He suits up and heads off, down the narrow footpath (framed by tall grasses) doused with predawn dew.

The moment he enters the misty forest, he's captivated by the soothing sound of the babbling brook, *God of the forest,* he thinks with smiling eyes.

Creekside, TJ stands at the water's edge, as the dawning sun glistens upon the rippling creek like sparkling diamond dust, as the distinctive aroma of morning mist invigorates the senses. Midmorning, TJ hurls a picture-perfect cast, snap dab in the middle of a shadowy pool, concealed beneath a cantilevering tree limb. He takes a prideful sigh and a cleansing breath, savoring the serenity of the moment until startled by the crackle of a twig snap, alerting him to the presence of another. Instinctively, he turns and looks left (upstream), in the direction of the sound.

He's surprised to see a boy he knows as Lopez. Lopez is an older kid who attends TJ's school. His first name is Ricardo; but for some unfathomable reason everyone simply refers to him by his last name, Lopez.

Lopez has a well-deserved reputation as a merciless bully, a troublemaker of mammoth proportions. He's taller than most in his grade. *The only advantage of being held back multiple times,* TJ snickers to himself.

He then hears a stone skim the water's surface downstream. With a quick twist of his head, he spots one of Lopez' accomplices, another big kid nicknamed Red. Red's a chubby chap. His pasty white complexion is peppered with rust-colored freckles, which frame angry green eyes. Red wears a scowl like a badge of honor, as if to forewarn would-be challengers. Like Lopez, Red too, is renowned as a notorious bully. TJ never understood why his nickname's Red because his hair was circus-clown orange.

Unable to shed his worrisome expression, a mild-mannered TJ just stands there, observably unsettled. He feels vulnerable, outnumbered and undoubtedly outmatched. Absent any viable option, he meekly utters, "Hi," in a timid, prepubescent tone, hoping to preempt something more perilous, as Lopez lopes his way.

"Whatta you doin here?" an agitated Lopez blasts in an intolerant tone, as if he had ownership privileges to the creek. His head swivels side to side, surreptitiously scanning the limits of the creek to be certain that TJ was alone.

"Flyfishing," TJ responds in a shaky voice.

"How come your line's yellow?" Lopez inquires, in a commanding tenure, flanked by a bewildered expression.

"In flyfishing, the line's buoyant, so it floats on the surface to present the fly," TJ timidly mumbles, loosely reciting what his dad taught him.

"Present the fly?" Red gruffly mocks with a contorted face, in advance of his hostile approach. "What the fuck does that crazy-ass shit mean?" Red heckles as he forcibly shoves an unprepared TJ, dropping him backwards into the cold creek shallows, accentuated by a distinguishable splash.

Both bullies share a sadistic laugh and a high five slap, at TJ's expense.

A wet and worried TJ guardedly stands.

"Let me see that shit!" Lopez demands, as he commandeers the flyrod from TJ's pliable grasp.

A comparatively, smaller TJ wisely complies without resistance.

After a few failed casts, a frustrated Lopez explodes. "*FUCK THIS SHIT!*" he yells, as he *SNAPS* TJ's rod over his boney knee and tosses its remnants into the creek, as the swift current sweeps it downstream.

TJ stands there on the verge of tears as both bullies casually saunter off into the woods.

Once out of sight, TJ dashes full sprint, down the narrow deer path that loosely lines the windy creek-bed. After a brief jaunt he spots and retrieves the broken rod, downstream.

After supper, Slater and TJ head off to their (cluttered) garage. Slater flips on the overhead light, repositions a couple of burdensome boxes, then rolls up the overhead door to introduce some cool evening air, as a chorus of crickets, serenade in the background. He improvises, using his shirttail to clean his obscured reading glasses, then carefully places the mangled rod atop his weathered workbench, in order to assess the required repair. He gently positions the fractured joint into a side-mounted vice-grip, then surgically inserts a small wire into the spine of the broken rod. Afterwards, he pours a touch or two of wood glue, before wrapping the repair with adhesive bonding tape. He then tightens the vice-grip, before wiping the residual overspill with a dampened washrag. "It'll need to set till morning. Unfortunately, it will never be as good as new; but it should work just fine," he assures. Sensing his son's humility, Slater offers a compassionate gaze.

"Thanks, Dad" TJ answers in a defeated tone.

"You're welcome, Son," Slater replies with sad dad eyes, as his son walks off, shoulders slumped, spirits down.

"Hold up a minute, T."

TJ stops and turns, facing the ground, too embarrassed to establish direct eye contact.

Slater approaches his troubled son and rests his right hand atop TJ's hunched shoulder. "Got an idea... How bout I show you some self-defense techniques this weekend in case bullies ever bother you again; nothing too fancy, just some of the basics?"

TJ lifts his once weary head, unveiling a welcomed sense of relief. "That would be really awesome," he enthusiastically replies.

The following morning, Slater and TJ arrive at the barracks, as Slater hoists up the corrugated metal, overhead door.

Once inside, he flips on the commercial gymnasium lights and plugs in the industrial sized floor fans, to help expel the dense humidity. "Okay, buddy, shoes off and hop on up into the ring," he instructs, pointing to the ring with a directive lift of his strong chin, as he forages through a tall pile of mismatched boxing gloves and assorted headgear, hoping to find something small enough to fit TJ. He soon locates and tosses a pair of gloves up into the ring. "Try those on, T," Slater calls out, as he climbs into the ring, headgear tucked under his arm as he laces TJ's gloves.

TJ looks down at the ratty gloves, then back up toward his dad. "These gloves smell like old cheese," he says, under his breath.

Slater lowers his head, takes a stiff whiff, eyes instinctively close as he stifles a gag. "That they do," he confirms, through a clearing cough. "Unfortunately, it's the only pair small enough to fit you, so you'll have to make do."

"Dad?" TJ sheepishly utters.

"Yes, Son," Slater replies while lacing TJ's gloves.

"What if I don't want to fight the bullies?" a notably nervous TJ innocently asks, anchored by a doubt ridden countenance.

Slater's thoughts internalize. He pauses to ponder the profundity of his son's question. He wonders if this might be too tall a task for his otherwise non-confrontational son. "Let's sit for a bit, T," Slater suggests.

TJ plops down onto the mat, skinny legs crisscrossed, attentive expression.

Slater rests on one knee, facing TJ... "No doubt, in a perfect world, the best solution would be to avoid bullies altogether," he explains.

TJ, a pacifist at heart, is a bit perplexed, but likes what he hears so far.

"Unfortunately, bullies are an inescapable reality. They're simply unavoidable. If a bully threatens you, you only have two choices. You can either stand your ground or run," Slater explains. "If you chose to run, that's like a green light to fight. If you stand your ground however, you send the message that you're not afraid. Be it the hungriest wolf or the meanest bully, neither wants to risk injury or defeat."

TJ returns an affirming nod, smiling up at his dad with trusting adulation as he apprehensively asks, "But what if the bully doesn't back down?" Face shadowed with doubt.

"That's why we're here today!" Slater emphasizes. "Ready to get started?" he asks, as he straps on TJ's headgear. "How does that feel?"

"Good," TJ answers, preoccupied with the springy ring while tossing mock punches and kicks into the air.

"Remember T, the skills I'm going to teach you over summer-break are *NOT* to be used offensively. In other words, *ONLY* use what I teach you in self-defense… we clear?" Slater categorically reinforces.

"Yup," TJ responds with an affirming nod.

After some light stretching, they commence with TJ's first session. "Let's start by finding your center of gravity. Tell me when you're balanced."

"I'm balanced," TJ quickly replies without hesitation.

"You sure you're balanced buddy?" Slater reiterates, knowing better.

"Yup," TJ answers, absent further consideration.

"Ok then, try not to move," Slater cautions, as he gently shoves his son who quickly falls backwards onto his butt, followed by a spontaneous giggle.

"Ok, partner, let's stand up and try that again."

TJ once again resumes a standing position.

"This time, I want you to spread your legs even with your shoulders, and bend your knees just a smidge," as he helps to reposition TJ's stance. "Ready?" Slater once again asks before he shoves TJ.

This time, TJ moves backwards a tad, but quickly recovers without falling.

"The second thing you need to remember, is to always protect your face."

They start off with some light sparring.

After a few minutes, TJ drops his guard.

"T, remember to protect your face, buddy."

"Why?"

Slater lands a subtle, yet stinging jab to TJ's nose and says, "So you don't eat a punch."

TJ pulls back in retreat. He covers his nose with his glove, as his eyes start to well with tears.

Slater's parental instinct is to embrace his son; but his inner warrior is ever mindful of the bigger lesson learned.

"Always protect your face pal. In the real world, bullies won't be sympathetic. Remember their goal is to hurt you. Understand?" Slater emphasizes, in a firm, yet compassionate tone.

TJ returns an acknowledging nod.

By the end of the first training session, TJ's surprisingly comfortable executing basic strike and kick combinations along with fundamental flips. Moreover, he seems to have enjoyed the sparring session far more than Slater had expected.

"Dad. Can we just do punches and kicks next time?" a sweat drenched TJ asks, between gasping breaths after an extensive two-hour session.

Slater smirks. "Sorry, pal. That would be nice; but unfortunately, you need to learn it all. You can't just pick and choose," he explains, while untying TJ's cross laced gloves.

"Why not?" TJ presses, in a disappointed tone.

"Well, in some situations punch and kick combinations could be considered excessive force. Unless you're in imminent danger, it's always preferable to submit your opponent, therefore diffusing the situation. Best to hold back punches and kicks until the situation escalates," Slater clarifies while removing TJ's gloves, again locking eyes with his son. "You might be surprised how effective submission holds can be. You have a menu of options, from old-school choke holds to debilitating pressure points, giving your opponent three options; tap, snap or nap." Slater laughs to himself, affectionately looking down at his son with a savoring smile, as an exhausted TJ heads off to shower.

"Kid's got a lotta potential," a familiar voice calls out from across the auditorium.

Slater turns to see his old pal and former recruit, Corbin Cole walking toward him. "Corbin! What a pleasant surprise!"

Old pals share a brotherly embrace.

"What brings you to these parts?" Slater asks through a welcoming smile.

"Was in DC for a boring FBI conference. Decided to hang back a couple days and visit some of my old cronies."

"How long you here for?"

"Unfortunately, I fly back tomorrow."

"Still livin the dream in Miami?" Slater asks, as he removes his gloves.

"Oh yeah. Love that city! All kidding aside, your boy's a natural," Corbin reiterates.

"Well, that's quite a compliment, coming from a warrior like you," Slater replies with a hint of apprehension in his tone. "Just not sure he's got the killer instinct. To be truthful, I think he's more of a pacifist. Gets that from his mom, I suppose... Lord knows, she was a gentle soul."

"Nothing wrong with that. This world could use some more kindness," Corbin reinforces.

CHAPTER 7

LATE SUMMER, EARLY morning. TJ (barely awake) sits at the kitchen table noshing on a boring bowl of cereal, while watching reruns on television.

Slater calls out from the adjoining room, "When you're done with breakfast, head on down to the barracks, new recruits are getting their first-hand to hand combat lesson today."

"*SURE!*" a reinvigorated TJ promptly replies as he snaps to, jumps up and dumps out his uneaten cereal, as he rushes upstairs to change.

"See you down there," Slater hollers as he exits the house.

Slater stands off to the side of the stacked bleachers in huddle with Lieutenant Evan Lauder, as Petty Officer Shane Griffin commands the ring in preparation for his first combat karate instruction.

New recruits assemble ringside wearing green shorts, tan tee shirts and cocky grins.

"Greetings, gentlemen," Shane annunciates, followed by a clearing cough. "Today's session is designed to help us to assess your fighting skillsets. Any volunteers?" Shane shouts out, scanning the crowd of new recruits for a taker.

A tall, slender, black recruit is quick to raise his hand.

"What's your name, soldier?" Shane snaps, pointing with his gloved right hand.

"Riggs... Ricky Riggs, Sir," the recruit respectfully replies.

"Grab some gear and hop on up soldier," Shane instructs with a bit of bravado in his mustered (tough guy) tone.

Riggs drops his shoes and armors up, while showoff Shane executes a series of mock punch and kick combinations, intended to impress (so he thinks) the new recruits.

Lauder turns toward Slater and whispers beneath his cupped hand, "Riggs is two-time, Jersey State Golden Gloves champ."

"This should be interesting. I'll put my money on Shane," Slater replies with a speculative smirk.

"Doubtful," Lauder responds. "Even money Riggs gives Shane a good old-fashioned beatdown," Lauder wagers with an extended hand.

"You're on. Bet ya a buck," Slater accepts with a confirming handshake.

Riggs enters the ring.

"You ready soldier?" Shane confirms before inserting his protective mouthpiece.

Riggs nods, unable to mask his predatory simper.

They soon square-off, testing one another's reach, while exchanging mild jabs. Some strikes connect while others are skillfully deflected.

After a couple minutes of light sparring, punches get harder as tempers soon flare, ultimately culminating into an all-out brawl.

After a few action-packed rounds, a sweat drenched, physically spent Shane gasps for air, anxious to call it quits.

Unfortunately, his wily-eyed opponent is just getting warmed up, as Riggs lands a *lights-out* uppercut, dropping Shane flat to the mat and out for the count.

Lauder blows his referee's whistle, collects his buck, and rushes ringside.

Slater follows, grabs a pair of gloves, drops shoes, and joins Riggs in the ring, as a limp legged Shane is ushered out by two new recruits.

"You good to go a couple more rounds, solider?" Slater asks, one glove on, as he tightens his second glove with his teeth.

Riggs responds with a smug smirk, followed by an outwardly brazen (debatably daring) nod, while motioning to Slater with his right glove, in a *bring it on* gesture.

Slater smiles, as he circles his cocky combatant.

Riggs controls center ring, arms nonchalantly dangle by his side.

"Understand you're Jersey State, Golden Gloves champ. Very impressive," Slater patronizes while stalking his prey.

Riggs remains emotionless, proffering no reaction. His arms casually slung at his side, demonstrating his utter lack of concern.

"You have a good sense of balance, nice combinations too. Always a good idea to keep your guard up, just in case," Slater baits.

Riggs bites. "Ain't no need to protect my face till I sense danger and right now I ain't sensin none," Riggs digs.

Slater turns, smirks then casually, delivers a wholly unanticipated, lightning fast, snap-kick, planting his rock-hard heel squarely into the bridge of Riggs' nose, knocking a dizzy and dazed Riggs backwards onto his butt as blood spews about the mat.

"How's that danger sensor working for you now, soldier?" Slater heckles.

New recruits elbow one another and sneer.

"Stings, don't it?" Slater presses in a taunting tone, as he circles a disoriented Riggs. "In martial arts, Mr. Riggs, unlike boxing, we have the luxury of using our legs which, as you just learned, are longer and stronger."

Shaken, but undeterred, Riggs stands. Carrying an angered expression, he advances, knuckles up now.

"Looks like you're sensing some danger now, huh solider?" Slater goads. "Bet you're plenty pissed off, embarrassed too. You should be," Slater provokes.

Riggs' face grows ever more enraged with each verbal taunt. Infuriated, he throws a wild punch which Slater easily deflects.

Riggs swings again.

This time Slater hooks his right arm under Riggs' punching arm, as he fluidly slams Riggs body onto the canvass, while quickly positioning his right knee into to the base of Riggs' neck. Slater then torques Riggs' arm upwards, burying his face into the mat as he casually turns to address his recruits. "I try to teach my men to be humble, yet confident. Never cocky or brash and never talk trash. Most importantly, don't allow anger to pilot your course and always, and I mean always, gentlemen, assume that your opponent is comparably equipped. If you employ these fundamental combat strategies, you should never be surprised or embarrassed." Slater stands, releasing a fully compliant Riggs.

Humiliated, Riggs stands then turns toward Slater with a respectful nod as he exits the ring.

TJ sits in the bleachers, wearing mile-wide smile, infinitely proud of his dad.

CHAPTER 8

IT'S THE LAST night of summer break. Tomorrow, the dreaded first day of school, as an overanxious TJ lays in bed, unable to fall asleep.

Slater quietly opens TJ's bedroom door to check in on his son.

"Hey, Dad!" TJ calls out from the darkened room, in a surprisingly perky voice.

"You're supposed to be asleep, pal. Remember you have school tomorrow."

"I know," TJ concedes.

"Night, buddy."

"Night... Hey, Dad?"

"*YES,*" Slater replies with a bluff of frustration in his otherwise even-tempered tone.

"Thanks for teaching me all that stuff this summer."

"You're welcome partner."

"Dad!" TJ once again calls out, intercepting Slater's exit.

"*YES...* T!" Slater answers, stifling a laugh.

"I just wanted you to know that you're my best friend."

Slater's heart melts. His face softens, eyes glisten with

emotion. "I love you buddy!" he replies, as he gently closes TJ's bedroom door.

The following morning, TJ boards his designated school bus. He stakes casual claim to a third-row window seat.

Within a few minutes they're off on a long, bumpy bus-ride to school.

That first day was particularly tough, especially after a long, lazy (and yes, oftentimes boring) summer break. The mere thought of getting up early, contending with testy teachers, boundless homework, and of course competitive classmates, only exacerbates an already stressful situation.

The ring of the dismissal bell that first day could not have come sooner, as a physically fatigued and mentally taxed TJ collects his books, exits his classroom and heads outside.

In no time at all, TJ acclimates to his new school schedule. Aside from being dreadfully dull, school's surprisingly tolerable and weekends off infinitely more precious. The only lingering dark cloud was Lopez. If bullying were an art form, Lopez would have rivaled Picasso. Unfortunately for TJ, Lopez was entirely unavoidable since they shared the same bus to and from school every day. Suffice it to say, Lopez was an inescapable blemish in TJ's otherwise unblemished life.

Lopez and his horde of hooligans would routinely search out trouble, nothing too outlandish, just a brazen disregard for even the most basic of rules. Lopez and his gang would (by way of example) urinate in the bushes, smoke pot on the bus, use foul language and wield knives. Lopez, the self-proclaimed ringleader, had an uncontrollable hair-trigger temper. In TJ's military mindset, Lopez was a ticking time bomb and TJ made a conscious effort to avoid Lopez and his explosive persona, at all costs.

It was the first home game of the season. TJ's team *The Cadets'* are hosting their archrivals, *The Cougars.'*

Slater, an incorrigible football fanatic, insists on making it a family event. TJ invites a few friends to tag along.

The stadium's bustling with a near-capacity crowd, as Slater and his crew settle for lower-level seats.

Later. The game's tied, fourth quarter, third down, two minutes on the clock and the ball's is on the one yard-line.

A loud *"HIKE!"* bellows from across the field, as the *Cougars* quarterback scrambles in the backfield. Unable to dodge a full-on rush, he fumbles.

The loose ball is quickly recovered by a *Cadet*, who runs it back for a touchdown.

The crowd rises in *ROAR*. Literally everyone in the stands is on their feet cheering.

TJ happens to glance down and notices Lopez and a skeletal crew of two, scurrying about beneath the bleachers, taking advantage of the standing crowd's preoccupation, as they steal (briefly unattended) purses resting on the bleacher floor.

TJ watches in disbelief, as one of Lopez' cronies, snatches his mom's purse out from under her feet.

Without hesitation, TJ slips between the bleachers and drops down onto hard packed soil, then sets chase after the quick footed culprit.

TJ soon catches and trips the thief, who drops his mother's purse, which TJ readily recovers.

Clutching his mother's purse, TJ heads back to rejoin his parents, until a lanky Lopez intercepts his departure.

"What's your problem, *PISS ANT*?" a decisively taller Lopez growls, followed by a two-handed shove and a challenging *let's go* glare.

"Your asshole friend tried to steal my mom's purse," TJ defends with unconvincing confidence.

"Oh, don't he look sweet carrying his mommy's purse," Lopez ridicules in an effeminate voice, as his entourage snickers in support. "Get outta here, *BITCH*!" Lopez blasts with a swift (humiliating) kick to TJ's butt.

Later, a deflated TJ waits at the bottom of the bleachers as the spectators slowly disperse.

From the dense crowd Helen eventually emerges. "Where'd you find my purse?" she frantically asks.

"It fell below the bleachers," TJ replies.

CHAPTER 9

IN THE MID-ATLANTIC, seasonal changes are generally subtle, arguably undetectable. The transition from fall to winter is typically demarcated by a dramatic drop in temperature, visually accentuated by the mass migration of southbound birds, whose abandoned nests pepper bare-limb trees.

This winter however, was uncharacteristically severe. Harsh howling winds and bone-chilling temperatures readily breach even the most insulated households, as once dormant furnaces are dusted off and fired up.

The season's first snowstorm was debilitating to say the least. Roadways were virtually impassable, cars buried beneath meter-deep snowdrifts with businesses and schools under compulsory closings. The relentless blizzard literally paralyzed Little Creek and greater Norfolk for days.

It was the morning after another midnight snowstorm, as TJ begrudgingly pulls a bundled Brandon in a hand-me-down, tomato red, toboggan, through the snow-covered streets. Destination, central base park where droves of kids sled the modest inclines.

By week's end most roadways are operational with businesses

and schools once again reopened, though remnant snowdrifts blanket the landscape and drape street-lined vehicles.

Monday morning, fast approaching 7 a.m. A flock of frozen faced middle-school students gather in huddle, clustered close in a futile attempt to block the relentless winter winds, while waiting for their notoriously late school-bus to arrive.

As usual, the boundless bus-stop bullies, blindly follow their lawless leader Lopez, in brazen pursuit of trouble. The hoodlums soon set their sights upon a harmless boy named Raymond, who stands off to the side keeping to himself, hands furled deep inside his fur lined pockets.

The hooligans exchange mischievous glances and sinister sneers, before unleashing a coordinated snowball assault.

Raymond instinctively turns, tightens and ties his insulated hood (attached to his navy- blue parka) in a seemingly success-ful attempt to protect his frostbitten face, which only serves to infuriate his antagonists.

The torment continues, as they chase Raymond through the knee-deep snow. Exhausted, he unwittingly submits to the hindering snow, as Lopez shoves him face first into the snow, then drags him by his legs like a human snow sled. His ruthless entourage cackles aloud, while Raymond (an ostensibly friend-less fellow) yelps for help.

None of the other kids, including a conflicted TJ, dare chal-lenge the older ruffians. Their torment unmerciful, their cruelty boundless.

Overcome with rage and unable to contain his mounting contempt, TJ (despite his dad's explicit instructions otherwise) blasts, "*ENOUGH!*" in a commanding tone.

Amazingly, the thugs halt their harassment; but quickly turn back and laugh it off as a baseless bluff.

An unrelenting TJ stands his ground, growing evermore enraged with each passing moment. His fingers instinctively curl into tight clinched fists. His heart beats faster, breaths shorter, eyes afire, face reddened with rage.

Armed with a daunting skillset, TJ boldly advances toward the cocky culprits, carrying an unflinching glare, as he sternly warns, *"LEAVE HIM ALONE... I SAID!"* more insistently this time.

Lopez, the unrivaled ringleader, intercepts TJ's poised approach with a menacing scowl, as he leans in, an Eskimo kiss shy of TJ's infuriated face. "And what the *FUCK* you gonna do about it, you little shit sandwich?" a fiery eyed Lopez's hisses.

TJ holds silent, figuratively biting his lip as Lopez sneers, turns away and tromps off.

Unable to suppress his disdain, TJ blurts, "Bust your nose! That's what I'll do!" he heckles with obstinate eyes.

Lopez spins in place, wearing a surly expression. Incensed that anyone would dare disrespect his top-dog status, as he hustles back in a raised fist approach.

At the precise moment Lopez unwittingly steps inside TJ's designated strike zone, TJ lands a bullet fast punch to Lopez' nose, knocking the utterly astounded bully to the snow-covered ground.

On the ground lay Lopez, head pounding, nose bleeding, ears ringing. Needless, to say Lopez was wholly incapable of proffering a meaningful counterattack.

Nearby, an overtly appreciative Raymond lay belly down, head up, offering a thankful sigh.

Lopez's posse just stands there, sharing bewildered expressions and worrisome glances.

Saved by the bus, TJ's quick to climb aboard, assuming his customary seat, amidst other underclassmen and nameless nerds.

Moments later, Lopez boards the bus, gloved hand pressed against his battered nose. He stops at row three, turns toward TJ and threatens, "After school, you're dead meat, asshole!"

The bus-ride to school that morning was a lonely one indeed. TJ's normal group of bus-buddies cautiously kept their distance, choosing to steer clear of Lopez's wrath. TJ felt contagious, ostracized and abandoned. Suffice it to say, he was surprised by the depth of Lopez's sphere of fear. TJ stares out the obscured window, in a troubled gaze. His left leg shakes uncontrollably. Understandably unsettled, his mind wanders, thoughts jumbled, *until now, I've only had sparring sessions with my dad, while wearing headgear and padded gloves. Far different, than a real life, toe-to-toe confrontation with a street thug like Lopez.* TJ ponders, desperate eyes, unable to shed his worrisome demeanor.

At school the word quickly spread of the impending fight like poison ivy in a bathtub. Seems everyone was talking about how Lopez was going to pummel TJ after school. Audible whispers and gawking glances exacerbate his classmates' ruthlessness. TJ's perplexed how the masses could so readily embrace a blatant bully, while shunning an otherwise innocent victim and (in his case) a Good Samaritan. His thoughts internalize, preoccupied with his impending confrontation. After all, this would be his first real life, street-fight. Maybe he should have listened to his dad's succinct advice, remained quiet, held back, minded his own business and had he done so, he would have averted this nerve-racking conflict. He's soon sanguine with his decision to stand up to a boundless bully, in defense of an innocent boy. He wonders, however, if this might be his destiny, to suffer physical punishment for ignoring his dad's cautionary warning. If that is his fate, he is prepared to accept it.

3:15 p.m. The blaringly *LOUD* dismissal bell sounds, as it does every day; but today's ring had a disturbingly different context. It was eerily reminiscent of the ringside bell at a boxing match, beckoning the next round, calling upon the combatants to meet center ring.

TJ robotically stands, exits his classroom and marches down the claustrophobic corridor, as snickering cynics abound. He ignores the boundless banter and proceeds in steadfast stride like a death-row inmate resigned to his sentence, headed to the execution chamber like a valiant warrior.

Outside now, he approaches the parade of soot covered, mustard yellow buses, stacked in queue, as relentless exhaust fumes cast thick grey clouds soon swallowed by the crisp winter air.

He spots his bus, climbs aboard and assumes his usual seat. Knees knocking, mind racing. *Settle down!* he tells himself, as he recites his father's words of advice in his head, *stand your ground... and never show fear.* He soon regains his composure, noticeably less tense, borderline calm; but far from confident.

Before long, Lopez and his flock of fools (tightly in tow) board the bus. Lopez, revitalized with a renewed sense of cockiness, snickers then slaps the top of TJ's head, as his (kiss-ass) companions howl in laughter. "You're dead meat mother fucker!" Lopez calls out, in route to the back of the bus.

TJ sits in silence, eyes straight ahead.

The bus-ride home that day was emotionally dreadful, seemingly shorter than normal and certainly faster than TJ had hoped.

The moment the school bus stops, TJ is among the first to exit.

As usual, Lopez and his clique lag back.

TJ walks a short stretch, then sets his schoolbooks atop the freshly shoveled sidewalk. He turns back toward the school bus (wearing a dogmatic expression) as students funnel out and onto the narrow walkway.

The instant Lopez comes into view, he sees TJ standing there, not running as Lopez had suspected (hoped). Instead, TJ remains poised, confident and battle ready.

A seemingly surprised Lopez swallows a big gulp of fear, as he steps off the bus and into the Lion's Den, where TJ waits, ready to *ROAR*.

At that ever-defining moment, TJ realized that his dogged stance had just unmasked his cocky foe's fear, further elevating his level of confidence.

Lopez and his entourage soon congregate, as ruthless bystanders hover, astoundingly keen to witness the carnage of battle.

The moment the school bus door closes, Lopez takes center stage, as he dramatically removes his coat, hoping to afford TJ an opportunity to reconsider and run. Lopez hands his ratty rag of a coat to one of his underlings, as the herd of spectators form a tight circle around the combatants.

Lopez turns toward TJ, wearing a dingy wife-beater and a threatening scowl, exposing his veiny arms and fiery-eyes. Wasting no time, Lopez advances with a wild glare, spewing trash talk, "I'm gonna kick your fuckin ass, *BITCH!*" Lopez hollers, fists clinched.

TJ stands readied, unyielding and unflappable, offering no verbal retort to Lopez' huff and bluff banter.

Lopez charges, swinging wildly, landing a handful of stingingly hard punches to TJ's unprotected face, followed by a powerful uppercut, knocking TJ backwards and flat onto his back.

Lopez turns toward the crowd, arms raised in strut.

TJ uses Lopez' premature victory lap to catch his breath and assess his injuries. His thoughts jumbled, hovering somewhere between fear and anger. He lifts his head and sees Lopez and the callous crowd starting to disperse. Unwilling to accept defeat, a once reluctant TJ stands, albeit unsteadied. Vision blurred, head spinning, his task evermore resolute, as he wipes first blood from his boyish cheek. The sensation of sticky blood between his thin fingers somehow resonated with him, summoning his inner warrior, awakening the savage inside. *So much for standing my ground,* he thinks to himself, indelibly awakened to the harsh reality that he has no choice but to fight to survive.

"*LOPEZ!*" TJ calls out, in a challenging tone. "Let's finish this!"

An astounded Lopez turns to see TJ standing there, reinvigorated and unafraid. Incensed, he charges toward TJ, as the crowd of merciless spectators egg him on.

Once again, the combatants square off in an impromptu fist pit, which quickly escalates into an all-out brawl, as the pair exchange pulverizing punches and blunt body kicks.

After several menacing minutes, a bloodied Lopez pulls back in retreat gasping for air, assuming a more protective posture as a pitiless TJ unleashes his fury.

Spectators cringe at the violent sound of TJ's cutting strikes. Each knuckled punch rips tender flesh, as Lopez' blood spatter peppers the virgin snow, exemplifying the harshness of his penance.

It doesn't take long for TJ to handily defeat Lopez. Incapable of proffering a fitting defense, Lopez lowers his lethargic arms in surrender. Exhausted, he unwittingly collapses onto the unforgiving sidewalk, resonating with a bone cracking *CRUNCH*.

After a long paralyzing pause, Lopez rolls onto his side, unable to stifle a pain induced moan. His confidence evaporated (poof) like summer rain on a hot asphalt highway. He lays there, coiled in retreat. After a few mortifying minutes, he grudgingly concedes defeat, as he mutters in plea, "Enough... you win."

The crowd just stares in disbelief, having witnessed the schoolyard bully endure a brutal beatdown and a downright thumping. All share expressions of open mouth awe, as the once rowdy crowd simmers to a quiet reverent hush. Having vicariously basked in the agony of another, they slowly disperse, show over.

TJ stares down at his nemesis with unsympathetic eyes. Sanguine that a non-violent resolution did not exist, he collects his schoolbooks and heads on home, leaving his passivity and Lopez, behind.

CHAPTER 10

IT'S A RELENTLESSLY rainy day in May, as a housebound TJ and his ever-present shadow, Brandon, ransack the family fridge. In tandem they stand, door ajar, eyeballing Slater's surprise (red velvet) birthday cake, craftily concealed on the bottom shelf, halfheartedly hidden behind a gallon of milk, and a wilted head of romaine lettuce.

"Out of there you two!" Helen yelps from across the room, in stern eyed bluff, defending her multi-layered masterpiece, smiling victoriously as the devilish duo darts off.

Tonight, was a special occasion, Slater's birthday, and Helen's sights were set on perfection.

Later, Slater arrives home to find a swarm of well-wishers, gathered in his honor (glasses raised in toast).

That evening, their tiny base home hosted wall-to-wall naval brass, with their respective rankings boastfully displayed on the sleeves and lapels of their navy-blue blazers for the envy of others (particularly their subordinates). Tonight, all ranks gather in celebration of Slater's birthday. Regardless of their seniority, all share a common respect for Slater, his quiet confidence and his authentically respectful demeanor.

At Slater's party, Admiral Zackery Dobson arrives, uninvited and wholly unexpected. A quiet hush blankets the once boisterous crowd, the moment Admiral Dobson's whispered presence is revealed.

All heads are directed toward the Admiral. Dobson's the undisputed top-dog, the big kahuna, a man everyone knows by name only. Dobson (ever the diplomat) shares brief cordialities, as he meanders through the less than obliging crowd, in route toward the birthday-boy.

He eventually weaves his way toward the kitchen, where Slater shares casual conversation and cold beers with fellow officers.

Dobson smiles and patiently waits.

Slater recognizes the Admiral and politely pardons himself.

He steps toward Dobson.

They shake hands.

"So, you must be the illustrious Slater Jensen I've heard so much about," Dobson annunciates, in an authoritative yet indulgent tone, coupled with unwavering eye contact and an inviting smile.

"Yes, sir, although I never thought of myself as very illustrious," an ever-humble Slater replies with inquiring eyes.

"Might I have a word with you in private young man?" the Admiral propositions with penetrating eyes, his right hand loosely grasps Slater's left shoulder.

"Certainly, Sir," Slater says, as they step outback.

The curious crowd watches with envious expressions.

Outside, the Admiral spares no time. "First and foremost, please allow me to apologize for interrupting your party unannounced. Let me be brief. The purpose of my visit this evening, concerns your service." He pauses for a moment, then continues. "The President himself has sanctioned me to engage the most fitting Special Forces Officer under my command, to oversee his recently proclaimed, *War on Drugs.*"

Dobson squints, both hands now rest atop Slater's broad shoulders. He leans in and details. "Having conducted a thorough inquiry, your name has repeatedly surfaced as a strong candidate. If such a position might be of interest, I would need to learn your decision immediately, because tomorrow would be your first official day on appointment."

Slater's eyes glisten with surprise. He returns a prideful smile and an affirming nod. "Indeed, sir. Yes sir. It would be my honor," Slater proudly proclaims, followed by a protocol salute.

"Appointment confirmed. Please have your family assembled by 0500 hours. A naval convoy will accompany you in route to your reassigned post." Dobson delivers, turns and walks off. He stops, pivots in place and adds, "And by the way, happy birthday young, man," followed by a respectful salute, before slipping into the night.

Pre-dawn, the following morning. Helen rustles TJ from a deep sleep. "T, gotta get up, honey. Our car's out front!" she gently coaxes.

"Okay," he mutters as he rolls over, pressing his face deeper into his plush pillow.

"T... Come on!" she repeats, louder this time. "Gotta go, sweety!"

"Alright," he placates in a muffled reply. He soon sits in stupor, planting his bare feet into the plush rug that borders his lower bunk. He takes a moment to oxygenate his adolescent brain, then hops up and heads off to the bathroom to brush his teeth.

He returns from the bathroom, gnawing on his toothbrush bristles. Still groggy, he plops onto his bed, then slides into a pair of jeans.

Like clockwork, everyone's ushered outside to the waiting SUV. Helen and Slater packed their limited belongings the night before, which consisted of clothes and personal trinkets. Furniture, linens and dishware are customarily provided by the Navy. Uniformed officers load their things with military precision.

With their belongings safely stowed they push off heading south, to a destination unknown (to TJ anyway). Their vehicle is flanked by twin camouflage HUMVEES, in traditional convoy fashion.

Slater sits upfront, reading glasses on, preoccupied with his new assignment briefs.

Helen rides in the back, bookended by the boys. She strokes Brandon's butterscotch blonde hair as he sleeps on her slender lap; while Rigby sprawls out on the rear windowsill, savoring the warm, early morning sun.

An ever-curious TJ stares outside, face pressed against the tinted window as they clip along, mentally tracing their route. He wasn't exactly sure what had happened or why they had to leave so abruptly; but his stepmom always told him that they could be reassigned on a moment's notice, as part of his dad's job.

The drive was unexpectedly long, a full day's travel. The skies darkened by the time they arrive.

A uniformed officer greets their late hour arrival with a quick salute. He soon leads the way, ascending a series of illuminated coral-stone steps, precisely positioned into the soft hillside lawn, ultimately leading to their new residence.

Slater carries Brandon (fast asleep) over his left shoulder, while the officers diligently unload their belongings.

In Little Creek, they resided in a narrow row-house, but this place was different. This house was a mansion-like estate, perched atop a prominent hill, surrounded by majestic oaks, draped in wispy Spanish moss, enveloped by a meticulously manicured lawn. The expansive front porch alone was literally larger than their home in Little Creek. By all indications, Slater had received a handsome promotion indeed. His new title was equally impressive, Captain Slater Vaughn Jensen. His assignment, to head a Special Task Force, to coordinate between the U.S. Coast Guard, and the DEA (Drug Enforcement Agency) with the daunting task of patrolling the Florida coastline for suspected drug traffickers, smugglers as it were.

CHAPTER 11

Sunday, 0700 (7 a.m.). An elongated golf cart pulls up out front of the Jensen's new residence. Its pilot, Chief Petty Officer Nicholas (Nick) Busser. His assignment; to provide the Jensen family with a brief tour of the Naval Air Station in Key West, Florida. Nick parks and patiently waits for the Jensen's to arrive.

The weather is picture-perfect, as Slater and his family emerge from their hilltop home.

TJ chases his mischievous little brother, as he darts between the thick oaks that dot the hillside.

Soon, all arrive curbside. Nick stands at attention, in full salute.

Slater salutes. "At ease."

Everyone climbs aboard.

Slater takes post upfront.

Helen hops in back with the boys.

With everyone safely aboard, Nick pushes off. They travel south, as Nick recites his semi-scripted narrative. "Base is located on Boca Chica Key and as you can see, Boca Chica is essentially an island. Bordered by the Gulf of Mexico to the west." He points to the right. "And the Atlantic Ocean to the east," he adds, with a leftward nod. "Truly heaven on earth!" he enthusiastically augments.

TJ sits to the left of Helen, eyes beaming with excitement. Helen seems equally excited, as she listens to Nick's narration, while clutching Brandon's belt.

Nick resumes his pre-rehearsed script. "Base is located about four miles north of Key West proper and is home to the Department of Defense, Homeland Security, The National Guard and several other Federal and Allied Forces," Nick narrates. "Base origin, dates back to 1823, when it served as a Naval depot, established to combat piracy throughout the lower Keys, in large part to safeguard wealthy shipping merchants, whose fleets operated in and around these waters." He turns toward Brandon and shares an interesting tidbit. "Many infamous pirates once sailed these seas, including the notorious Black Beard."

Brandon's eyes are aflame with intrigue.

For the next few minutes, they drive in silence, all savoring the impeccable weather and incomparable vistas.

Slater seems content, relaxed. He likes it here, more than he had expected.

After a short trek, Nick continues. "Base was expanded during the Mexican/American War of 1845, then again during WWI, but ultimately decommissioned in 1917." Nick stops to point out a school of dolphin feeding near shore. He slows and pulls onto the road's shoulder. "It's not uncommon to see dolphin and other marine mammals," Nick notes.

"*WOW!*" TJ yelps, as he leaps out of the golf cart to gain a better vantage, as Helen snaps several photos.

After a few captivating minutes, they once again push off. "Base was eventually reopened, just prior to WWII, to accommodate Naval submarines, Naval Air Station housing, WWII destroyers, sub-patrol craft, amphibious aircraft and satellite surveillance squadrons. Today, base hosts Navy strike fighters, U.S. Marine Corps, U.S. Air Force, Air Force Reserve, National Guard fighter and rescue squadrons, among several levels of training detachments," a winded Nick concludes.

With the tour now complete, Nick heads back to drop Helen and the boys off at their new residence, before shuttling Slater over to the marina, where he's scheduled to meet up with the local Sheriff Lloyd Dean, for further debriefing.

They soon arrive at the marina. The off-duty Sherriff is already there, standing beneath a tattered canvas awning.

Running late, Slater hops out of the moving golfcart. "Thank you again, Nick," Slater says, followed by a hurried salute.

"My pleasure sir," Nick replies as he drives off.

A stickler for punctuality, Slater walks briskly toward the plain clothes, big boned Sherriff, who sports a scruffy beard and a wide, welcoming smile.

"Sorry I'm late," Slater apologizes mid-approach. "And thank you again for agreeing to meet on a Sunday, by the way. I certainly understand how precious days off are," Slater conveys, with a reassuring smile and extended hand.

The pair shake hands and exchange respectful smiles.

"Lloyd Dean," the Sheriff introduces.

"Slater Jensen. Pleasure to meet you."

They head dockside and soon step aboard Lloyd's idling skiff.

Lloyd assumes helm then pushes back from the narrow berth, masterfully spinning his little rig seaward.

Slater leans against the padded standing seat, savoring the moment as the pair cruise down the (uncharacteristically choppy) inlet at a slow, puttering pace. He turns toward Lloyd and speaks above the engine murmur, "I think it's important to understand local law enforcement's perspective on how drug trafficking has impacted their community," Slater says, with a sense of camaraderie.

"Well, you certainly came to the right guy," Lloyd reassures, momentarily turning toward Slater as they exit the inlet. "I grew up here… Born and bred," he boasts, unable to mask a prideful smile. After a brief reminiscent pause, he continues. "This place used to be a tropical paradise."

"Used to be?" Slater interjects, head cocked with an inquisitive countenance.

"Before the drugs and all the crap that comes with it," Lloyd explains, eyes ahead as they turn northward, now traveling parallel to the shoreline.

They soon cruise at a faster clip, conversation challenged by the straining engine, rushing wind and bow battering waves.

Slater looks eastward, out toward the endless Atlantic and smiles to himself.

After a long, bone jarring journey, they eventually come upon an elevated bridge span. Lloyd throttles back, as his tired skiff drifts shoreward.

Lloyd points up toward a long stretch of bridge, as a band of bikers roar northbound. "That's a big part of the problem right there," Lloyd reveals in a troubled tone. "When drugs hit our shores, bikers followed like grizzlies feastin on salmon," he spews. "These banditos are downright bad for business. It's like renting a beachfront bungalow riddled with roaches," he anecdotally adds. He repositions his Ray Ban sunglasses behind his thick, sunburned neck, as he pans the scenic limits he calls home, with unfiltered eyes. His attention redirects back toward Slater. "With bikers comes trouble. Their mere presence frightens tourists away," Lloyd conveys, as a painstaking look occupies his ruddy face. "Local law enforcement has been requesting Federal intervention for over a decade. Glad Reagan finally heard us…

Last year alone, we had four shootings, countless stabbings and eight rapes. Six of those rapes were children, including the rape and murder of my predecessor's boy." He footnotes through an emotional gulp. "Tourists found his naked corpse in the mangrove shallows on Christmas Day."

FLASHBACK...

> *An emotionally distraught tourist gives Police his statement, while his wife comforts their traumatized children.*
>
> *Meanwhile, forensic teams scour the crime scene.*
>
> *Off to the side parking lot, a burly Sheriff sits inside his patrol car, windows up, head down, as he sobs uncontrollably, over the inconceivable loss of his only son.*

"My Lord!" Slater emotionally responds, expression etched in awe. "I can't even imagine."

"I know! It's incomprehensible," Lloyd concurs.

"No wonder he retired."

"Wish that were the case, sadly he took his life. Hung himself the day after he buried his boy," Lloyd solemnly conveys. "He was my mentor," Lloyd emotionally punctuates. "Before the bikers, the worst thing we had to contend with was an occasional Friday night fist fight between drinking buddies, which would either end in a stern warning or a night in the drunk tank to sober up. I know you got a job to do and that may not include cleaning up my hometown; but I just wanted you to know that drugs impact a lot more than the addicts. It also affects local, residents and our tourism industry too," he shares, unable to squelch deep rooted resentment.

"You have my word. I'll do everything in my power to help out where I can," Slater reassures.

"What precise role do the bikers play in the drug trafficking world?"

"Not exactly sure about their direct connection. Pure speculation on my part; but I think they provide distribution and protection functions. You know, escorting loads off island." Lloyd pauses, then adds, "And they make no effort to disguise it either... They brazenly own the road. It's not uncommon to see a handful of bikers escorting a northbound, commercial van... Hell, if I had a buck for every-time I witnessed that scene, I'd be one rich son of a bitch."

Both men share an impromptu chuckle.

"Do they have a base of operation in the Keys?" Slater inquires with a curious furl of his brow.

"You're looking at it!" Lloyd responds. "Rumor has it, they rented the marina straight ahead, inland a bit," Lloyd reveals as he carefully navigates the narrow channel, framed by encumbering mangroves. "When you travel these backwaters, local knowledge is essential, sandbars and mangroves can get you stranded right quick," Lloyd cautions, as they draw deeper into the aquatic jungle. "This gang's local chapter is based in Hollywood, Florida, between Miami and Ft. Lauderdale. They generally commute in small groups of five or so bikers, which we affectionately refer to as packs."

Engine off, his skiff sets adrift. Lloyd grabs hold of a cantilevering mangrove branch, with his plate-sized hand. With a firm tug, he effortlessly pulls his watercraft under cover, as the outflowing tide softly slaps his fiberglass hull. "Over there," he whispers, pointing with a tilt of his head toward a tired looking metal building, perched near the water's edge. "That's the marina, we think the bikers use as their stash house.

"Have you ever raided the facility?" Slater asks.

Lloyd turns to Slater and smirks. "We're not Fed... Around

here, we need a thing called probable cause… You give me probable cause and I'll give you a grade 'A' mother fuckin raid," Lloyd crows. "They may look like uneducated bastards; but if you even look at em cross-eyed, they'll lawyer up right quick."

Slater (sympathetic of Lloyd's plight) nods.

Lloyd continues, "After old man Dowd died, the marina stood vacant for some twenty plus years. During that time, the state revamped their conservation laws. Long story short, the state imposed, restrictions on dredging and unless you had an active marina you weren't eligible to obtain a dredging permit… without dredging rights, the sandbars eventually filled in and closed off the channel we just traversed."

"Not sure I'm following," Slater concedes. "Why would bikers, or the Cartel for that matter, want to operate an inaccessible marina?" Slater probes through a perplexed expression.

Lloyd smirks, then answers, "Once again, this channel is way too shallow, and far too narrow for most boats. Years ago, it was wide enough to accommodate large cargo vessels; but today nothin' larger than a small skiff like this or a flats boat, can pass through. What you said earlier is spot on. Under normal circumstances, a marina could never make money if it were only accessible by narrow beam boats with shallow drafts. It would be totally infeasible to operate; but if you wanted to operate an illegal drug operation, restricted accessibility would be an asset," he finishes with a cynical sigh.

The proverbial lightbulb goes off in Slater's head.

Lloyd elaborates. "We believe the bikers use flats boats to retrieve drug shipments from the *go-fasts* that anchor off-shore. That way they're able to easily slip in and out of the marina shallows, which would obviously impair police pursuit. After they drop their cargo, they load it into the commercial vans and head north, to a variety of distribution locations."

"Any idea who owns the marina?"

"That's the million-dollar question… When the Dowd kids grew up, they also woke up to the harsh reality that they inherited a worthless marina." He laughs aloud. "Hell, they were probably elated to learn that their otherwise obsolete marina was desirable for drug runners. Not entirely sure if the Dowd kids still own it or not. From what we can tell, it's controlled by an offshore entity whose mailing address is a big Miami law firm. As you know, they have a fiduciary not to reveal that information."

Late day, back at base. Lloyd drops Slater off dockside.

Slater hops up onto the old grey dock. He turns back toward Lloyd (still aboard his skiff) and reiterates, "Once I get settled in, let's revisit an offshore intercept strategy with Fed sanctioned support. Between your 24/7 surveillance and our federal authority to institute random search and seizures, we should be able to shut down their operation posthaste," Slater assures, closing the conversation with a casual salute.

A grateful Lloyd nods then hollers out, as he reverses from the slip, "That would be a wonderful day my friend… By the way, you should try the *Sea Shanty* for dinner. It's about ten miles north. Best seafood on the island," Lloyd follows with a *thumbs-up* gesture.

"Sounds great," says Slater, as he waves and walks off.

Early evening. Slater and Helen corral the kids as they head off base in their government issue vehicle, destination *Sea Shanty*. Everyone seems excited to try Lloyd's recommendation.

After a short, uneventful drive they arrive. Slater turns left into a jam packed, graveled parking lot, shortly before 5:30 p.m. After an exhaustive search, he eventually discovers a sliver of a space, sandwiched between two thick pick-ups. Everyone carefully exits, so not to ding the neighboring vehicles.

All head toward the rusty-roofed restaurant.

I could get used to this weather, Slater thinks to himself, sporting a big grin, as the late day sun casts an amber hue.

A rambunctious Brandon breaks from the pack and makes a beeline for the side canal.

"*CAREFUL!*" Helen nervously yelps through a stern-eyed stare.

Slater notices a sizable crowd congregating out front, so he hustles over to add his name to the long waiting list.

After an hour plus passes, the bright-eyed hostess announces, "Jensen, party of four?"

A famished Slater leaps up and off the wood bench, with a prompt raise of his hand and hollers, "Here!"

The young pink, haired hostess escorts them out back to the scenic rear porch. Their table faces a picturesque canal, framed by a collage of wild mangroves, as a fitting end to another day in paradise. Off to the side of the covered dining deck, a husky assistant chef, outfitted in traditional chef garb (checkered pants and a white mandarin collared shirt) squeezes through a narrow screen door, which softly closes behind his lumbering exit. He steps out onto the rustic side deck, struggling to balance a large grey tray, heaped high with fish scraps. He sets his tray to rest, atop the warped wood railing, which frames the dining deck. He wipes his brow free from sweat, then indiscriminately tosses remnant fish scraps into the dark canal, as a school of fish and a handful of sizable sharks compete in a feeding frenzy.

Later. The Jensen family surrenders their forks, having devoured the last bite of the *Sea Shanty's* renowned key lime pie.

As they exit the restaurant, they're shocked to see overflow vehicles lining the apron of US1, as far as the eye can see.

The tropical vibe soon disrupted by the incongruous *ROAR* of menacing motorcycles, as a band of bikers, spill into the parking lot like a pack of predatory wolves.

Helen's maternal instincts kick in, as she quickly shepherds the boys into the car.

Slater remains poised as he leans against the back of their vehicle, gnawing on a complementary toothpick while the motley bikers roll on by, wearing gang colors and provocative stares.

Slater returns a neutralizing smirk, followed by a quick flick of his pick.

CHAPTER 12

DAYBREAK. SLATER PACES the raw concrete floor of the central barracks compound, eager to address his new troops.

TJ watches from the otherwise empty bleachers.

Before long, Slater's troops assemble, awaiting further instruction. All wear military issue, tan tees, green trousers and shiny black boots.

"At ease, gentlemen," Slater authoritatively directs, as his troops respond by repositioning their arms (hands interlocked) behind their backs.

His squadron consists of fifty-five, hand selected, topdrawer Navy SEALs (the proverbial *crème' de la crème*). Under his command is a fleet of ten, high performance vessels (aquatic missiles, if you will) with a crew of five per boat with five rotating reservists, atop a talented team of marine mechanics.

His troops stand readied, notably skilled and refreshingly eager.

Ensign Riley indiscriminately tosses headgear and mock (rubber) knives to four random SEALs.

Slater kicks off his shoes and climbs up and into the ring. Once inside, he turns and instructs, "Those of you holding headgear and mock knives, please join me in the ring. The rest of you kindly observe," as four unwitting participants enter the ring. "I know the group of you are well-versed in hand-to-hand combat, however it's my objective to introduce you to some foolproof strategies, designed to help you survive virtually any life-threatening situation with a high probability of success." He narrates through a penetrating stare. "Over the next few weeks, I will demonstrate a variety of martial art disciplines, including Maui Thai kickboxing, Brazilian Ju Jitsu and Aikido, coupled with some old-fashioned street brawling techniques. These skillsets may not tender a Black Belt designation; but make no mistake gentlemen, you will be bad-ass mother fuckers by any definition," Slater emphasizes with redirected eye contact, as his troops exchange prideful smiles. "More importantly, you will have the necessary skills to prevail and if need be, *KILL*." Slater finishes in a solemn tone, anchored by a stone-eyed stare.

Slater steps back, then turns to face his mock assailants. "Attack at will," he instructs, as he assumes a free hand, (weaponless) defensive posture.

The troops advance in a coordinated effort, mock knives raised, poised for attack.

One of the four attempts a calculated swipe at Slater's ribcage. The combatant's attempt is effortlessly deflected, as Slater skillfully twists his arm and flips his assailant onto the mat with a resoundingly loud thud.

A second combatant takes advantage of Slater's brief preoccupation. His attack is also easily thwarted with a quick kick to his mid-section as he coils in moan.

Now equipped with a mock knife of his own, two down and two remaining, Slater assumes an offensive posture as he quickly mock-slashes a third opponent, then drops, rolls and stabs the fourth and final combatant mid chest. The entire combat sequence is completed in under a minute.

After a few grueling weeks of intensive combat training, his troops are bruised, battered and eager to advance to the less physically demanding, firing range. Here the troops have an opportunity to hone their shooting skills.

The troops peel off into three squadrons, rotating between high power pistols, long-range (sniper) rifling stations and ultimately advancing to the ever-popular, automatic weapons range.

The third and final leg of training returns the sailors to the sea. Slater stands dockside as he addresses his troops. "Once again gentlemen, I know the group of you are equipped to perform a variety of aquatic maneuvers. That said, this open-water segment shall focus on the identification, interception and apprehension, of the ever-elusive, well-capitalized, drug runner. Make no mistake about it, these banditos are heavily armed and highly incentivized by a limitless supply of Cartel cash. To these hardened smugglers the stakes are high. A single load can yield tens of millions, and they're prepared to defend their coveted cargo, sacrificing life and limb, as an occupational prerequisite," Slater emphatically details, serious tone, eyes scanning his troops for confirmation.

As expected, the first few missions were fraught with disappointment; but after a few arduous sea trials, Slater's troops grow more comfortable with the task at hand. At the conclusion of an exhaustive training session, his troops' skillsets have been markedly honed. Spirits rebound, when Slater rewards them with a short furlough, affording them some well-deserved time, to rest up for the *big day*. The *big day* is to help promote the President's *War on Drugs*, by demonstrating a series of oceanic maneuvers.

The late day sun threatens to set, as Slater's troops congregate at a local haunt, *The Islander,* for dinner and drafts.

Slater's unannounced appearance comes as a welcomed surprise. His squadron stands in unison, in a respectful raise of their amber ale mugs.

Slater joins his men at an elongated table. His foamy beer promptly delivered. He stands and toasts, "To a fine group of courageous young men. I am honored to serve with you." Mug's clang, bonds form.

The following day, Slater and his sons spend the afternoon snorkeling the bountiful reefs.

By day's end, the trio arrives home.

"Supper's getting cold," Helen whimpers, though happy her boys have returned safely.

"Mom, we saw a bunch a fish and a humongous stingray!" Brandon excitedly relays, as he dashes into the kitchen (boyish arms spread wide, exaggerating the stingray's breadth).

"Wow, that sounds wonderful," Helen placates, as her delicate fingertips frame his pink cheeks. "Looks like someone forgot sunscreen," she remarks, flanked with a perturbed simper, soon dampening to a playful pout.

An otherwise oblivious Slater is preoccupied with a platter of freshly baked tater tots.

CHAPTER 13

THE LONG AWAITED, *big day* has finally arrived. The event's emboldened by the President's last-minute decision to attend, coupled with his commitment to perform a brief christening ceremony.

Five of the ten vessel fleet are moored dockside, unmanned, engines off. Their sleek design is arguably inspired by the notorious Cigarette racing boat, distinguished by its nine-foot beam, shallow draft and thirty-nine, foot length. Suffice it to say, these boats can plow through ocean waves like a lethal torpedo. Unlike the fiberglass hulls of its pleasure boat counterparts, these military-issue vessels have metal hulls, painted navy gray with black tubular framing, powered by trip 350s (delivering 1,050-HP), with a top speed in excess of 93 MPH (so they say).

Showtime's fast approaching. The President and his entourage are already on base, exchanging niceties with the naval brass.

Meanwhile, Slater and his squadron assemble dockside for a last-minute briefing. His troops stand readied, garbed in Kevlar vests, flat metal helmets, blackout face paint and (unloaded) automatic weapons.

Slater stands before his men, pausing briefly to collect his emotion, then addresses, "You've worked long and hard to get here, gentlemen. You should be very proud, individually and collectively. Today, is *YOUR* day. Make your country proud out there. Let's saddle up," he finishes in an inspirational, authentically heartfelt delivery, followed by a congratulatory gaze and a reassuring nod.

His troops' eyes glisten with pride as they salute their leader, then disperse to board their respective vessels.

An ecstatic TJ steps aboard the lead vessel, soon strapped into a starboard, standing seat, behind helm.

Soon, the President is escorted dockside, accompanied by an ever-alert suit and tie entourage while hovering helicopters provide supplemental surveillance.

Encumbered by a snug fitting (customized) helmet, TJ's unable to hear anything but indistinguishable murmur. He watches, keen eyed as the President (clutching the traditional bottle of champagne) steps dockside to christen the hull of their vessel.

The crowd *CHEERS*, as the President waves to masses of well-wishers, positioned across the inlet.

On cue, engines power up, idling loudly as the deafening sound reverberates across the narrow channel.

Dockside, Slater salutes the President, then turns to rejoin his team, as he climbs aboard the lead vessel.

Onboard. Slater retrieves his radio handset, then checks his SAT signal. He nods to the khaki clad dockhands, as they tie off and salute, freeing the lead boat, as it slowly reverses from its sleeved berth.

Center bay. Slater's lead vessel slowly pivots in place, now facing due east toward the open ocean, as the other four vessels stack in single file formation, behind Slater.

Slater scans the crowd for Helen (his biggest fan). He spots her holding Brandon. He waves with a loving smile.

Helen, normally reserved, is flush with emotion. Her eyes well with pride, as she waves excitedly.

Slater speaks into his radio handset and instructs, "South course V." He pauses for a moment as the engines throttle up, piercingly loud, creating an overwhelming sense of anticipation.

TJ's eyes scan the shoreline across the inlet, as swarms of onlookers flash their cameras, as American flags flail above the sea of heads, honoring their warriors. He feels patriotic, ever so proud of his dad, his troops, and their mission, tasked with ending the drug related bloodshed that's plagued the streets of Miami for so many years.

Slater nods to Lieutenant McQueen (Mac) directing him to bury the hammer.

Mac returns a spirited smile as he gladly obliges his Captain's request.

BANG, BOOM they *BLAST* off, exploding down the inlet like a thoroughbred racehorse, bursting free from the starting gate on race day.

The G forces literally thrust an ill-prepared TJ backwards, pressing him against the standing seat. His boyish cheeks flap in the pressing wind as they accelerate through the calm inlet, in search of open water.

Engines roar at ear-piercing octaves. The excitement's contagious, as a sea of spectators wave them on.

They soon hit wave one at the mouth of the inlet, pounding the hull with a thunderous *THUD*, launching them airborne as Mac throttles back to avoid throwing a prop. Their landing is accentuated by a loud, bone jarring *THUMP* as they rapidly regain liquid traction, throttles once again buried as they breach the second wave like an arrow through an overripe apple, soon penetrating the vast girth of Mother Ocean.

Once again, they accelerate full throttle, soon eclipsing moored spectator boats.

Before long, they're several miles offshore, helicopters hover above trying to keep pace. The waves notably taller, four to six footers, Petty Officer Conroy apprises as their lead vessel slices through them like a sharp-edged, razor.

An ever-resolute Slater commands helm. "Pivot south," he orders above the blaring engine roar and splashing seas, as their vessel spontaneously turns onto its starboard side, dropping their once vertical standing position, fully horizontal.

The tip of TJ's right ear literally skims the cutting sea. His equilibrium's askew. Overcome with the sensation of nausea, he vomits into the raging sea.

They eventually level out, tracking due south at supersonic speeds. TJ feels better, having purged a burdensome breakfast.

"Show me some wings," Slater commands as the trailing boats create an inverted "V" formation behind his lead vessel.

The other pilots (now in view) respectfully nod. Their camaraderie's infectious as their vessels effortlessly pierce smaller wave sets now.

"Let's give em what they came for gentlemen!" Slater shouts, eyes ablaze. "Cross cut four," he orders, as the four flanking vessels instantaneously respond, performing a highly synchronized, crisscross pattern behind Slater's lead vessel.

"Split four!" Slater directs above the pounding seas, as the four vessels wing-off, passing their lead vessel at incomprehensible speeds, then split off, two westward toward the shore, then north, while the other two head eastward toward the open sea, then north.

Within a matter of minutes, all four vessels complete a circular pattern, eventually rejoining the lead boat, demonstrating the incomparable maneuverability of these high-performance vessels, and the unparalleled skillsets of Slater's talented team.

CHAPTER 14

PRACTICE DRILLS, SOON replaced by real life missions. True to his word, Slater's first appointment includes a surveillance team, tasked to provide offshore support for the Sherriff's crew of two, (who occupy a small skiff) anchored at the throat of the narrow channel (which leads to the suspected, biker-based marina).

1:21 a.m., Slater's team drifts offshore, as the subtle seas gently slap their boat's bow.

A burly (baby-faced) black recruit introduces himself to his assigned partner, hand extended, amiable expression. "Buster," he greets, followed by an awkward chuckle.

"Spence," a comparatively scrawny chap replies, through pensive eyes.

"Where you from?" Buster inquires, in an oh-so Southern accent, framed by an authentically kind smile.

"Born and raised in Pittsburgh PA, Steeler's country!" Spence proudly replies.

"How bout, you?" he asks.

"Florida boy," Buster boasts. "Gainesville. Gator country, you know, University of Florida, damn near the belly of the state.

Always wanted to live by the beach, so I guess you might say I'm one happy camper," Buster blurts, sporting a big, honest grin.

A distant rumble interrupts their conversation.

"You hear that?" Spence asks in an alarmed tone. Both men pause to listen, as the faint, distant roar grows progressively louder.

Aided by night vision goggles, Buster confirms an approaching *go-fast*.

Spence promptly notifies the Sheriff's inlet team via a secure transmission frequency. "*Go-fast* inbound," he relays.

"Roger that!" the Sherriff's team excitedly responds, hovering close to the channel, concealed beneath dense mangroves. They soon detect the soft hum of twin flats boats negotiating the narrow channel, lights off, undoubtedly in route to meet up with the inbound *go-fast*.

Within minutes the bad-guys rendezvous, engines off as they hurriedly transfer the coveted cargo. Unbeknownst to the banditos, the offshore team stealthily advances, with the assistance of night vison.

Suddenly, bright transom lights illuminate the drop scene, intercepting the handoff. "Hands up or we'll open fire!" the neophyte crew commands, with youthful bravado, automatic weapons drawn and trained on the stunned smugglers.

The Sherriff's crew soon summoned, as they quickly advance, sirens blaring, blue lights flashing.

Sandwiched, the bad boys surrender without resistance. They take no chances, hands held high, as they swiftly submit.

Within no time, police and DEA swarm the marina and detain a handful of bikers, before scouring the marina for evidence, to no avail.

Daybreak. "Fuck!" a frustrated Lloyd barks.

"Don't get discouraged." Slater reassures. "The good news is, we intercepted a handoff, and they obviously got the message. There's always another day my friend."

Thereafter, the Sherriff's Department maintains a 24/7 surveillance, which proves to be an effective deterrent.

That weekend, Slater makes good on his promise to explore Old Key West with his family. Early Saturday morning they head off. As they leave base, Slater observes a handful of bikers following closely, too close for his liking.

After a mile or so, Slater makes the last-minute decision to pull into a roadside convenience store, ostensibly to get gas.

He's relieved when the bikers drive on by. He takes the opportunity to top off his tank, while Helen grabs a couple bottles of water and a bag of corn curls.

Within a few minutes they merge back onto US1, heading south. Around the bend, he spots a band of bikers, parked in the middle of the otherwise quiet road, blocking both lanes of travel.

In his rearview mirror, he notices another pack of banditos accelerating behind him.

Bookended by bikers, Slater slows to a controlled stop. Ahead, an enormous biker casually dismounts his Harley, as he nonchalantly removes his Nazi styled helmet revealing a clean-shaven head. His thick neck is enveloped by a series of interlocking swastika tattoos. He sets his helmet atop his cowhide seat, then steps toward Slater's vehicle, unable to conceal a distinguishable limp.

"Lock the doors. My gun's in the glovebox," Slater informs, eyes upon the advancing biker.

Frightened, Helen compliantly nods.

"Everything will be okay, I promise," Slater assures as he exits the vehicle.

The pair meet midway, standing less than a meter apart. Slater (an otherwise tall man) is dwarfed by the uncommonly large biker.

They share brazen stares but no words.

The biker breaks silence. "My employers don't like people fuckin in their business," the burly biker opens, then turns to spit a wad of dark brown, chewing tobacco.

"Is that a threat?" Slater qualifies through an unflinching tone.

"Nope," the big biker answers with a sketchy grin. "Actually, they wanna hire ya to help keep their business safe," he explains.

"So, you're bribing me?" Slater clarifies, with a (*you must be kidding me*) sneer.

"Just trying to find common ground, my friend. You know, a win/win."

"First of all, you and I are anything *BUT* friends. Furthermore, you can tell your employers to pound sand... Now get your scooters outa my way, before I run em over," Slater growls as he returns to his vehicle.

After a long, eventful day touring historic Key West, the Jensen family packs it in, and heads home.

As they pull up to their house, Slater observes something nailed to their front door. He parks off to the side of the house. "Wait here. I need to check something out first," a preoccupied Slater advises.

"What's wrong?" Helen asks, in a fretful voice.

"Give me minute!" Slater reiterates, as he heads toward the front of the house, shocked to find a raccoon tail nailed to the front door. He quickly removes the tail and tosses it into the shrubs, then calls for backup.

"Grayson. Dispatch Security to our place, ASAP! I need help clearing our house," he directs.

Minutes later, two uniformed officers arrive.

Slater points to the severed raccoon tail lying on the ground. "That was nailed to our front door," he informs in a troubled tone.

They enter the grand-foyer, and within short order complete a thorough room-by-room sweep of the first and second floors.

Slater periodically calls out for Rigby, to no avail.

They reconvene out front.

"A local biker outfit threatened me earlier today and our pet raccoon seems to be missing, disturbingly coincidental… Here out, please ramp up security at our place. I'm concerned that our offshore surveillance may have ruffled some biker feathers."

"Will do!" the officers respond in unison, followed by protocol salutes.

"Thanks, gentlemen," an appreciative Slater replies, as he heads back toward his car.

Helen rolls down the passenger side window. "Slater what's going on, you're scaring me," she nervously asks.

"Sorry. All good. You know me, just overly cautious. Couldn't find Rigby though," he preemptively alerts.

"You know him, he comes and goes through the dog door. He's probably foraging for grasshoppers," Helen surmises, unaware that the coon tail had been nailed to the door.

Later, approaching 11 p.m. Brandon's in bed, fast asleep. TJ's in his room, headset on, listening to music, while Helen draws a warm bath.

An emotionally spent Slater looks to unwind as he pours a shot of vintage Vodka. He opens the freezer to grab a couple cubes and is incensed when he discovers Rigby's tailless carcass, strategically positioned in the ice tray with a crack pipe in his mouth. Without hesitation, he removes the ice tray and places Rigby's remains outside in a large trash bag, before scouring the bloodied tray with ammonia and rinsing it with hot water. Afterwards, he returns the thoroughly clean tray to the freezer, to avoid alarming Helen.

The following morning, Slater drives fast-paced down the dusty dirt road that leads to the biker-based marina.

He blasts through the main entry, between tall chain-link gates and parks out front, as a cloud of trailing dust accentuates his hurried pace.

Harleys proliferate the parking lot, as a handful of burley bikers, eyeball Slater's brazen approach.

Slater exits his vehicle, opens his trunk and grabs the plastic trash bag (containing Rigby's remains) and marches inside, unannounced and unintimidated, like an army of one.

Inside, he tosses the trash bag on top of the head hooligan's makeshift desk (positioned in the center of the otherwise empty room).

"I wonder what this might be," the grubby thug quips with a sarcastic smirk, framed by a scruffy grey goatee.

Slater steps closer, both hands firmly pressed atop the flimsy desk. He bids a menacing stare and warns, "Next time you scumbags want to send a message, you know where to find me… and if you *EVER* involve my family or my home again, this place burns in a blaze and I'll use your little *DICK* as kindling," Slater spews, fiery eyes as he turns and tromps off.

Unable to conceal his consternation, the bewildered biker boss offers no retort.

The giant biker (Ox) who confronted Slater the day before,

intercepts Slater's departure, thick arms crossed, wearing a brazen stare.

"Underestimating me would be unwise," Slater confidently informs.

"*OH YEAH?*" the big biker challenges.

"Here's the problem… When you were a kid, you were probably bigger than most other kids your age, so you mistakenly thought you were tough. Fortunately, it only takes one good beat-down to correct that misconception."

"Bring it, tough guy," Ox spews, as he steps toward Slater.

"*OX!*" the biker boss authoritatively blurts.

The big guy complies, as he begrudgingly steps aside.

"You should buy a lottery ticket, cause today's clearly your lucky day, dickhead!" Slater mocks.

CHAPTER 15

In addition to his stateside responsibilities, Slater's tasked with restoring diplomatic relations in crucial South American countries, while orchestrating joint intercept strategies with Bahamian authorities.

In his absence, Helen's head of the household. A job she readily embraces. She's more than capable of giving orders, albeit in a gentler fashion. By all accounts, she's a strong role model and a true constant in TJ's life.

Helen celebrates Slater's return with a heaping bowl of Scungilli (conch) Fra diablo, atop homemade squid ink pasta, sprinkled with a hint of cayenne pepper, topped with aged, Manchego cheese.

After supper, TJ delivers his empty plate to the sink, before heading off to study for a science quiz in the adjoining room.

Slater and Helen linger in the kitchen, laughing, relishing their reunion, their spark forever lit.

The distinctive ring of Slater's SAT phone disrupts their moment. He's quick to answer. His facial expression transitions from jovial, to focused. "Give me five," he responds in a decisive tone, as he hustles upstairs to armor up. From the top of the steps, he calls out. "T, wanna tag along?"

TJ turns toward Helen with a beseeching gaze.

She instinctively shakes her head, '*no*' then begrudgingly concedes, with an affirming nod, and a concessionary smile.

"*YES!*" he exclaims, as he folds his schoolbooks, grabs his helmet, and slips into his custom Kevlar vest.

Within minutes, the duo is out the door and whisked off in a waiting golfcart, destination dockside.

Their boat stands fueled and idling.

Their team, already aboard and armored up.

TJ pushes past two poised warriors. Their expressionless faces are blackened with camo cream. No eye contact proffered. No words shared.

Engines rev as they push back away from the dock, soon spinning in place to face the throat of the darkened inlet.

BOOM, they *BLAST* off, leaving a sizable wake in their narrow path.

As they exit the inlet, their vessel's propelled airborne, launched by an unexpectedly large, incoming wave. TJ braces for impact as the metal hull comes crashing down with bone crunching consequences, compounded by a sharp, unanticipated turn. Unlike daytime demonstrations, this evening's venture offers no forewarning. This real-life mission is more like a Disney ride through the hallways of Hell. TJ tries to gain visual perspective, but the pitch-black skies are less than obliging, bad news for TJ (incorrigibly prone to motion sickness). He grows more nauseated with every unexpected twist and turn, as he turns his head to vomit into the sea.

Before long they're far offshore, seas more forgiving now as they track due east toward the open ocean, painlessly piercing successive sets of waves, roughly two footers. Engines deafeningly loud, speeds unimaginable.

Slater remains positioned at helm eyes glued to the moss green computer screen.

Suddenly, a night image of the *go-fast*, comes into view, courtesy of the surveillance plane soaring above (equipped with night optics). Slater relays the *go-fast's* speed and heading, in order to calculate precise intercept coordinates. "They're six miles out tracking south/southeast at approximately 68 MPH," Petty Officer Saga reports above the pounding seas.

Slater's eyes remain fixated on the computer screen, as they steadily gain on the *go-fast*.

"At this course and speed, we can expect intercept in approximately 11.4 minutes," Saga calculates.

Slater nods.

Acutely aware that they're being pursued, the *go-fast* suddenly changes course and veers due east, making a beeline for the Bahamas.

Slater's crew stays close, running a parallel track.

Several minutes pass. They're hot on their heels and quickly closing in.

Unexpectedly, the *go-fast* opens fire as a barrage of bullets, pelt their metal hull, accentuated by the disturbing sound of piercing pings. Fortunately, Slater and his crew escape without casualty.

"Throttle back," Slater orders. "Request permission to return fire," Slater shouts into his handheld SAT phone.

After a brief delay, NAS Jacksonville 4th Fleet responds, "Permission granted."

A stern eyed Slater offers a *go nod* to his crew.

Emotions run high. Patriotism is infectious.

Ensign Nolan Bishop is quickly strapped into the gunnery

(machinegun) post, strategically positioned within the boat's hollowed bow.

"Full-throttle," Slater instructs, as they once again *BLAST* off, soon gaining on the bad guys.

"Welcome to America, mother fuckers!" Slater (unable to contain his adrenalin) hollers into the night skies, "Range?" Slater calls out.

After a brief pause. "Range confirmed," Saga relays.

"Fire at will," Slater instructs, as gunnery sergeant Bishop unleashes a firestorm of fury.

TJ closes his eyes and covers his ears, in a failed attempt to muffle the disturbingly violent rattle of gunfire.

The *go-fast* crew is quickly annihilated, as the bad boys' boat putters to a slow, mid-sea, roll.

"Light em up," Slater directs, as T-top mounted floodlights illuminate the *go-fast*.

No sign of life as a dense, dreary grey cloud of artillery smoke looms, hovering above the lifeless vessel.

With practiced precision, Slater's team guardedly boards the *go-fast*, guns readied.

TJ stays back, still processing the reality of this life ending mission. It's an emotional moment to say the least. Four men, likely dads, died that night, to protect a load of cocaine that didn't even belong to them. It seemed so devastatingly senseless to TJ. He was understandably conflicted. It was hard to feel proud at such a somber moment. By choice, this was his first, and final, real-life mission.

CHAPTER 16

MORNING. TJ's FIRST day at his new school. He's understandably apprehensive, better said anxious, as he navigates unfamiliar hallways.

His new school hosts a modest 130 students, compared to his Virginia school's enrollment which exceeded 2,200. No doubt, things are dramatically different here. Even the kids seem different, curiously casual, and refreshingly cooler (hip as it were). There's no semblance of a dress code. Most sport short pants, with flip-flops. Long hair was the unspoken norm.

In Homeroom, TJ assumes one of two unoccupied seats. All eyes upon him. New kids were an oddity in the Keys.

At lunch, TJ sits alone at an elongated table, observably disinterested in his foul smelling, cafeteria crud.

A disheveled (happy faced) husky fellow sits across from him. "You gonna eat that cookie?" he boldly inquires, pointing to TJ's plate with a lift of his dimpled chin.

TJ looks down at his plastic plate. Using a flimsy fork, he does a bit of exploring and ultimately discovers a chocolate chip cookie, smothered beneath a puddle of thick, putrid grey gravy, overflown from his open-faced, processed turkey sandwich.

"No. You can have it," TJ gladly offers with a slide of his tray the other boy's way.

"Thanks, dude. You the new kid?" he mumbles, mouth full of food.

"Yeah," TJ awkwardly responds.

"Where ya from?" the burly boy asks.

"Virginia," TJ timidly replies.

"That's cool." He nods. "I'm Gilly."

"TJ."

Another boy soon arrives, carrying a stacked lunch tray. He sits across from Gilly to the right of TJ.

"This is Fitz," Gilly introduces.

"What's up?" Fitz follows with an obligatory nod and a half-hearted smile.

"TJ," he replies, more assuredly this time.

"He's new," Gilly apprises.

"Nice," Fitz adds in a debatably disinterested tone.

Within short order, TJ readily assimilates into his school as a welcomed addition to the student body, now 131. To his surprise, typical sports (otherwise common in mid-Atlantic), like baseball, basketball, football, and the ever-coveted lacrosse, took a subordinate seat to surfing, snorkeling, and snorting. You read that right, *snorting*. The genesis of Slater's reappointment had found its wicked way into the nostrils of babes. Turns out the Florida Keys was more than a drug drop depot.

Fortunately, TJ steers clear of the cocaine crowd (rightfully rebutting blow), but willingly partakes in an occasional hit of weed, as an inescapable *rite of passage*. In all events, TJ's new school pals are a welcomed surprise. Alas he has civilian roots.

Months later. The school bell sounds, as students swarm the concrete corridors, in mass exodus.

A long-haired (nearly unrecognizably) TJ, fusses with his locker combination.

"Dude!" a jovial Gilly shouts in advance of his amiable approach.

"Sup, bro?" TJ replies, employing local lingo.

"You goin fishin with me and the Fitzter tomorrow?"

"Fer sure," TJ responds, while callously stuffing his schoolbooks into his undersized cubicle.

"8 a.m. Point Pier, marina," Gilly bellows as he shuffles off, down the hallway.

The following morning, Helen, hair pinned up in an impromptu (nest-like) bun, drives an overtired TJ to meet up with his fishing buds.

She parks dockside, eyes pan the limits of her cluttered car. "Where's the lunch box I packed for you and your thermos?" a frantic Helen asks, while rummaging through her backseat.

"Mom chill, I'm totally fine," TJ huffs, as he exits her silver Subaru.

"What do you mean fine?" Helen presses with a questioning expression. "How will you be fine in the middle of the ocean, with no food or water?" she asks through the open passenger window.

A flush faced TJ hustles back, hoping to allay Helen's trepidation. Left-hand pressed atop the passenger side door, he lowers his head, tucks his hair behind his ear and *calmly* reassures. "Mom, we're fishing the flats. Flats are shallow waters near shore, one foot deep, max. I assure you I'll be fine," he respectfully replies. "Bye," he grudgingly bids, with a frustrated shake of his adolescent head.

Helen watches as he walks off, ostensibly consoled.

She sits for a bit, before driving off, smiling to herself. She's happy for her stepson, ever mindful, that she too, was once a teen.

"T-man," Gilly greets, from the far end of the sundried dock.

They meet midway, slap hands and bump chests.

"You're gonna really dig this shit dude, it's so fuckin cool out there," Gilly yelps. "The water's crystal fuckin clear and the Fitz Mister is a master of this shit, he'll totally dial you in," Gilly visually embellishes, while noshing on a folded (mustard and marmalade) waffle.

"That sounds cool," TJ eagerly replies.

Moments later, Fitz rounds the bend in his yellow hull flats boat, aptly named, *Mellow Yellow,* leaving a modest wake in his path.

As Fitz approaches the dock, he instinctively taps neutral and free hands the steel wheel, piloting the small craft to a soft, synchronized dockage.

Gilly and TJ climb aboard, as the threesome push off.

Gilly grabs a breakfast beer from the rear cooler. "T, wanna beer?" Gilly shouts (head buried inside the ice-filled cooler).

"No thanks, I'm good."

"Fitz?" Gilly yaps.

"Maybe later," Fitz appeases, followed by a roll of his eyes. "Who the fuck drinks beer at 8 a.m.?" Fitz whispers as he and TJ share a stifled laugh.

"Heard your old man's top dog on base," Fitz blurts, above the smooth purr of his near noiseless, 60-HP outboard.

"I guess so," TJ answers, followed by a modest shrug of his boyish shoulders.

"Cool," Fritz responds, as they briskly clip down the narrow canal, soon startling a gaggle of roosting birds, as they burst into synchronized flight.

"You're gonna love it here, dude. Nowhere on earth like it," Fitz pledges.

With the broad bay now in sight, Fitz throttles back, spinning the chrome wheel as he twists his head side to side to visually assess his surroundings. "We're gonna start off here at the mouth of the mangrove, to catch the outflowing tide. Hopefully, we can snag some Reds, that's Redfish," Fitz clarifies as he locks eyes with TJ. "If we're lucky, we might spot some tarpon or bonefish, both good fighters. If we're super fuckin lucky, we might even hook a Snook."

"Hook a Snook?" TJ repeats, through a befuddled expression.

A flabbergasted Fitz turns toward TJ. "You serious? You never had Snook?" he probes.

"Don't think so," TJ responds.

"Don't think so?" Fitz glibly mimics. "Dude, if you ever tasted Snook, you'd never fuckin forget it, it's the best eatin fish on earth," Fitz asserts, as he skillfully pilots his small craft between treacherous tree limbs (remnant reminders of hurricanes past), that encumber passage.

Once inside the broad bay Fitz kills his engine and trims his prop up and out of the water, setting his skiff adrift. He then lowers his bow mounted, electric prop into the knee-high waters, as he stealthily traverses the open flats. "Gilly, cover me at helm, I'll take tower," Fitz delegates, as he ascends the elevated platform (positioned above the outboard engine) to gain better vantage of the enveloping shallows.

After a few uneventful minutes, Fitz spots something in the water. He calls out, "Blacktip, ten o'clock," as Gilly veers left.

TJ stands ready to cast, as he scans the transparent waters. "I see em."

"Hit it, dude!" Fitz directs.

TJ casts, then quickly recoils his line, repositioning his fly within the angulating shark's path.

"Awesome cast dude," Fitz praises.

STRIKE ON, as the four-footer hits his line with startling ferocity. TJ instinctively yanks his rod back to set his hook, as the adolescent shark breaks surface, launching airborne, in a futile attempt to escape the grasp of the forbidding hook, as TJ's pole bends near ninety degrees. The fight lasts a solid five minutes, which seems like an eternity. The shark eventually tires, as TJ reels him portside.

Fitz (wearing a protective metal-mesh glove) skillfully removes the set hook, releasing the young shark. "Nice job!" followed by a congratulatory high-five.

It's nearly 7:00 p.m., by the time the boys roll in, as the late day sun hovers above the distant horizon.

Helen and Gilly's mom, Rita, have been anxiously awaiting their late hour return.

The moment Helen sees the boys round the bend, her worrisome expression softens to a convivial smile.

CHAPTER 17

It's a chilly Friday night (*by Floridian standards, anyway*), as TJ and his new crew congregate beachside, encircling an impromptu bonfire. They share warm beers and cigar-sized blunts, while the ocean surf softly splashes upon the sugar-sand shore.

Lilly, a local, leggy legend (the girl every boy would love to date) takes a selective seat next to TJ, atop a putty grey, Sable Palm log.

An inebriated classmate (seated on the other side of the waning bonfire) disrespectfully rants (loud enough for all to hear), "Lilly, get your sweet ass over here!"

An intrinsically chivalrous TJ stands and commands, "Watch your mouth," in a puffed chested, cautionary tone.

The random boy wisely complies without rebuttal.

TJ retakes his fireside seat.

"Thank you," Lilly mouths, tossing an interested glance, one a blind outfielder could catch.

TJ blushes, and shyly looks off.

His timidity spikes her already keen interest, as she extends her delicate hand. "I'm Lilly by the way," she suggestively whispers.

TJ (smitten by her innate beauty) replies, "TJ."

Days later. TJ musters the courage to ask Lilly out on a date.

Before long, they're going steady.

Lilly's older and (yes) overly protective brothers, Reed and Julian, put TJ through a rigorous vetting process, and ultimately give their approval. Lilly's brothers had dropped out of high school in order to take over their father's commercial fishing business, after his arrest. Seems their dad Bertram, used his boat for more than fishing. The lure of Cartel cash was hard to ignore in the Keys. Beyond accomplished anglers, her brothers are also proficient free divers.

It's early evening and everyone's out back, hanging out.

Lilly's eyes half-mast, as she bogarts a solo blunt.

Reed attends to the fiery BBQ, while Julian and TJ chill dockside, sharing a couple of cold brews and light conversation.

"You a diver?" Julian inquires, with a contagious smile.

"You mean Scuba diving?"

"*FUCK NO!*" Julian jabs, as he leans forward. "Scuba's for pussy tourists, I'm talkin about freediving, dude," he enthusiastically clarifies.

"No... Never been," TJ reveals, followed by a soothing sip.

"You should come with us. We're gonna bag some bugs, tomorrow."

"Bugs?" TJ questions with a confounded countenance.

"Dude, how long have you lived here?" Julian teases. "Bugs are Caribbean lobsters. You know, spiny lobsters. They don't have big ass claws like Maine lobsters, so they look like fuckin bugs," he explains. "It's cool how they migrate in single-file formation, along the ocean floor. Anyway, we're super stoked. Just make sure you're here by 5 a.m.," Julian qualifies.

"Count me in," TJ affirms, with a raise of his beer.

"You'll have a blast," Julian assures with a wide, toothy smile, and a tip of his beer bottle.

Next morning, 5 a.m. Helen drops TJ off out front of Lilly's house. Out back, Julian and Reed prepare for their predawn departure. The big boat's moored dockside, as its aged, twin diesels idle to an unsteadied rhythm.

"Morning!" TJ calls out in a raspy (early morning) voice, announcing his predawn arrival.

Julian looks up toward the darkened dock. "What's up?" he replies from the boat's beamy stern, as he tosses TJ a dive mask.

Unprepared, TJ fumbles the catch.

Julian chuckles, as he flings a pair of dive fins, which flop onto the dock. "Try those on for size," he quips,

"You ready to snag some bugs, big guy?" Reed calls out, as he emerges from below deck, wiping his greasy hands (having fussed with the old diesel engines).

"You bet!" TJ enthusiastically responds, while trying on his dive fins.

Shortly before sun-up, the trio ties off and plows down the narrow canal, through the open inlet toward Mother Ocean.

Reed commands helm of their old Down-Easterner, affectionately named Dora's Dream, after their great grandmother. Their vintage vessel's a family heirloom, handed down through three generations of commercial anglers.

Julian's posted at aft, coiling the dampened spring lines.

Well beyond inlet limits, Reed revs the old girl's engines, eventually topping twenty knots, as he cautiously navigates obsolete channel markers, which fail to accurately depict uncharted sandbars.

As soon as they reach the open ocean, Reed activates his

sonar fish finder, to help identify their migratory quarry. Before long Reed shouts out (above the old engine's grumble). "Bugs a bottom!" he yelps, as he slips into neutral.

Julian rushes bow-ward, his body suspended over the protruding bow rail as he visually surveys the crystal-clear waters below, soon signaling Reed to reverse the old lady, to set the plunging anchor.

Later, engines off, the threesome suit up and drop in, soon skimming the ocean floor.

TJ (initially uncomfortable with the daunting depths) frequently resurfaces to grab a gulp of air. After a few uneventful dives, he starts to enjoy the bountiful voyage. After plucking a bagful of bugs, he reenters the water for a second and final round.

Having snagged his limit, an oxygen-deprived TJ starts to ascend, when he feels something coarse (akin to sandpaper) bump the back of his left leg. Eyes widen when he sees a nosey nine-foot, Lemon shark looking to steal a meal.

TJ drops his bag of bugs and scurries (fins flapping) toward the surface. Head above water, he floats.

Reed to the rescue as he tags the snoopy shark's snout with the multi-prong tip of his trusted (but rusted) Hawaiian sling, sending the opportunistic predator scurrying off to the shadowy depths.

The threesome float in huddle, heads bobbing above the slow ocean roll as their snorkels dangle.

"I'm so done with this crazy shit!" a panicked TJ declares between gasps of air and unintended swigs of salty seawater.

"You gonna let a little nine-footer run you off?" Reed teases.

"Damn right!" a frantic TJ fires-back.

"Dude you need to get the bag of bugs you just dropped," Julian jests.

"No fuckin way!!"

The brothers roar with laughter, as Reed drops down below surface to retrieve TJ's bugs.

Early evening, a physically exhausted, emotionally spent TJ returns home and presents Helen with his bountiful catch, which she broils and serves over a bed of risotto.

After a sun-filled day, and a belly full of succulent Caribbean lobster, TJ heads to bed.

Mid-summer. Lilly introduces TJ to hashish. He ultimately concludes that it's simply too potent for his liking.

Unlike TJ, Lilly relishes the added potency. It allows her to escape reality, she readily reveals.

Before long, Lilly's usage becomes more frequent, notably excessive and arguably problematic. By all accounts she's a chronic user, better said an incorrigible addict. Lilly gets high multiple times a day and simply zones out. At some level Lilly's untamable wild side affords TJ an opportunity to pause and self-reflect.

By the close of summer, TJ ends things with Lilly (who had since dropped out of school), having succumbed to the insatiable allure of yet harder drugs. Coke and meth became her drugs of choice, propelling her to spiral out of control into an irreversible downward descent.

Before long, she'd taken up residency at a sleazy motel in a sketchy part of town, selling her body and soul to help sustain her habit.

Her family was understandably devastated. Her brothers inconsolably distraught. Their efforts to intervene staunchly rebutted.

Having witnessed this tragedy first-hand, was a constructive, eye-opening experience for TJ, now evermore reverent about his dad's mission, and the addictive consequences of coke.

Though emphatically committed to staying clear of the hard stuff, TJ was nevertheless undeterred when it came to his recreational usage of pot, growing ever more lackadaisical with his indulgence. On occasion, he'd brazenly smoke a joint in his bedroom (window open of course), with a small (nickel bag) stash on deck, under his mattress.

It's late evening, fast approaching midnight. TJ's in the family room, sprawled out on the soft sofa, lights dimmed, watching television, while munching on a bag of sourdough pretzels and humus dip.

Helen enters the room, flips on the light, carrying an enraged expression and a small bag of weed in her grasp, "What's *THIS?*" she shrieks.

TJ (in a cannabis coma) sits up, *ever so slowly*. "Relax, it's all good," he reassures in a red-eyed reply.

"What do you mean *ALL GOOD?*" Helen growls with unforeseen ferocity, in her otherwise even-keel demeanor. Infuriated, Helen (ever so tired of TJ's rebellious behavior) tosses the bag of pot onto the sofa. "Get this garbage out of here. How dare you bring illegal drugs into our home. How utterly disrespectful, particularly since your father's job is to oversee the *War on Drugs*! Your dad will deal with you when he returns," she scoffs, as she storms off.

TJ promptly snaps to and sobers up.

Days later, Slater returns from his trip.

A deliberate knock upon TJ's bedroom door, interrupts his studying.

"Come in," TJ answers in a semi-submissive tone.

Slater enters. "Heard you've been grounded," Slater casually notes, as he plops atop TJ's unmade bed.

"Yup," TJ answers, swiveling in his seat to face his dad, as he tucks his long hair behind his left ear.

"Yup... Is that all you have to say?" Slater grills.

"Sorry," TJ concedes, facing the floor.

"Let's take a walk, son," Slater suggests, in a firm yet compassionate tone, as he exits the room.

TJ folds his book and follows his dad outside.

Out front. They walk side by side, slow paced through base.

After a brief silence, Slater initiates conversation, "Life is a gift, T... How we live life is a decision." He pauses to afford TJ a moment or two to digest his words, then continues. "In life we have one tool for many tasks." Slater once again pauses, hoping to trigger TJ's curiosity.

After a brief delay, TJ (still staring down toward the ground) sheepishly asks, "What's that?"

"The ability to make good choices," Slater articulates as they continue to walk. "Every day we're confronted with choices and somewhere amongst that long list are choices regarding drugs." Slater pauses, then proceeds. "Personally, I'm not particularly wound up about pot. From what I've learned after taking this job, pot may actually have more benefits than consequences." Slater snickers. "Unfortunately, it's classified as an illegal drug and possession, use and/or distribution are criminal offenses. That in and unto itself, is all the reason we need to steer clear of weed. The harder drugs, like coke, meth, heroin, and the like, are materially worse and of course also illegal, and highly addictive. You should know that better than anyone, T. After all, you had a front row seat when Lilly's life imploded," an empathetic Slater, convincingly analogizes.

"I know," TJ acknowledges. "But how can you say pot is okay when you arrest smugglers?"

"Well. My mission is to intercept *cocaine* smugglers. That said, if we unexpectedly seize a load of marijuana, we'd certainly make an arrest and confiscate their product and cash. There again, my personal perspective is irrelevant. I have a job to do, and that job is to stop illegal drugs of any kind, from hitting U.S. soil. Technically, if I were to catch you, my own son, with a bag of weed, I'd be legally compelled to arrest you as well. You understand that don't you, Son?"

TJ ponders the sobering reality of Slater's narrative. He looks up at his dad, carrying a distressed face and asks, "Would you really?"

Slater lets TJ's question go unanswered, leaving room for doubt in his inquisitive mind. "If and when pot is ultimately legalized, I might even share a joint with you; but today it's not, so we won't," Slater joshes.

"I can't picture you smoking weed," TJ says, unable to suppress his smile.

They both share a lighthearted laugh.

"That would be an interesting sight indeed," Slater concedes as he places his left arm around his son's slumped shoulder, pulling him in close. "Next time, T, let's try to make better choices. Okay, pal?"

"Will do," TJ replies, head and spirits lifted.

"Okay then," Slater concludes, as they turn to head home.

CHAPTER 18

It was about two years into the President's *War on Drugs*, when surface intercepts started to taper off. From all indications, the bad guys had grown wise to the DEA's coastal dragnet, somehow able to predict shoreline vulnerabilities, allowing smugglers to slip in and out of select ports virtually undetected.

In response, the DEA decided to revamp its intercept strategy by adding more undercover operatives while revitalizing their fleet.

It was a typical Tuesday, when two U.S. Customs Agents drop in on Slater.

The front desk clerk summons his presence.

Within a couple minutes, Slater enters the small reception area where the Customs Agents sit in wait.

"Captain Jensen?" the senior officer greets, as he quickly stands. "Sorry for dropping in unannounced," he apologizes.

"Not a problem," Slater responds with a welcoming smile.

The two shake hands, then Slater turns to shake the subordinate officer's hand, as he half stands, before retaking his seat. "I just wanted to let you know that we dropped the new prototype into the water. She's moored dockside. Officer Briggs is aboard as we speak, preparing her for sea trial. I was hoping that you and Lieutenant McQueen might find time for Officer Briggs to familiarize you with the new launch," the senior officer informs, with an infectious smile.

"Sounds great. I'll dispatch Mac to see what his schedule looks like."

"I fully expect you to be thoroughly impressed with the vast technical advancements, not to mention the significant upgrade in power and stealth," the subordinate officer (still seated) eagerly interjects.

"After your sea trial would you be kind enough to deliver her to Port Everglades for technical vetting?" the senior officer requests.

"Certainly."

"If your team fancies her performance and provided the technological evaluations prove favorable of course, we expect to deliver a replacement fleet by year's end."

"Fabulous," Slater finishes, as the Customs Agents bid farewell.

Within the hour, Slater and Mac arrive at the marina.

"Welcome aboard, Captain. Officer Jessup Briggs at your service," Briggs greets in full salute. "As you can see, we've retained her uniquely narrow, nine-foot beam, but modified the hull configuration to help enhance acceleration by reducing drag, aka water viscosity," Briggs explains, trying to dumb down the technical verbiage. "Other notable features include a quantum leap in horsepower," Brigg's brags as he heads toward helm. "She also offers some impressive technological advancements including preprogramed trim tabs, capable of evaluating wave height and separation."

"Very impressive! Can you walk me through the instrumentation panel?" Mac (the team technician) requests.

After a thorough briefing, the gents are anxious to let her loose.

Later, Briggs stands dockside (once again) in full salute, as Slater (positioned at helm) skillfully reverses from her narrow berth.

Mid-bay. Slater spins the old girl eastward. Beside him, trusted Lieutenant McQueen. Their mission is to *let the little lady run.*

They putter through port, slow rolling over a series of incoming waves, as Mac acquaints himself with some of the new prototype's nuances.

Shoreside, spectators soon swarm, drawn to the deafening vibration generated by the quad 450s.

Both men seem eager to sea-trial their new and improved (higher horsepower) launch, dubbed *Lady of the Night*, with a purported top speed, of 110 mph. Goggles on, it's *Ladies' night out*, as the boys *BLAST* off toward the deep blue sea, soon hitting wave one, a solid five-footer, launching them airborne as Mac throttles back to protect her props. *THUD*, they land, ocean spray douses the pair, who share gluttonous grins as they thrust through, successive wave sets in their water-rocket.

Outside the inlet, they pivot north clocking 107 mph (but who's counting). Adrenalin's high as they share mile-wide smiles, destination Port Everglades to berth the beast.

By the time they approach Lauderdale, the skies have darkened.

"Wanna grab a couple drafts and a bucket of the world's best stone crabs, before we dock her?" Slater shouts out, above the thunderous engines.

"If I said no, I'd be an utter fool," Mac jests as they enter Port Everglades.

They soon travel north, through the intracoastal waterway at idle speed, respectful of the *no wake* zones.

Ahead, Slater spots the omnipotent *Jonny's Stone Crab* sign, brightly illuminated on the west side of the intra-coastal, as he effortlessly completes a seamless dockage, sandwiching their svelte vessel, between two mega yachts.

Mac tosses the bowline to the attentive dockhand, then hops dockside to help tie off stern.

As they head off toward the restaurant, Slater slips a respectable tip to the attentive dockhand.

A curious crowd gathers and gawks at the gunmetal grey, military launch.

Meanwhile, Slater and Mac successfully pirate a dockside two-top and order up a couple cold drafts and a bounty of (jumbo) stone crabs. Slater's military instincts kick in when he observes a few tattooed ruffians, a table or two away, exchanging nervous glances. His suspicion elevates to high alert when they request a check, in advance of their food.

Slater stares back, turning up the heat, as the fidgety four pay cash and dash, hustling dockside toward their gaudy *go-fast.* Slater's eyes follow the sketchy crew as they hurriedly board their boat.

He sets his untouched draft to rest then stands, "Cover me," alerting an otherwise oblivious Mac (preoccupied cracking a crab claw).

Slater approaches the *go-fast.* "Nice boat," he compliments.

"Thanks," one of four curtly replies, hoping to discourage further dialogue.

"Gentlemen, with your permission I'd like to come aboard to inspect your watercraft."

"What for?" the captain snaps back in a gruff, confrontational tone.

"Because I have reason to suspect that you might be transporting illegal contraband, that's why," Slater decisively responds.

The motley crew exchange pensive glances and jointly determine that it's time to go, as one powers up, two and three push back, as four shuts the door with a sawed-off shotgun pointed at Slater.

Within seconds the bad guys back out and blast off, streaming southbound, down the intra-coastal waterway like a rifled bullet.

Mac at helm, powers up.

Slater hops aboard as the pair push off, in hot pursuit.

Restaurant guests gather dockside as the spectacle unfolds.

It's readily apparent that the *go-fast* is no match for their new launch, as Mac steadily gains on the hombres, soon trailing a boat length behind.

Slater uses the handheld intercom, "Pull over, or we'll open fire!" he warns.

The *go-fast* captain ignores Slater's warning, as one of his cohorts fires repeated blasts from a semiautomatic weapon, as bullets ping the bulletproof windshield of Slater's pursuit vessel.

The banditos make a last-minute decision to hook a hard right, as they plow down a narrow side canal, pushing 60mph plus.

Mac rides their tail, as their collective wakes thrust moored boats into the unforgiving seawall.

Ahead, the *go-fast* barely slips beneath a low, fixed bridge.

Mac makes a quick calculation and follows suit, losing his transom in the process. A causality of war, he justifies.

Trapped within a dead-end cul-de-sac, the bad guys soon

slow, as they methodically spin their vessel to face Slater and Mac.

"Block their exit!" Slater calls out as he grabs a high powered (military-issue) rifle, holstered at helm.

Mac quickly spins their boat sideways to preempt the outlaws' escape.

Curious homeowners soon appear as the show unfolds.

Slater stands portside, grabs his handset and warns, "You have nowhere to run. The authorities have been summoned, therefore a land escape, will be equally impossible."

Police soon converge (guns drawn) in the backyards of canalfront residences, ushering homeowners back inside their homes.

Desperate, scared and absent of any viable options, the bad guys decide to ram Slater and Mac's boat to facilitate their getaway.

BOOM, they blast off, straight toward Slater & Mac.

Slater readies his rifle and takes steadied aim. "When I signal, pull forward and hug the western seawall," Slater calmly instructs. His left eye travels the barrel of his high-powered rifle, as the bad guys plow toward them.

Slater tickles the trigger and fires a single, rifled shot into the forehead of the *go-fast*, boat's captain, as first blood splatters onto their plexiglass windshield.

"FORWARD!" Slater shouts.

Mac responds immediately, as he thrusts their vessel toward the western seawall, while the *go-fast* races toward them, soon clipping the tip of their portside engine, as they ricochet into the seawall, hurling its occupants airborne, as their battered boat bursts into flames.

A quick count reveals two down and two afoot.

Mac swiftly reverses toward the eastern seawall, as Slater (gun shouldered) leaps ashore, after the fleeing banditos.

"Halt!" he hollers, as one of the culprits turns and opens fire.

Slater drops to one knee, aims and returns fire. Another bad guy down.

Slater's up, in pursuit of the last man standing.

The search continues into abutting backyards. Slater cautiously advances, rifle raised while his eyes gradually adapt to his darkened surroundings. Alerted by a noise emanating from a neighboring house, he pauses and drops, stealthily crawling on his stomach. He again hears the noise, resembling the sound of a chair being moved. He turns to see the silhouette of the last hombre, taking cover under the adjoining home's rear porch.

"Hands up!" he commands.

The bad guy stands and discharges successive rounds.

Slater returns fire, piercing the perp mid-chest as he stumbles backwards. After a brief recovery he again stands, albeit unsteadied and raises his weapon.

This time, Slater preempts his assault with a fatal blast, hurling the hombre's body through the sliding glass door, as he lay inside the house, bleeding out.

CHAPTER 19

Washington National Airport

IT'S 11.41 A.M. when Slater's flight touches down (ahead of schedule).

He's greeted by Officer Louis Decker.

Later, they push off, destination Pentagon. Slater rides in the back of a black, Government-Issue SUV. His worn, canvas overnight bag rests on the seat next to him. Conversation discouraged. Slater looks right, across the Potomac at the Washington Monument. He carries a warm smile, validating his commitment to his country.

They soon pass the Arlington Cemetery to the left. Slater stares somberly at the countless white tombstones that blanket the rolling hillside, memorializing the patriots who bravely gave their lives to defend our nation. He thinks about his dad and his undaunted patriotism. He regrets their argument.

Their pace soon slows to a crawl. Snarled in traffic, Officer Decker blasts his loud siren, followed by a fast flash of his distinctive bright blue lights, as civilian vehicles quickly clear a path for their government sanctioned vehicle.

Inside the Pentagon. Slater undergoes a series of rigorous screenings, ultimately greeted by two (expressionless) officers who escort him down a seemingly endless, ill-lit corridor, terminating at a small, nondescript metal door.

One of the officers knocks, then opens the door, cueing Slater's entry with a directive nod.

Once inside the dwarf-sized chamber, Slater takes the last remaining seat inside the musty, windowless room.

Unfamiliar faces proffer obligatory smiles, as awkward minutes pass painfully. Once again, conversation's discouraged, cell phones silenced.

Agony averted by the welcomed sound of the doorknob twisting.

In walks a distinguished, high-ranking officer, as he swaggers toward the podium. His perfectly combed, winter-white hair complements his pearly smile, yet fails to conceal his hardened, military persona.

He assumes a familiar post behind the veneer podium. He takes a moment to position his briefs for his ease of reference, eyes directed upward as he addresses his invitees. "Greetings and thank you all for coming on such short notice," he conveys with unscripted sincerity. "My name is Admiral Dietrich Halsey. On the Hill, I'm *Hey Dieter*." He softly smiles.

Attendees unify in chuckle.

"In a bit, I'll afford the group of you an opportunity to introduce yourselves; but for now, I'd prefer to get to the issue at hand." Glasses on, he forces a clearing cough, refers to his notes, then proceeds. "From all accounts, the President's *War on Drugs* started off as a resounding success… In the first year alone, we observed an estimated 37% reduction in cocaine stateside. Both air and sea intercepts proved remarkably effective. As you know, the barometer of success is gauged by the street value of the product, measured by fundamental supply and demand factors. Limited supply translates to higher prices and vice versa," Dieter loosely narrates, aided by visual hand gestures. He pauses, rubs his strong chin, then continues. "Of late, there's been a dramatic drop in that stat, evidenced by a surplus supply, supported by a surprisingly low street value," he narrates, oversized hands clutch the outer edges of the flimsy podium. "From that disappointing data, we can only draw two inescapable conclusions, either we have a turncoat amongst us, or the bad guys have simply outsmarted us, *ONCE AGAIN!* No doubt, the Cartel is continually trying to reinvent themselves by honing their smuggling methodologies, while routinely substituting trafficking routes," he elaborates, finishing in frown.

Dieter reaches inside the podium drawer and retrieves a small, hand-held remote. He initiates the wall mounted television screen, then turns off the lights. Using a red laser pen, he points to the South American coastline, overlaid with a series of alternate smuggling routes, delineated by dotted yellow lines. He points to the Bahamas and narrates. "Of late, there's been an increase of product routed through the Bahamas. Unfortunately, many Bahamian officials are Cartel sympathizers, aka co-conspirators," Dieter reveals through a somber expression. "Who says money isn't the root of all evil?" he adds with a disappointed shake of his head. "Sources tell us the Cartel's Bahamian distribution strategy involves a combination of land and offshore air drops. The offshore drops are business as usual. GPS coordinates, readily relayed to the *go-fast* operators, who swarm like bees to honey, to *hook and book*"...

"In addition, our Cartel pals have endless vessel options." He changes the computer image to display a submarine afloat mid-ocean, unloading cargo onto an open hull, *go-fast.* "Of late, we've observed a noticeable surge in submersibles, which, as you might imagine, are next to impossible to detect and track."

Dieter changes the computer screen. "For bigger shipments, they favor the cargo freighter."

Change of screen. "For smaller loads, the common commercial fishing boat, will suffice."

Change of screen. "Or the go-to, cruise liner."

Change of screen. "And let's not forget, the ever popular, pleasure yacht… "Bottom line people, the moment we learn about plan '*A*' they go to plan '*B*' or simply skip to plan '*C*' and so on… It's like chasing a ghost… In the final analysis, we've wasted countless resources, running up sand hills," he regrettably concedes with a furled brow.

Dieter steps away from the podium and turns toward his attendees, and elaborates. "To compound matters, we've recently learned that the Cartel has adopted an expanded distribution network with drop sites extending beyond the Keys and Miami, to include Fort Lauderdale, Sebastian inlet and in some cases as far north as Jacksonville and Savanah, Georgia." He turns towards his attentive attendees and concludes. "The purpose of today's briefing is to unveil a revised strategy… Instead of pursuing the ever-elusive smugglers, our revamped strategy redirects our efforts toward choking off their distribution network. Clog the pipeline as it were. This mission, (affectionately dubbed *Snake's Head*) is highly classified and only shared with those within the confines of this room." He reads the facial expression of each attendee, to visually convey the importance of their strict compliance.

All attendees respond with affirming nods.

"Our primary target, Don Marco's eldest and slimiest son, Paquito, who's been tasked with overseeing their stateside distribution. Our objective, to infiltrate his inner circle using a well-vetted informant." Dieter pauses, unable to squelch a gloat-ing grin. "I'm pleased to announce, that we've identified such an individual. A true insider, who has the uncontested ability, to proffer our undercover operative unfettered access. This surpris-ingly eager individual is in protective custody as we speak. With such an introduction, we should be able to effortlessly penetrate and unravel their distribution network. In summation, we've abandoned our random intercept tactics, while redirecting our efforts toward shutting down the Cartel's distribution pipeline, essentially *cutting off the proverbial head of the snake* if you will." He finishes with a hopeful gaze.

The screen now reveals a massive pleasure yacht, cruising at sea. "Speaking of snakes," Dieter mocks, as he zooms in on a small framed, pale complected, physically unfit man, basking in a large Jacuzzi, (perched at the ship's beefy stern) enveloped by a gaggle of tawdry women. "Allow me to introduce you to Paquito, street tag Pinky. Unlike Don Marco's other children, Pinky grew up stateside, with his embittered mother, Emmanuelle (Don Marco's first of five ex-wives). Not sure if Pinky even speaks Spanish. Regardless, he undoubtedly takes after his papa. They're both ruthless psychopaths, who have quite literally killed their way to the top, leaving a swath of carnage in their wakes. Make no mistake about it, Don Marco and his baby boy Pinky, are formidable foes by any measure. To underestimate either of them would be a drastic miscalculation," Dieter conveys, through a penetrating stare.

He transitions back to Pinky's photo. "In addition to being a notorious Drug Lord, Pinky is also a high-profile Ecstasy dealer. He's also been arrested on multiple counts of rape. It's no surprise that all of his victims were high on *X* during the alleged rapes. Apparently, he expected sex for *X*. Charges ultimately dismissed for lack of evidence, no doubt a direct result of his daddy's expansive reach and thick wallet."

Dieter zooms in on Pinky's boat's beamy aft, aptly named, *X to Sea*. "As you can see, he's certainly not bashful."

"What's the backstory on the name Pinky?" a random attendee blurts.

"Before overseeing distribution, Daddy put his scumbag son in charge of one of their low-level casinos in Atlantic City. Pinky's a short-shit, barely five-foot tall, plagued by a colossal Napoleon complex… Anyway, he has issues with tall men. Hates them with a vengeance. If a tall casino patron even looks at him crossways, Pinky has him escorted to the backroom, where he has one of their pinkies snipped off with a cigar cutter. Rumor has it, that he has a cigar box in the back freezer, full of pinkies, hence the name."

The computer screen now reveals an aerial perspective of Pinky's palatial (waterfront) estate. "The Pinkster lives large, no low-key, under the radar for this pompous prick," Dieter vents with unrestrained disdain in his tone. "Sorry," he quickly apologizes.

The group enjoys a tension breaking chuckle.

The computer screen zooms in, providing a tight shot of Pinky's ostentatious mansion. "His place, his *PALACE,*" Dieter embellishes, "is flamboyantly perched at the northern tip of Star Island in Miami. In recent years, Pinky gladly overpaid to tear down his abutting neighbors' homes in order to control the entirety of his cul-de-sac. No doubt this tiny turd thinks he's pretty, cagey. Fortunately for us, he's not as smart as he otherwise thinks."

Dieter continues, "Pinky's stepsister Anna, married an opportunistic dirtbag named Jorge Ramirez, who operates a phony chiropractic practice. Turns out, it's no more than window dressing. A front to launder drug money. A total sham. Bottom line, Jorge and Pinky are thick as thieves. Together they oversee the Cartel's distribution network. Sources reveal that their long-range plan is to expand overseas. Long story short, we apprehended Ramirez last Sunday, on a quiet back road with an undercover operative, no eyes. Before we could even charge him, he coughed up a full confession. He flipped faster than a paper-thin griddlecake." The group roars in laughter. "He practically begged to be an informant," Dieter mocks. "After a two-hour interrogation, Ramirez rolled on Pinky and his entire crew. Under the supervision of a court appointed Public Defender, he agreed to testify at trial in return for a five-year plea, followed by witness protection, with a new identity minus the wife." Dieter laughs. "Probably cheaper than a divorce. Bottom line, he's the perfect informant."

Dieter stops, turns back toward the table and elaborates. "Here's the plan. Ramirez introduces our undercover operative to Pinky as a long-time confidant. Pinky embraces our undercover with open arms. Our undercover's backstory needs to be totally untraceable, rooted in an obscure overseas connection. Initially, we contemplated a Russian connection; but quickly concluded that Don Marco and his elites already have ties to the Russian underworld, so we settled on a Dutch Mafia script."

He directs his attention toward Slater. "Captain Jensen… I understand you speak fluent Danish. Might you be interested in heading this assignment?" Dieter asks.

"I'd be happy to," Slater eagerly responds. "This mission's been under my watch from the get-go and at some meaningful level I feel responsible for its waning success," Slater apologetically replies.

"Wonderful. Let's continue that conversation later. For now, I'd like to brief all attendees on our precise plan. The best way to hook a big fish, is to use big bait. Given Pinky's insatiable appetite for money, we decided to bait our hook with greed.

Accordingly, our undercover operative is going to place an outlandish street order, fifty million dollars to be precise. Once agreed, they'll schedule a drop and we'll be there to execute a coordinated takedown."

Later, Slater phones home to inform Helen that he needs to remain in D.C. for a couple of weeks to prepare for his undercover assignment. No further details are provided.

CHAPTER 20

WEEKS WHISK BY. Slater returns to Florida to perform his undercover assignment.

Plain-clothed Feds pick Slater up at Miami International.

They drive off in a Lincoln Town Car. Agents ride up front, Slater in the back.

The driver maintains a watchful eye in his rear-view mirror for any indication of a tail.

The front seat passenger sits sidesaddle, as he instructs, "Here's the skinny. You reside in Penthouse B." He hands Slater an envelope, containing the room key and script. "The valet is your backup in case things turn squirely. His undercover name is Franco."

Slater places the unsealed envelope inside his duffle bag.

Before long, they approach a luxury condominium tower on Biscayne Bay. They pull under an extravagant porta cache and park.

The driver turns to face Slater, lowers his sunglasses and instructs, "Ramirez is scheduled to arrive tomorrow, 5 p.m. At

4:50 p.m. call Franco to bring your car out front." He pauses and asks. "You can drive a shift, right?"

"No problem," Slater assures, with a confident (*you must be fuckin kidding me!*) smirk.

"Ramirez will meet you in the lobby. Again, act as if you're old acquaintances, you never know who might be watching."

Slater nods, then exits.

The front seat passenger lowers his window and calls out, "Don't get too used to the lifestyle."

Slater ignores his taunt as he heads toward the entry.

He enters the building, then proceeds through the (perfectly appointed) lobby toward the elevator shaft. He enters the ornate elevator and presses PH-B.

After a hastened ascent, the elevator opens directly into the luxurious Penthouse. Wall to wall windows reveal sweeping vistas of Biscayne Bay and the endless ocean beyond. A mesmerized Slater drops his shoes, pours a Brandy and flops onto the over-sized sofa, as he savors the moment.

The following afternoon, Ramirez arrives as scheduled. He and Slater meet in the lobby. As scripted, they pose as old acquaintances sharing a big hug and familiar smiles.

Franco pulls their car out front.

The pair push off, soon crossing Mc Arthur Parkway as the late day sun hangs low. They roll large, in an open T-Top, Ferrari 308 GT (courtesy of the U.S. Government). The temperature, a warm 76 degrees.

They travel due east. Slater eventually downshifts to navigate a left turn, over an arched fixed bridge into prestigious Star Island.

Pinky's playhouse is pretentiously positioned at the tail-end of the private peninsula, no interconnecting cross streets, just one way in and one way out.

They pull up to Pinky's gaudy gates (at the throat of the cul-de-sac). Slater presses the buzzer repeatedly to no avail. Eventually, the gold-leaf gates swing open as Slater advances his vehicle and parks out front.

Inside the expansive, open two-story foyer, Slater and Ramirez stand, hands raised, pockets emptied as they pass through a commercial grade, metal detector.

Ramirez (a known entity) avoids supplemental frisking.

Slater (a fresh face) undergoes a quick frisk, by a pair of mindless muscle-heads. The duo brandish shouldered pistols and skintight tees, to accentuate their bogus (steroid induced) biceps.

"Clear!" one of the juice jocks heralds in an embellished baritone voice, as Slater and Ramirez proceed inside, past a long line of scantily clad, coke-whores snorting snow.

An ever-alert Slater scans the limits of the residence in utter disbelief. The first floor is entirely open, not a single interior partition, except for a lone boxed bathroom, as drug slugs congregate in disconnected clusters.

To his left, he observes a random couple having oral sex on the skanky crushed velvet sofa, while a flamboyant, gay male (dressed in a leopard leotard) roller skates around them, culminating in a tight circle (tantamount to a freestyle figure skater), hands raised to accentuate the speed of his controlled spin.

To his right, he notices an emaciated, brindle, Cane Corso (revered drug-dealer dog) barking incessantly, amid countless piles of foul, smelling feces. His movement restricted by an inhumanely short, rusted chain, secured to a structural column. His undersized water bowl, bone dry.

They proceed out back. Poolside now. A similar scene plays out here, as near nude stripper-types cluster in the poolside shallows, while *wannabe*, drug thugs bounce offbeat, to home-grown, crap rap.

"Over here!" Pinky calls out, from the moored yacht's elevated aft deck.

Ramirez returns an acknowledging wave, as he and Slater ascend a teak ramp (framed by taut wire cable railings), to the boat's starboard deck.

They're greeted by a small Asian male, wearing a shoulder holster and a stern stare, as he escorts them back to where Pinky entertains his harem of whores.

Pinky (a runt of a man) holds court amongst a throng of thongs, as bawdy dancer types vie for his attention (drugs), while stoic bodyguards (carrying semi-automatic weapons) take strategic post.

Pinky sports a weathered sombrero, a sweat drenched silk shirt and a pair of camo shorts (exposing his pasty white legs) accentuated by tasteless black socks, sleeved inside a pair of dingy white sandals. Pinky remains seated, no proffer of a handshake, either a reflection of his lack of etiquette; or (more likely) his insatiable need to establish control.

"Sit! Sit!" Pinky gestures with his tiny, callus-free hands in a downward motion, as Jorge (Ramirez' first name) and Slater (masquerading as Johan), take side by side seats.

"Go, go," Pinky impatiently shoos his clad-less companions in a frustrated tone, as they coquettishly eye Slater, as they depart.

"*NO*, you stay!!" Pinky insists, hand clasping onto the bikini bottom of a young (probably teenage) girl, arguably the prettiest of the bunch.

She pauses, frightened eyes, but wisely complies.

Pinky tugs, pulling his unwitting playmate onto his lecherous lap, soon sedating her with *X*, Y and Z, as she willingly snorts a long line, instantly high and conveniently compliant.

Pinky (seemingly oblivious to the presence of others) gropes her near naked body, soon shoving her head into his sweaty crotch, loosely covered by a small beach towel. Head back, he moans with pleasure followed by a long cleansing breath.

Jorge and Johan sit there, in utter disbelief, thoroughly disgusted by Pinky's barbaric behavior.

Jorge, hoping to break the awkwardness of the moment, commences with scripted introductions, motioning to Johan, "Pinky, I would like to introduce you to Johan Vander Plough, a trusted friend of mine... I first met Johan about ten years ago through Pepe Villa (a recently deceased, Venezuelan Drug Lord). Johan represents a well-respected European family, based in Denmark. His employers have literally controlled the European prostitution industry for over a century."

Johan nods, affirming the accuracy of Jorge's introduction.

"Prostitution. My favorite sport," a perverted Pinky proclaims.

A notably nervous Jorge, leans in toward Pinky and whispers "Johan's client is interested in purchasing a sizable shipment of coke and I thought this might fit well with our plan to expand into Europe." Jorge finishes with a suggestive furl of his eyebrows.

Pinky just sits there as a vacant stare occupies his pudgy, unshaven face. His thoughts unrevealing. He's either pondering Jorge's proposal, unwittingly disinterested or he's slipped into a temporary coma. He soon snaps to, sporting a cocky grin as he lifts and lights a thick Cuban cigar. He takes a prolonged drag, then blows successive (near perfect) circles into the air. It's unclear whether he's humoring himself or attempting to show off. Impossible to tell what goes on in the mind of a moronic psychopath. Pinky remains uncharacteristically quiet, conspicuously disengaged. He leans forward and callously grabs an oversized clump of caviar with his stubby fingers and places a mound atop a thin wafer, which he ravages it in a singular swallow. Remnant morsels cling to his beard stubble. He leans back, smiles, then proceeds with an impromptu interrogation. "So, *JOHNAN*, you live in Denmark?"

Johan pauses before responding, then in a pre-rehearsed Danish accent, answers, "I actually grew up on a houseboat, on the *Brouwersgracht* Canal, in the *Jordaan* district of Amsterdam." After another short pause, Johan continues. "For the past eleven years however, I've been stateside, chasing the American Dream, as they say," he convincingly finishes with a forced smile.

"So, you speak Dutch, right?" Pinky, tests.

"Danish actually," Johan corrects, *"Selvfogelig" (of course),* Johan authenticates.

"So, *JOHAN*, what exactly do you do for this '*well-respected*' (Pinky emphasizes with air quotes) European employer of yours?"

"He's an enforcer," Jorge nervously intercepts.

"What do you mean, when you say *ENFORCER?*" Pinky repeats, his interest piqued, curiously awaiting Johan's reply.

"He handles the rough stuff," Jorge anxiously answers.

"For fuck-sake, Ramirez, I asked the fuckin Dutchman!" Pinky reprimands in an irritated tone, open palm directed toward Johan.

"Jorge is quite correct, among other ancillary responsibilities, such as third-party negotiations, similar to my capacity here today," Johan calmly responds, in an embellished (broken English) accent.

"So, what exactly do you enforce?" Pinky prods (pressing Johan to state the obvious).

Johan pauses and with a penetrating stare, replies, "If someone fails to live up to their end of an arrangement, I'm generally called in to encourage their compliance."

"Woo!" Pinky mocks, hands raised as he sarcastically repeats,

"*ENCOURAGE THEIR COMPLIANCE!!* now that's a polite way to say you kick some fuckin ass," Pinky pokes.

After a deliberate pause, Johan humbly replies, "Something like that." Followed by an unflinching gaze, designed to convey his frustration with Pinky's antics.

"So, you must be a badass mother fucker," Pinky asserts through a smartass smirk.

Johan just sits there, expressionless, without reply.

Pinky leans forward, eyes directed at Johan. "You know who I am?" Pinky asks, with an overwhelming need to feed his insatiable ego.

"Yes. You are a man named Pinky," Johan responds, contrived accent, pretending to be perplexed by Pinky's preposterous question, as he stifles a laugh.

"Something funny?" Pinky presses in a challenging tone, fueled by deep rooted insecurity.

"No, nothing. So sorry," Johan apologizes.

"No, no. Let's hear it, so we can all enjoy a good fuckin laugh," Pinky pounces.

After a brief pause, Johan replies in his rehearsed accent, "Your name, that's all. It's just, how you say, unusual."

"*UNUSUAL?*" Pinky pushes, in a testy tone, "Unusual, nice or unusual stupid?" Pinky persists.

After a brief ponder, Johan replies in goad, "If I had to pick one of the two, I suppose I would have to pick unusual, *STUPID.*" Johan assuredly answers, in a calculated attempt to piss off the Pinkster.

Pinky remains seated, though visually perturbed by Johan's unbridled brazenness. Unable to conjure an apt response, pinky pauses in protest, carrying a dumbfounded expression about his mortified face. He draws another long drag from his thick cigar, then punts. "Now that's an honest fuckin answer." Pinky punctuates, with a forced smile, masking his fuming temper, eyes surveying the deck to measure the reaction of his entourage.

"Let's drink to that," Pinky suggests, as he waves his steward over with an exaggerated twirl of his index finger.

The deck steward promptly tenders three chilled Mojitos. Conversation suspends, as the three sip their refreshing drinks.

Pinky's playmate is fast asleep, more likely unconscious.

Frustrated, Pinky shoves her from his lap, as her limp (drug induced) body flops onto the unforgiving wood deck, as a stream of saliva bubbles from her adolescent mouth.

Johan, (Slater/an innate protector), finds it challenging to witness such abuse. His instinct is to intervene, but he knows that's not an option.

Unaffected, Pinky resumes. "So, Johan, how tall are you, six three, six four?" Pinky randomly asks, tapping his cigar ashes into an oversized conch shell.

"Six four," Johan answers, followed by an obligatory sip of his mojito.

"That's a respectable height," Pinky acknowledges with a decisive nod. "For me, I got fucked in the height department." Acknowledging the obvious, followed by a contrived, self-deprecating laugh. "But the way I see it, I make up for it in other areas. Like brains and money. See, I'm pretty fuckin smart, plus I got a shitload a cash," Pinky boasts, prideful smile, arms raised, as he looks around for his entourage's endorsement.

"That you do," an edgy Jorge chimes in, fearful eyes, hoping to sooth any remnant tension.

"Then there's my fuckin attitude," Pinky footnotes, sitting back, indiscriminately flicking ashes onto the unconscious girl's (near naked) body. "I got a badass attitude… so I'm told," he egotistically adds. "But then again, I got the muscle ta back that shit up. Know what I'm sayin, Dutchman?" Pinky rhetorically asks.

Johan returns an observably disinterested smirk.

Pinky proceeds. "Basically, when I want shit done, it gets fuckin done." Hands raised above his head in a "V" formation, followed by a snap of his fingers. "Like that!" He finishes with a bluff of bravado.

Johan dismisses Pinky's narcissistic rant with a condescending shake of his head.

Jorge injects a nervous laugh.

"You followin what I'm tellin you, Dutchman?" Eyes remain trained on Johan's response.

Johan leans forward. Through a frustrated expression he asks, "Where is this conversation going?" he baits in a provocative tone.

Pinky takes the bait and bites. "This conversation is goin wherever the *FUCK* I want to take it, you, arrogant Dutch douchebag," Pinky spews, glaring eyes, angered expression, as he blows a large plume of cigar smoke directly into Johan's face.

Johan pulls back, though unable to dodge the cloud of smoke. "I ask because I have limited time and as you can appreciate, time is a valuable commodity, irrespective of the fact that I'm sweating my ass off listening to your boring bullshit," Johan concludes.

Pinky's eyes redden with rage. He's uncontrollably livid. Unable to bridle his overwhelming disdain for Johan, Pinky literally *LEAPS* out of his seat and tosses the remains of his mojito into Johan's face. "Maybe that will help cool you off, you disrespectful, prick!" Pinky scolds.

Jorge quickly stands, in a failed attempt to defuse the situation.

"Sit the *FUCK DOWN*, Ramirez!" Pinky snaps, fiery eyes.

Jorge willingly obliges.

Johan remains seated, surprisingly collected, as he calmly wipes remnant mojito from his face and shirt.

"So sorry I'm fuckin boring you," Pinky scolds, neck veins pulsating. "Like I said, asshole, all I gotta do is snap my mother fuckin finger and any one of my men, will gladly toss yer ass overboard. You, cocky mother fucker," an enraged Pinky blasts.

Pinky's entourage closes in, anticipating an impending confrontation, awaiting further instruction.

Johan offers an unflinching stare. "I'd be most interested to meet such a man," Johan dares, throwing down the proverbial gauntlet.

"*WHO THE FUCK DO YOU THINK YOU ARE?*" a perplexed Pinky hollers, standing over Johan, who remains seated and entirely unintimidated.

Johan slowly unfolds from his chair, standing now, dwarfing a disproportionately small Pinky. "I respectfully suggest that you take your seat, little man," Johan warns.

On cue, Tiago, a muscular, dark-skinned Latin man, wearing tuxedo trousers, suspenders and no shirt, intercepts Johan's advance with panned fingers.

Johan instinctively reacts, as he grabs and snaps Tiago's right middle finger backwards, with a bone-cracking crunch, dropping Pinky's bodyguard to his knees, as he bellows in blood curdling pain.

All on deck, particularly Pinky, are in absolute disbelief, as Pinky's bodyguard is effortlessly eradicated.

"Get up you, pussy!" Pinky berates.

A humbled Tiago slowly stands, nods to Johan, and walks off.

A speechless Pinky spits in Tiago's face. "Get outta my fuckin sight you pathetic piece a shit… Wimp ass bitch," Pinky abashes.

The big man tolerates Pinky's rant, as he walks off, cradling his broken finger.

"Let's move this conversation below deck," a perky Pinky suggests, in a refreshingly respectful tone.

Below deck, Johan slides into a semi-circular, bench seat which envelopes a high-gloss, cherry-top table.

Across the room, Pinky pours himself another mojito. He motions to Johan with a lift of an empty glass.

Johan shakes his head, *no*.

Pinky flops into a burgundy beanbag (facing Johan) noisily slurping his drink through (you guessed it) a pink straw.

Visibly shaken Jorge remains standing.

"So, *Mr. JOHAN*, how can I be of assistance?" a wholly humbled Pinky inquires.

"My employer is interested in purchasing five-thousand, kilos of pure, uncut blow and we will pay the price for purity." Johan relays.

Pinky's beady eyes beckon with greed. "What's your time-frame?" he asks.

"Soon, next week, soon," Johan details.

Pinky (still overwhelmed by the large quantity and quick timing) chokes on his drink. Through a clearing cough, he replies, "You know you're talkin north a $50 mil?" Pinky confirms with a curious expression.

"I can do the math, thank you," Johan curtly rebuts. "I have a cargo container, dry docked at Port Everglades, scheduled to depart for Europe next Thursday. If you can make it happen, let Jorge know. If not, another time perhaps," Johan says, stands and leaves.

That following morning, Jorge's cell phone rings. It's Pinky.

Federal agents (monitoring Jorge's calls) motion to him with succinct hand gestures, directing him to answer. They listen in, while recording the conversation.

"Hello," a notably nervous Jorge answers, eyes upon agents for further directive.

"Jorge?" Noise in the background encumbers reception, some words inaudible.

"Can you speak up?" a jittery Jorge asks.

Pinky pauses, then continues in a louder, stern tone. "Ramirez… I need to hear you tell me that this mother fucker is for real, cause if he ain't, and this shit goes south, I will fuck you up bad," Pinky threatens.

"I already told you; I've known Johan for nearly ten years. He's a standup guy and his employer is for real. Don't insult me, dude, we're family," Jorge convincingly concludes.

"NO! We're not family, Ramierz, you just happened to be married to my slut stepsister."

The Feds smile, with a *thumbs-up* gesture, acknowledging Jorge's credible performance.

Silence on Pinky's end.

Jorge listens intently.

After a brief delay. "Okay, let's do this!" Pinky confirms, then hangs up.

The buy is on. The plan is for Pinky's crew to deliver the product to Port Everglades.

7 p.m. *Buy time.* Pinky and his crew pull up to the Port Everglades' entry, in a pretentious two-tone (black and gold) Rolls Royce, with a white commercial van (transporting blow) in tow.

An undercover DEA agent (posing as port security) greets their scheduled arrival. He approaches Pinky's ride with an elongated flashlight.

Pinky lowers his (left/rear) window. As instructed Pinky says, "Here to see the Dutchman," with a cocky countenance.

The security guard lowers his head and uses his flashlight to quickly assess the confines of Pinky's vehicle. He steps back and signals the other guard (also a DEA agent) with an affirming nod, as the entry gate opens. "Straight ahead, first left gentlemen," he advises, gesturing with a twist of his flashlight.

Pinky's window rolls up, as his Rolls, rolls in.

Johan and a crew of two, stand center yard.

Pinky and his entourage drive into the shipyard, stop midway and park. Pinky waits a few minutes before exiting, instinctively scanning the limits of the otherwise vacant lot.

Pinky's driver, a humbled Tiago (broken finger in a brace), exits the vehicle, opens Pinky's rear door, then walks a few steps behind Pinky, as Johan's associates proceed toward them.

Johan stays back.

On cue, Pinky and his men raise their hands, as one of Johan's men frisks them, while the other brandishes a semi-automatic weapon.

Afterwards they conduct a thorough search of Pinky's vehicle, then proceed toward the van.

At Pinky's prompt, the van occupants hop out to oblige the same drill.

After a few minutes, Johan's men offer an *all-clear*, gesture, signaling Johan to advance.

As Johan approaches, Pinky (wearing a contrived smile) extends his stubby arm.

Johan rejects his invitation to shake.

Embarrassed, Pinky's quick to retract his gesture, face flushed with unfamiliar humility.

Unbeknownst to Pinky, strategically positioned rooftop

snipers encircle the scene. Their high-powered rifles remain trained on Pinky and his crew.

All congregate at the back of the van, both doors remain fully ajar.

Johan's tester, wearing blue plastic gloves, facemask, and goggles, reaches inside. He selects a random test brick, buried amongst the tall, tightly packed stack of blow. He makes a small incision, then collects a thimble sized sample, which he carefully pours it into a tall test tube. He shakes the tube, which soon reveals a bright blue color. He offers an affirming nod, confirming purity.

Johan raises his right arm above his head and with a subtle wave of his hand, a nondescript vehicle (parked near the periphery of the lot) accelerates toward them.

The driver stops and pops the trunk, revealing several suitcases, crammed with cash.

Pinky's men count their bounty. One man tests random bills for authenticity, a second counts aloud, as the third enters his verbal calls into a handheld calculator. Within a few minutes, Pinky's men confirm the agreed sum.

"So, where's your container?" Pinky asks.

Johan points to a burnt orange cargo container, positioned off to the side of the parking lot.

"Load em up," Pinky instructs, as he once again scans the limits of the parking lot, while his team repositions their van next to the cargo container.

Pinky's crew hops out and quickly forms a makeshift assembly line, to transfer the product from the van, into Johan's container.

SUDDENLY, the container door *BURST* open, as several heavily armed DEA agents wearing flat jackets and helmets quickly apprehend Pinky and his sketchy crew, without resistance.

Slater fires off a quick text to Dieter. "*The snake is in the bag.*"

CHAPTER 21

Big Pine Key, Florida.

IT's A BLINK of the eye shy of 2 a.m. on a hot and humid, August eve. The broad bay is unusually tranquil, as the still waters mirror the hazy, halfmoon. The unspoiled silence, soon disrupted by the threatening growl of an inbound *go-fast*.

From the black abyss bursts a bright blue bow. Its captain (an older, thin framed, pirate-eyed, Latin chap) throttles back, as he approaches the mouth of Big Pine. Engines off, he floats in wait. Sweat beads atop his leathered brow as an unlit cigarette stub dangles from his crusty lips. He nervously surveys his expansive surroundings. He knows too well, the consequence of capture.

Time passes slowly, as his crew of two bookend his center helm position, on this balmy breezeless night. The eerie quiet, occasionally disrupted by surfacing fish. The plan, loosely hatched, is to rendezvous with three flats boats, piloted by Cartel crewmembers. Their task, to transport the product to a predetermined drop spot. Destination unknown to the *go-fast* boat's captain and crew.

To the Cartel, fragmented knowledge is a sound occupational precaution.

Far beyond the scheduled drop time, the captain spots the triple flash of a distant spotlight, signifying the Cartel's belated approach.

Before long, the three flats-boats come into view, as they putter in queue, toward the waiting *go-fast*.

The calm waters help facilitate a seamless handoff. The *go-fast's* hull is emptied in minutes. The flats boats sit low, barely an inch above the water's surface, weighed down with cargo. Piled high, they push off and head back toward the inlet.

As instructed, the *go-fast* crew waits, engines off, until they receive an, *all clear* signal from the flats' crew.

Before long, they see the triple flash of the trailing boat's spotlight, as the flats-boats veer off into the brackish backwaters. Without hesitation, the *go-fast's* captain, powers up, spins around and *BLASTS* off, roaring away, into another nameless night.

Meanwhile, the flats boats skillfully traverse the muddy mangroves, through low tide tributaries (too shallow for police pursuit). Obstructive branches are easily eradicated with a single slash of their honed machetes, as the three travel tight. Their destination, a mile or so downstream to meet up with a local biker outfit to exchange cargo for cash.

The bikers' van is already in position, parked inside a small clearing, enveloped by moss-laden oaks. They sit in wait, windows down. After a few, mosquito menacing minutes, they spot the incoming flats boats, as they announce their arrival with a triple flash signal.

The flats-boat crew tosses their lines, as the biker's promptly pull them ashore.

SUDDENLY (lights, weapons, ambush) strategically positioned floodlights illuminate the drop scene, rendering bikers and Cartel crewmembers, temporarily blinded and wholly vulnerable, to a well-orchestrated bombardment of firepower.

Within seconds, seven lay slaughtered, their carcasses line the shallows of the mucky embankment. The dense summer air reeks with the smell of gunpowder, peppered by the rancid stench of death.

Mid-morning, the following day. Investigators tape off the crime scene.

Slater accompanies a veteran CSI agent, tasked with overseeing the investigation, as a team of forensic experts methodically comb the crime scene for clues.

"Owen Richards." The lead CSI agent obligingly introduces.

"Nice to meet you... Slater Jensen."

The pair shake hands.

Slater watches as Owen (wearing plastic gloves) examines a shell-casing, sleeved atop an unsharpened pencil.

"What do you think happened here?" Slater inquires.

"Not sure," Owen cautiously responds, while panning the clearing.

"A turf war, amongst rival factions would be my guess..." Richards speculates. "The puzzling part is the collateral damage."

"Collateral damage?"

Richards turns toward Slater. "Three of these corpses were Cartel... Killing a competitor is one thing... Killing Cartel is bad business... ill thought and fatalistic," he explains with a seasoned sneer. "One thing I've learned over the years, is that nobody fucks with the Cartel and lives to brag about it."

CHAPTER 22

MONTHS LATER. IT's a week shy of another Caribbean Christmas. The midday sun's masked by dense cloud cover as Slater travels north to participate in a mandatory debriefing in Ft. Lauderdale.

Later, Helen makes plans to head off base to do some last-minute Christmas shopping. "T, I need you to tend to your brother while I'm gone. I should be home by supper, if not, I have stew in the crockpot," she instructs while rummaging through her purse, in search of her car keys.

"I can't. I'm meeting up with some friends," TJ snaps back, with teenage obstinacy.

They're a Navy family and in the Navy, an order does not invite debate. Helen spins in place, now facing TJ with glaring eyes, no words needed.

TJ quickly comports.

3:10 p.m., Helen pushes off on her Christmas outing.

TJ evaluates the risk of sneaking off and returning undetected. He decides to go for it. Before departing, he collects his dad's military issue backpack to tote his dive gear.

3:22 p.m. TJ leaves base afoot, with Brandon in tow. Destination, Summerland Key, to meet up with his school chums to free dive for lobster. With a clumsily stuffed backpack casually slung over his left shoulder TJ and Brandon trek north, on the east side of US-1, (which traverses the length of the Florida Keys). TJ walks backwards, right thumb up, in hope of soliciting a ride.

With countless miles of interconnecting bridges between a series of small islands, hitchhiking became a reliable, arguably inescapable mode of transportation.

Almost immediately, a dingy white commercial van slows, a short distance ahead of where the boys are walking. The illumination of the van's brake lights signals a prospective ride, as the vehicle abruptly pulls off road and onto the sugar-sand shoulder that frames this narrow stretch of US-1.

The obliging front seat passenger hops out and slides the side panel door open for their ease of entry.

The boys hustle up and quickly climb inside.

Once aboard, the front seat passenger is quick to close the rear sliding door, before hoping back up front.

Inside the van now, TJ instinctively surveys the sparse surroundings. *Odd for a commercial work vehicle to be empty inside,* an unsettled TJ ponders. He would have felt more comfortable having accepted a ride from a family on vacation. The sliding door handle is also missing, which in and unto itself is disturbingly suspicious and understandably unnerving. Grateful for the ride, he squelches further feelings of uneasiness and allays his straggling concerns.

Brandon and TJ sit atop a corrugated steel floor, backs pressed flat against the side of the van, as the driver merges back onto US-1.

"Where you boys headed?" the driver asks, beady blue eyes peer into his rear-view mirror.

"Summerland Key," TJ responds with a touch of trepidation in his tone.

His attention now redirected to the front seat passenger (a skinny tweaker type). His left bicep hosts a crude indistinguishable jailhouse tattoo. TJ watches as he fiddles with something between his bony kneecaps, just beyond his restricted view.

The driver on the other hand, is an enormous, baldheaded chap, with a series of (interconnecting) swastika tattoos encircling his abnormally thick neck. Unbeknownst to TJ, he's the same biker who had threatened Slater long ago.

"You dudes smoke weed?" the front seat passenger asks in a raspy (smoker's) voice.

"Of course," TJ boldly replies, as the front seat passenger passes him the crusty blue bong.

TJ takes a long hit, inhales, then starts to cough (uncontrollably). *I've smoked my share of weed; but this stuff seems oddly chalky, with a chlorine-like aftertaste,* he thinks to himself.

Later, a buzzed TJ notices a sign for Big Pine Key. In a panicked voice he yelps, "Hey, we passed Summerland Key. You need ta pull over and let us out!" he demands through a troubled tone.

The driver and front seat passenger share sadistic simpers, ignoring TJ's request.

"Hey, you *NEED* to stop this van *NOW!*" TJ demands.

The front seat passenger turns toward TJ and with a penetrating stare warns, "And you *NEED* to sit back and shut the *FUCK UP!*" while pointing a loaded, snub nose revolver at TJ's face.

5:17 p.m. Helen returns home. Frantic that the boys are gone, she phones Slater on his SAT phone.

Slater (still in a meeting, in downtown Ft. Lauderdale)

notices his silenced phone vibrating. He steps outside to answer. "Hello," right hand covering his open ear, to help muffle background noise, left ear pressed into the receiver.

"Slater, it's past suppertime and the boys aren't home. I specifically told TJ not to leave base. That kid needs to learn to listen," Helen hysterically rants.

"It's okay, calm down," Slater reassures. "If they aren't home by sunset, call me right away. Don't worry, I'm sure they're fine."

Long past dusk, nothing from the boys.

Slater's phone rings. He sees his home number. Now he's concerned. "Hello," he nervously answers.

"Slater, they're still not home," Helen relays, crying now.

"Okay, I'm on my way," Slater replies. He turns toward his team. "Sorry, I need to push, family emergency," he reveals, in exit.

As Slater drives southbound, he phones one of his officers. "Galen, Jensen here. Both of my boys have gone missing, which is highly abnormal. Do me a favor and contact FHP and the Sherriff's Department. Ask them to dispatch an APB and to please ignore the 24-hour *missing person* protocol."

"Yes sir!" Galen responds, as he promptly notifies State Trooper headquarters and police stations statewide.

7:18 p.m. A rookie State Trooper on routine patrol in Big Pine Key, cautiously sips a piping hot cup of watered-down (yucky tasting) coffee, as he listens to a radio alert.

"Attention all officers, be on the look-out for two boys, ages ten and fifteen. They went missing earlier today, between 3 and 5 p.m. near Boca Chica, Key. We have reason to believe they may have been abducted. Given the timeline, they could have traveled a considerable distance by now. The older boy is tall, athletic built, approximately six feet tall with medium length, brown hair. The younger boy is approximately four and a half feet tall, with dirty blonde hair. These kids belong to one of our own, so please keep an eye out for anything suspicious."

The groggy-eyed Trooper, (anxious to wind-up a double shift) makes a final pass through the belly of Big Pine. He travels brisk paced along a lonely stretch of lightless two-lane road, framed by a wall of unmanaged mangrove. The temperature's uncommonly cold for the tropics, mid-forties. He clips along then slows, having spotted a commercial van, suspiciously parked down an unpaved sideroad. He stops, then reverses his patrol car to improve his vantage. He maneuvers his hood mounted spotlight to illuminate the seemingly abandoned van. *Why would anyone park on a dirt road, in the middle of nowhere, especially on such an uncommonly cold night?* He wonders, with a bemused expression. He decides to take a closer look, as he zips his state issue, fleece lined (basic brown) windbreaker. He gulps the remainder of his diluted coffee, before abandoning the comfy confines of his warm cab, engine idling.

Outside the patrol car, the young trooper grudgingly braves the cold, as he proceeds toward the van, which appears to be surreptitiously camouflaged beneath low hanging tree limbs. He uses his flashlight to help navigate mud-free passage. The startlingly loud crackle of lightning electrifies the once-darkened skies, unleashing a barrage of grape-sized hail, sending the young trooper scurrying back to the security of his patrol car.

Inside the van. The ferocious bombardment of hail pelts the thin tin roof, rousing a fuzzy minded TJ. He lays there shirtless, mind numbingly encumbered, face down on the musty metal floor. Overcome by an insatiable urge to expunge surface grit from his parched tongue, he starts to gag, then ultimately vomits.

Inside the patrol car. The rookie trooper savors the welcoming warmth of his cozy cab, briskly rubbing his frost-bitten hands together, as he waits for the hailstorm to pass. Before long, he makes the unflappable (albeit ill-considered) decision to push off, clock out and head home to dry off.

Inside the van. TJ shivers uncontrollably. Time passes without measure, as he eventually falls asleep only to be awakened by the fierce snap of lightning and the threatening growl of reverberating thunder. With mustered determination he tests his weary eyes, in a futile attempt to survey the limits of his hostile confinement. He takes deep cleansing breaths, to help soothe his overwhelming anxiety. In a brief, moment of lucidity, he makes the hardened decision to lever an escape, as he feverishly kicks the handle-less door, to no avail. Helpless he sits, carrying a defeated expression. Thoughts of escape quickly vanish, as the side panel door abruptly opens, introducing an unwelcome wave of bone-chilling air, as the front seat passenger reaches in and grabs TJ by his hair, then drags his unresponsive body, dropping him onto the cold, damp ground.

Outside now. "Get up!" his captor yells.

Disoriented, TJ struggles to stand.

"Move it, you little prick," his captor berates, with a forceful shove.

TJ stumbles but quickly recovers.

Growing increasingly irate, his captor kicks him in the buttocks to compel his compliance, as the pair proceeds down the narrow dirt road into the eerie dark forest, toward a destination unknown.

The dirt road soon morphs into a crude, nearly indistinguishable footpath, hindered by low-lying branches and protruding thickets, making it virtually impassable by vehicle.

TJ's tempo, hastened by his captor's periodic shoves, as the persistent rain blurs his already compromised vision. Overcome with thoughts of survival he wittingly prepares for the unexpected.

Successive lightning strikes pound the ground beneath his feet, which (for a brief, moment) illuminate his hostile surroundings, while highlighting his horror.

Once again, his captor grabs him by the hair, as he directs him toward a distant candlelit lantern, obscured by the relentless rain.

As they draw nearer, TJ hears his younger brother's unfiltered screams muted by the pelting rain, soon fading to a waning whimper. Closer now, he's able to distinguish the blurred silhouette of the driver as he towers over Brandon's listless body, his boyish arms shackled to a thick tree, trousers loosely bundled around his ankles.

TJ watches in horror as the demonic driver violently penetrates his brother's exposed rectum with flesh slapping thrusts. In that instance, rage replaces fear. *"STOP IT!"* TJ screams.

The culprit halts his sexual assault as a steady stream of blood trickles down his brother's youthful thigh. The driver stands upright like a monstrous ogre amidst the Florida jungle. Steam emanates from his nakedness, exacerbated by the frigid rain. He proffers a demonic stare, followed by a sadistic simper, as if to offer a perverted prequel of what TJ was about to encounter.

TJ stands there frozen in fear, body quivering mind racing.

"Untie this little bitch!" the driver commands.

His accomplice, in a moment of lapsed judgement, releases his grip on TJ's hair leaving him unattended.

Without equivocation, TJ seizes the opportunity and dashes full sprint through the dense dark forest, as unforgiving tree limbs slap his frozen face. *No time to turn back to see if I'm being pursued,* he reminds himself with refreshing soberness, as his heart races. After several fast-paced minutes he slows his hastened gait. He takes refuge behind a large tree. Exhausted, he drops down, and listens. All seems quiet. *Best wait until daylight,* he tells himself, knowing his survival depends upon someone seeing him on the highway during daylight hours. His body begins to shake uncontrollably, as he surveys his surroundings in search of shelter from the cold. In the distance, he spots an exposed root ball, attached to the large, freshly fallen tree.

Moments later, he feverishly claws a small tunnel under the moss-covered tree and climbs inside.

Once inside, he remains motionless yet keenly alert, body trembling from cold and fear. He shoves his dirty fingers inside his mouth to help stifle the sound of his chattering teeth. Still alarmingly cold, he reaches out and scoops a patch of loose moss to cover his exposed torso, in hope of retaining body heat. Still shivering, he curls into a tight fetal position, soon warmer. Unable to sleep, he continues to listen intently for his pursuers. His heart leaps at every unidentifiable sound. He digs into his pocket to retrieve a half stick of gum which he quietly unwraps. Hand shaking, he places the gum into his parched mouth. He chews slowly, as the juices come alive, quenching his palate like a well-seasoned steak, conjuring warm memories of home and safer times as he eventually dozes off.

Sunrise. The soft morning sun filters through the exposed root ball like a signal from Heaven, gently rousing TJ from a contorted night's sleep. He feels warmer, safer, summoned to get up and start moving again, as he decides to abandon the security of his small, hand carved cave. Before emerging, he cautiously pokes his head outside of his makeshift burrow, scanning the forested floor for signs of his captors.

Once outside, he stands and stretches his rigid body. His

eyes soon acclimate to the bright sunlight as it pierces the dense forest, expelling the evil that existed the night before. He moves slowly, cautiously heading off in search of the highway home.

In the distance he hears the faint hum of vehicular traffic. He turns and heads in the direction of the noise.

Beyond the wooded limits, he notices a paved roadway. Hovering within the protective cover of the forest he crouches down, periodically glancing out toward onto the road, on the lookout for oncoming vehicles. He soon spots a red sedan rounding the bend. Instinctively he abandons the security of the forested canopy, in a futile attempt to flag them down.

They see him, quickly turn their heads and speed on past.

Discouraged, but undeterred, TJ continues to trek south-bound (gauged by the morning sun).

In time he grows more brazen, walking along the road now, hoping to capture the warming sun's rays.

A few minutes later, he hears another vehicle approaching. He quickly dashes into the forest and ducks for cover. He crouches down and peers through the branches. He sees a mid-sized car headed his way. Once again, he rushes out toward the road's edge, wildly flailing his arms. To his surprise, it's a police vehicle.

As soon as the observant officer spots TJ, he pulls off onto the shoulder of the road.

Seems the police have been looking for Brandon and TJ all night, at his parents' behest.

Turns out the prior sedan had alerted the police to his whereabouts.

As TJ runs toward the patrol car, the officer exits his vehicle to greet him with a warm, wool blanket and a reassuring smile.

Gasping, TJ hurriedly relays what had happened, triggering the reality of the situation, as an uncontrollable stream of tears wash over his weary, dirt ridden face.

Once inside the patrol car, TJ feels safe, reinvigorated.

The officer's a burly fellow with a ruddy complexion and tight yellow crew cut. He dispatches backup.

Before long, two other patrol cars arrive.

Soon all push off. TJ rides shotgun in the lead vehicle. They travel slow paced, while TJ scans the forested limits hoping to identify where they entered the woods. After several minutes, they come upon a rutted side road. "Stop!" TJ yelps.

Fresh tire tracks support TJ's recollection.

Paramedics soon join them.

All exit their respective vehicles then follow TJ into the woods. The policemen brandish pump-action shotguns while the paramedics tote emergency medical gear.

Emboldened by their presence, TJ feels invincible as he leads the charge, retracing his path, following broken branches and muddied footprints.

Ahead he sees the open clearing (now illuminated by the mid-morning sun). He pushes further, faster, his heart pounds with apprehension.

Closer now, he spots Brandon's naked, lifeless body, lying face down in a shallow mud puddle, discarded like yesterday's trash. He stops, as the policemen and paramedics push past him. TJ watches as the EMTs flip Brandon over onto his back, before connecting him to a portable resuscitator. He jumps at the disturbing sound of the electric shock paddle. Within a few ago-nizing minutes the EMTs abort their rescue efforts, pronouncing Brandon dead.

TJ stands there with a bug-eyed expression, unable to over-come his self-imposed guilt. Unwilling to comprehend that his beautiful baby brother is gone. His grief inconsolable, his pain insurmountable, his accountability irrefutable. He cannot begin to rationalize what had happened. One thing, however, is resoundingly clear, had he followed his mother's explicit order to stay on base, Brandon would still be alive, back home watching cartoons, and eating Fruit Loops.

Slater's cell phone rings. "Hello?" he anxiously answers.

"Captain Jensen... My name is Officer Bruce Evans." After a brief gap in conversation. "I'm calling to apprise you that your son TJ has been located. He's safe and unharmed. I am however, saddened to report that your younger son, Brandon did not make it, sir."

An otherwise invincible Slater drops the phone and falls to the floor, hands pressed against his forehead, as he sobs uncontrollably.

Later, Slater arrives at Big Pine Key. He approaches TJ, wrapped in a thick wool blanket, in the back of an illuminated ambulance. He embraces his surviving son. "You okay, son?" Slater asks in a quivering voice.

TJ nods, hugs his dad and weeps.

After a brief reunion, Slater's ushered over to the crime scene, as a forensic team scours the area for clues.

On an idle gurney lay Brandon's corpse, snuggly sleeved inside in a child-sized body bag. The supervising officer unzips the black bag so Slater can identify his son. Slater's a seasoned warrior who has seen it all; yet he struggles with the barbarity of what his child had endured.

The following morning. FBI agent Corbin Cole (Slater's longtime friend) and his associate Agent Douglas Reese, appear at Slater's front door.

Slater greets his old pal with an emotional embrace.

"I'm so sorry for your loss Slater," Corbin conveys in a solemn tone, mournful expression.

"Thank you… Please come in," Slater invites with an open arm gesture.

Corbin and Doug enter, then follow Slater down the hallway toward his study.

On the back porch, Corbin observes an understandably distraught Helen, carrying a somber expression.

"I apologize; but Helen's simply unable to participate today. As you can imagine this has been incredibly hard on her," Slater explains, as they step inside his study.

"Of course," Corbin compassionately replies.

"TJ," Slater calls out.

TJ soon joins them in the study.

"T, this is my longtime friend Corbin Cole and his associate Doug Reese. They're with the FBI. They have a few more questions for you son."

Corbin stands and shakes TJ's hand. "Hello, TJ."

"Hello." TJ shyly replies.

Everyone sits.

"I know you've been through a lot, and I know the sheriff's department has already interviewed you; but I just need to ask a few more questions, if you don't mind."

Head down. TJ nods, no words.

"Did you know your assailants TJ, or have you ever seen them before?"

"No. Never." TJ categorically replies.

"Can you describe them and their vehicle?

TJ pauses, then proceeds, "The driver was a really big, bald guy with a buncha tattoos. The passenger was tall too, but skinny with a long ponytail. Their van was empty inside and the door handle was missing," he adds.

"Did you witness the assault on your brother?"

TJ nods affirmatively, then begins to cry.

Corbin pauses then concludes. "I think we have all we need. I'm so sorry that you had to go through this horrible, tragedy son."

TJ exits the room.

Slater closes the door behind him.

"What are your thoughts, Corbin?" Slater inquires, as he retakes his seat.

"Well. What's most disconcerting is that this incident occurred at the precise location of the recent Cartel blood-bath, which leads us to believe this may have been retaliatory in nature."

"Retaliatory?" Slater questions, in a befuddled tone, trailed by a puzzled gaze.

"To your knowledge was the Cartel/biker massacre sanctioned as a covert mission?" Corbin boldly inquires.

"As you can appreciate, I'm not at liberty to discuss classified missions, particularly covert assignments. That said, to my knowledge, the Cartel/biker massacre was likely a rogue attack. In fact, CSI agent Richards told me that he suspected a turf war between rival factions," Slater adds. "Who knows, maybe the Cartel blames us. I can't speak to that."

"My immediate concern is for your safety and the safety of your family. We're not sure this ends here. With your permission I'd like to dispatch a security team to maintain 24/7 surveillance."

"I appreciate the offer; but we'll be safe within base limits," Slater assures.

CHAPTER 23

CHRISTMAS NEVER CAME to the Jensen household that year. It skipped right on by, like any other day. Their Christmas tree remained unlit, presents unopened and the holiday spirit, hopelessly lost.

Slater took to task handling Brandon's funeral arrangements. At Brandon's funeral, it was truly gut wrenching to witness Brandon's school friends, ever so curious as they stare down into Brandon's small casket. It's disheartening to bury someone so young. They laid Brandon to rest in the Base cemetery. It was unsettling to see the dates of his short life, chiseled into his shiny, grey granite headstone. Slater remains brave for both Helen and TJ; but suffers in silence.

Before Brandon's body is even cold in the ground, Slater's summoned on assignment. Had he had an ordinary job, he would be home on grievance leave; but he was a warrior, and a warrior must always be battle ready.

Helen had been a stranger to sleep for days. In Slater's absence she (a self-proclaimed teetotaler) sought refuge in cheap Scotch and unbranded Brandy. Inside the living room she sits, lights off, staring out the front bay window into a dark, empty night. TJ knows deep in his soul that he's to blame. It was a terrible burden to bear and at his young age even harder. It was particularly difficult to be home, alone with his mom and her grief-stricken wrath.

Riddled with self-imposed guilt, TJ sheepishly approaches his embittered stepmom in a futile attempt to pierce her shroud of pain, in hope of alleviating, or at least neutralizing the tension that existed between them.

He gently rests his hand atop her tired shoulders.

Helen swiftly rebuffs his gesture with a stiff shrug. She swivels in her seat to face him, contorting her soft facial features into a hateful scowl. Irate, "How dare you!" she scolds in a soft; but nonetheless enraged tone. "You took my son from me… My baby boy," she lashes out, through a pain stricken, expression. "You ignored my explicit instructions to stay on base and worse yet, you made no effort to help your brother. Instead, you ran like a spineless coward," she gruffly concludes.

Understandably taken aback, TJ gasps. As bad as he feels he's stunned by her unrestrained reaction. No doubt he'd been reckless with Brandon's safety, albeit unwittingly; but it was never his intention to abandon his brother and run like a coward. In his eyes, he did everything possible to seek help. Nonetheless, her words resonated with him, compounding his inescapable guilt. His brother had been in his charge and his negligence had subjected him to suffer an insidious rape and senseless murder.

Helen's vengeful eyes bore right through him. "You're dead to me… unalterably dead!" she reiterates as she exits the room in ruthless contempt.

Helen's unscripted words are indelibly etched in TJ's adolescent mind. Their relationship irreparable.

It is New Year's Eve morning. The day Helen left that is. TJ watches through his bedroom dormer as the base shuttle pulls up out front of their home shortly before dawn, which in and unto itself was glaringly odd.

He abandons his warm bed, opens his bedroom door and watches as Helen juggles two sizable suitcases and a shouldered purse, down their circular stairwell, absent a final farewell. Under normal circumstances he would have tried to intercept her departure, had his prior attempt to console her pain not been so angrily rebutted. He knew deep down in the bowels of his being that she was right. *I understand her leaving a wretch like me, but why my dad? He certainly didn't deserve to lose his soulmate. Especially on the heels of Brandon's death. After all, he did nothing wrong. For God's sake, he was a decorated hero, worthy of her love and support,* TJ thinks to himself.

Later. "Helen… I'm home," Slater calls out in an embellished gleeful tone, to help lighten Helen's inescapably somber mood.

Desperately ashamed, TJ intercepts his dad's unanswered calls. "Dad," TJ mutters softly. "Mom's gone," he informs, absent further explanation.

Oddly, TJ's words resonated with his father. Slater seemed to understand. Suffice it to say, Slater was surprisingly, unsurprised. He stood there for a moment, before heading off to shower and change, gently closing the bedroom door behind him.

Before long, Slater reemerges seemingly unaffected, markedly refreshed and notably reinvigorated. "Let's grab a couple burgers at McDonalds," (TJ's favorite, haunt) Slater suggests with a bold sense of newness in his tone. Strangely, Slater never mentions Helen again. It was almost eerie, as though she never existed. Bizarre to think that someone he loved no longer existed in his mind or his heart. Stranger yet, how he could fully absolve

TJ and continue to love him and watch over him as if he were an innocent participant.

Sadly, they never heard from Helen again, EVER! Had she passed, that would have been awful; but at least they would have had closure, a gravesite at the cemetery to visit. This was different, more difficult to accept for TJ anyway. She simply left, vanished. Her whereabouts would forever remain a mystery. In the final analysis, TJ accepts the hardened fact that he and he alone, was responsible for the totality of this tragedy which ultimately fragmented their family and for that reason, it would be his destiny to shoulder this burden.

CHAPTER 24

SUMMERTIME. SIX MONTHS following Helen's unexpected departure, Slater elects early retirement. There's no formal ceremony customary for retiring officers, especially distinguished ones like Slater. Curiously, it was just over, done. His uniforms readily discarded, exchanged for civilian attire which includes an awful assortment of brightly colored, Hawaiian shirts.

Slater, unbeknownst to TJ, purchased a small beachfront bungalow in a quiet, virtually unspoiled spot, known as Sombrero Key (a modest drive north of base). Anxious to show TJ their new casa, the pair travel north.

After a short scenic drive, Slater slows then turns onto an elongated sugar sand driveway (lined by curvaceous coconut palms). At the end of the narrow drive sets a charming, quintessential cottage. The cottage is painted *happy* yellow, which helps to disguise its grave state of ill repair. The old roof is authentic (thigh rolled) red-clay, barrel tile. More than a handful are broken, the balance concealed beneath a carpet of green moss. Regardless of the gross state of neglect, the location is undeniably idyllic. Needless-to-say TJ is beyond enamored by the new place; but cannot help but feel underserving of such goodness.

Slater's excitement is contagious. His demeanor, refreshingly child-like, revealing a seldom seen lighthearted side.

TJ's spirits soon lift in tandem.

Slater waves him outback onto an *oh so* tropical, pecky cypress porch, a mere tumble to the beach. The exterior walls are adorned with a splattering of colorful seashells and sporadically placed, sundried starfish. They stand side by side, in unspoken awe as the turquoise waters gently caress the sugar sand shoreline. "This is the most amazing place I ever saw," TJ blurts... "Dad, can we afford a place like this?" TJ asks with buoyant eyes.

"Well, it will take most of my pension; but the short answer is yes," Slater proudly proclaims with a playful muff of TJ's bushy hair.

"What happens if there's a big storm or a hurricane with humungous waves?" TJ asks.

"That's what makes this place so special," Slater notes as he points. "We're protected by that coral jetty over there."

"What's a jetty?'

"They're generally coral formations, designed to protect the beach and beachfront residents from bad storms," Slater explains.

By week's end, father and son take occupancy. Wasting no time, they set out to tackle the long overdue repairs. Slater's responsible for the exterior, while TJ handles the interior.

TJ's immediate task involves ripping up the old musty carpeting and dragging it curbside, for trash pickup. Afterwards, he methodically preps the walls for painting, a more tenuous task than he initially thought. The interior walls of the cottage reveal thick layers of authentic, old-world plaster which absorbs fresh paint like a bone-dry sponge. After several arm breaking coats, the long neglected interior springs to life with a confluence of tropical colors, as accented by subtle-tone terrazzo floors which span the interconnecting living areas. TJ's particularly fond of the sunken family room, which centers on a large coral fireplace, framed by antique white walls. The kitchen however is differentiated by wide plank, Dade County yellow pine, floors.

The exterior windows are old, salt encrusted, hand cranked jalousies. Most are inoperative, rusted or camouflaged beneath invasive vines.

Generally, speaking the cottage was fundamentally uninhabitable. Renovating the old place however, turned out to be much more than a self-repair project. It evolved into a father and son bonding experience. After all, this was the first home they ever owned.

Slater and TJ make routine trips to the local hardware store, periodically trekking further north to Miami to get some of the bigger building supplies. They work tirelessly, day after day, side by side, wielding hammer and saw from sunup to sunset, all summer long.

TJ's especially fond of lunchtime, when he and his dad sit out on the coral jetty, ravaging atypically thick deli sandwiches while sharing meaningful conversation.

Slater, an old salty at heart, savors the sea.

Unfortunately, TJ's happiness comes at a price. His joy forever burdened with guilt. Had it not been for him, his stepmom and brother would be here too, to share in all this goodness. Nearly every day he thinks about Brandon and how he always looked up to TJ and trusted him. TJ also laments about his stepmom's rash, seemingly inexplicable exodus.

"I don't think I'm worthy of my name," TJ blurts, between bites.

"Why?" Slater probes after swallowing a mouthful of roast beef.

"I certainly wasn't *God of the forest* the night I left Brandon in the woods to die," TJ emotionally purges.

Slater pauses and with a compassionate expression adds, "You were a young boy, T. Don't be so hard on yourself. There was nothing you could have done. Going for help was the appropriate response," he reassures.

Head down, TJ counters, "I should have been braver. I should've fought to save my brother."

"Against two grown men?" Slater challenges. "That would not have ended well! Had you done that I would have lost both of my sons. You had no choice, T!" Slater rebuts.

TJ feels better now. His dad's words are cathartically freeing. He knows his dad honors the warrior's code which views death as an inevitable part of life. Moreover, his dad never blamed him because of that fatalistic belief. TJ can only speculate that his dad didn't want to sacrifice two sons over the loss of one. From where TJ stood, Slater was a uniquely forgiving father who loved him unconditionally with undying devotion.

After a modest pause, TJ redirects the conversation. "Dad weren't you an undefeated fighting champion or something?"

Slater chuckles then modestly clarifies, "I suppose I won a couple base tournaments; but I'm certainly no champion. Make no mistake about it, I took my share of beatdowns along the way," he humbly concedes. He pauses. "Many years ago, during a routine training session, a cocky new recruit challenged me to a bare-knuckle brawl." Slater reminisces with observable regret.

"What'd you do?"

"I ignored protocol and foolishly accepted. We stood toe to toe for more than fifteen minutes until he finished me with a *light's out*, uppercut. I was out cold!" Slater reveals.

"Were you hurt?"

"Only my ego!" Slater confesses, flushed face. "I learned an invaluable lesson that day."

"What was that?" TJ probes.

"There's always a tougher puppy in the pound," Slater shares.

"Ironically, the man that kicked my butt that day was my FBI pal Corbin. He's truly one of the few people I thoroughly trust. "

At the close of summer, the old place sprang back to life. It was revitalized, inspiring and most importantly, theirs. Above the coral fireplace mantel, hangs the Viking sword that had been handed down through multiple generations. A symbol of their Nordic heritage. "One day that sword will be yours, T, and one day you'll pass it on to your son," Slater proudly proclaims, with a paternal smile and a one arm hug.

"You ever use the sword?"

"No." Slater responds with a chuckle. "It's for inspirational purposes."

"Huh?"

"When I was a little boy, probably five or six, I got a bike for Christmas. I was riding it around the block when the neighborhood bully pushed me off and took it."

"What did you do?"

"I ran home crying. My dad asked me what happened, so I told him. My granddad overheard the conversation and chimed in. He pointed to that sword and said, "Our ancestors lived and died by the sword. So, stop your crying and go get your bike back," he staunchly conveyed in a firm tone.

"What did you do?"

"I went and got my bike back!" Slater replies with a reminiscent smile.

CHAPTER 25

THAT FALL, TJ enrolls in the local high school with barely a dozen students per class. An ever-amiable TJ, forges friendships fast.

Living off base turned out to be a welcomed surprise. If TJ and his new pals weren't surfing post storm waves, they were fishing the still water flats or freediving the bountiful reefs. Like his former schoolmates, most of his new pals were cool, non-confrontational and non-judgmental kids. Not a single overachiever amongst them. TJ found most of his classmates to be uniquely humble, and enviably content. He thirsted for contentment, a seemingly irretrievable void in his life. TJ, unlike most of his peers, was ambitious. Deep down, he had an inextinguishable fire in his belly. He felt as if he had something to prove, most likely to himself.

TJ's undisputed best friend was a mellow fellow named Dillon, aptly nicknamed *Chillin Dillon*. By all accounts, Dillon's a template for the rest of TJ's pals. He's a tall, lanky sort, with broad shoulders, content smile, bronzed skin, bushy blonde hair and hopeless eyes. TJ and Dillon are kindred spirits. They're virtually inseparable. Dillon, an only child, considers TJ the brother he never had. And TJ (at some level) views Dillon as a replacement for the brother he lost.

Dillon's on deck to inherit his family's languishing, offshore fishing business, if it can hang on that long. In recent years, the fishing industry had experienced some dramatic setbacks, more anglers chasing fewer fish.

It's the summer after TJ's sophomore year of high school.

"T, I'd like you to find a part-time job this summer," Slater casually notes. "It's important to understand the value of a dollar," he adds.

"Sure," TJ readily replies in an obliging tone.

Unlike TJ, Dillon didn't have to look for summer work. Every summer he worked with his dad. He did it all, from hoisting commercial fishing nets at sea, to deckhand duty on evening fishing charters. Dockside, he'd work for tips, fileting fish for charter guests, as they watch in wonderment, as Dillon wields his filet knife with surgical precision.

In the Keys, summer jobs were scarce, good summer jobs virtually non-existent. Local *help wanted* ads include a fishing boat first mate, a dive boat crewman, a flat's boat guide, a boat rental coordinator, several hotel bellhops and last, a busboy position at a local restaurant, called the *Beach Bum.*

Absent the necessary skillsets to secure more meaningful employment, TJ eagerly accepts (when presented with) the busboy position, at the *Beach Bum.*

The owner/operator of the *Beach Bum* is a likable chap named Ernie, who hails from Belize. At six years of age, Ernie lost his left forearm to a shark attack in three feet of water. Had it not been for his father's quick reaction and paternal instinct, the shark would have surely pulled him out to sea.

Story told, Ernie's dad literally leaped on top of the ten-foot bull shark and dug his fingers into the shark's eyes, until he released Ernie.

After that near fatal incident, their family decided to move stateside.

As a teen, Ernie also worked at the *Beach Bum*, essentially doing TJ's job for his then boss, Clem Boggs.

After Clem's unexpected passing, his son, Clem Junior inherited the business. Unfortunately, Junior was nothing like his hardworking father. Instead, he was a raging alcoholic, compulsive gambler, and notorious skirt-chasing womanizer.

Rumors soon circulated that the *Beach Bum* was indebted to the hilt. Seems Clem, Jr. financed the business, then refinanced the real estate with another bank, took all the cash and ran off to Aruba with Ernie's fiancé, Delores.

The banks subsequently foreclosed, repossessing the real estate, while shutting down the business.

Ernie, a trusted, longtime *Beach Bum* employee, had the gumption to meet with both banks. He ultimately restructured the loans, which afforded him the time to turn the business around.

Today, Ernie's the proud owner of the *Beach Bum*. In the final analysis, he may have lost a forearm and a two-timing fiancé; but in the end, he gained a thriving business and a well-deserved reputation, as a highly respected local entrepreneur.

Ernie scheduled TJ for a full day's shift (11 a.m. to 11 p.m.), with a handful of mini breaks in-between.

10:30 a.m. TJ arrives early (as instructed) for a pre-lunch orientation.

Ernie greets him at the hostess stand.

"You ready, big fellow?" Ernie asks, sporting a welcoming grin.

"Yes, sir," TJ respectfully replies with a soft smile, trying desperately to avoid staring at Ernie's missing forearm.

They soon transition toward the main dining area, lights off, tables empty.

"Here's the lowdown," Ernie narrates. "We have 225 seats, a full bar and a billiard area." He turns toward TJ and emphasizes. "In the dining area, our goal is simple, turn tables. Every hour, I want to see a new butt in every seat. Although we make good money selling food, our real profit comes from pouring liquor. Way *MO* money," Ernie funs with a contagious smile. Ernie points toward the pool tables. "Different than the dining area, we encourage our bar patrons to linger, hence the rationale for the pool tables. Remember linger longer, drink more," he paraphrases with a confirming gaze, right hand resting atop TJ's left shoulder. "In short, your job is to make sure the tables in the dining area get bussed quickly... Fair enough?" Ernie asks.

"Fair enough," TJ repeats, with an affirming nod.

Ernie then escorts TJ back into the kitchen. "This is where we make magic!" Ernie boasts.

"Magic my ass," the cynical head chef teases.

The assistant cooks share a spontaneous laugh.

"Gang, this is TJ, he's our new busboy," Ernie introduces, his right (full) arm slung around TJ's shoulder, as his left limb dangles beneath his rolled shirt sleeve.

The kitchen crew (preoccupied with lunch prep) offer half-hearted smiles.

Suffice it to say, TJ's first day was unexpectedly hectic.

"TJ! Tables fourteen and twenty-two need bussing, *ASAP*," Kendra, a lifelong employee snaps in a perturbed tone, flanked by a frustrated shake of her leathered face.

TJ hurriedly responds, toting his large grey bus tray from table to table, soon in sync with the rhythm of the restaurant.

Eventually, TJ's pals would stop by to play pool, while TJ works.

On occasion, Ernie would turn a blind eye and allow TJ and his buddies to have a brew or two (once TJ finished his shift of course). Ernie knew the boys lived a short walk down the beach, so he'd periodically relax the rules.

Before long, it became a Friday night ritual, for TJ and his friends to hang out and drink up. On rare occasions, TJ would overindulge and swagger on home, pop a breath mint and head to bed.

One night, TJ and (his best bud) Dillon, occupy a small table in the poolroom (after TJ's shift) to down some drafts while munching on a basket of over-fried conch fritters. They're minding their own business, just shooting the shit, when a few (unfamiliar) beer-bellied bullies, decide to fuck with them.

"You ladies on a date?" One of the four foreigners goads (referring to the boys' long hair), loud enough for other patrons to overhear.

TJ and Dillon ignore their inebriated taunts until one of the brash bruisers, hustles over and commandeers the stool next to Dillon. He reaches out and starts to stroke Dillon's hair with his large, callused paw, while his comrades roar from a nearby table.

"You sure got a pretty hairdo sweetheart," he presses.

His pals egg him on with raised beer mugs.

A nervous Dillon tries to reposition his stool to no avail.

TJ on the other hand is steaming mad, yet mindful that the odds are strongly stacked against them. He wisely simmers down.

The four are formidable, burly chested chaps, with big beefy arms.

The resident bully continues his relentless quest to humiliate Dillon.

Finally fed up, Dillion stands to confront his antagonist, who effortlessly shoves Dillon, thrusting him into a neighboring table.

Infuriated, TJ instinctively steps between them. "Enough, you fuckin asshole!" TJ snaps, scowling expression, literally nose to nose with their adversary.

The big bully offers a smartass-smirk, followed by a lights-out punch, dropping a comparatively smaller TJ to the floor.

Pat (the big boned bouncer) leaps over the bar, "Back off, asshole!" he commands, through a threatening glare.

The cocky culprit raises his husky arms in mock surrender, as he casually saunters back toward his entourage, with a departing chuckle.

Brenda, the busty barmaid, phones Slater.

By the time TJ opens his eyes, Slater's already there. "You okay, son?" Slater confirms, in a concerned tone.

"Yeah," a groggy TJ replies, vision blurred, ears ringing, nose bleeding.

Ernie kneels next to TJ, pressing a wet bar towel to his battered nose.

Slater stands and calmly asks, "Who did this?" while scanning the crowded bar.

"Those four over there," Dillon interjects, pointing with a sideward nod.

Slater looks and sees the four fools playing pool, seemingly unaware or unconcerned about his summoned presence.

"The ones playing pool?" Slater confirms.

"Yeah," Dillon reaffirms.

Ernie and Dillon help TJ up and into a seat.

Without a moment's hesitation, Slater confronts the four-some. He snatches their cue ball from play, disrupting their game but gaining their attention. "Which one of you imbeciles thinks it's okay to strike a minor?" Slater inquires, in a thunderbolt tone.

The cocky culprit saunters over toward Slater, pool cue in his clutch. "And who the *FUCK's* askin?" he demands, in a confrontational demeanor.

"I'm his father!" Slater reveals through an unflinching stare.

The fat-faced culprit turns toward his crew, then back toward Slater. "Unfortunately, *DADDY*, yer boy was being a disrespectful little shit, so I gave em a lesson in manners."

Once again, his cohorts unify in laughter, this time at Slater's expense.

"At the moment, I happen to be in the middle of a game of pool, so unless you got somethin else to say you best be on your way, sweetheart," he spews, followed by a condescending, shooing gesture with the tip of his cue stick. The brazen bully leans in, inches from Slater's face. "I suggest you return the cue ball and get the *FUCK* outta my face; before I put a hurtin on your old ass!" he threatens, with a psychotic smile.

Slater smiles, "Unfortunately, you leave me no choice," he proffers, through a deadeye stare, and an even-keel tone. "Why don't you and your girlfriends meet me out back, so we can finish this conversation," he challenges as he nonchalantly rolls the cue ball back onto the green felt tabletop, before heading out back.

Within minutes the bar patrons spill outside onto beach like ants on a lollipop.

Inside the bar, the bullies just stand there, as dumbfounded expressions consume their once brazen faces. They share sobering glances, perplexed how one would dare challenge four. They soon muster their booze-inspired courage, set their pool cues to rest and reluctantly accept Slater's challenge.

The bullies' countenances flatten as they amble outside, as

the beachside crowd chants Slater's name, while Ernie and Pat, push through the shoulder-to-shoulder crowd.

Ernie clutches a thick wood bat, boasting its share of battle scars, while Pat stands ready with wild-eyes and curled fists, ready to back Slater up.

Slater on the other hand is surprisingly relaxed, as he casually removes his topsiders, then methodically cuffs his khaki trousers, before rolling up his denim shirtsleeves, exposing his bulging forearms.

His adversaries quickly coalesce, a seemingly safe distance from Slater's unflinching post.

"Who wants to swallow some teeth?" Slater threatens in a fiery tone, as he brazenly advances in unfettered strides toward his unwitting opponents.

One might rightfully wonder why Slater (in-light of the daunting odds) seems so confident. But there was something about his demeanor that suggested a hidden fury, an unspoken firestorm that was about to be unleashed.

Without warning, the biggest of the bunch rushes straight into Slater's iron fist, as he flattens his first foe.

Slater resumes his advance.

The remaining three cling to their gang inspired courage, as they orchestrate an ensemble attack.

Slater *LEAPS* airborne, torquing his body clockwise like a twisting tornado, hammering his foot into the side of the second combatant's head, dropping him to the ground like a sack of rocks.

Without missing a beat, Slater pivots toward the third thug and literally neutralizes his attack with a series of lightning fast, blood splattering blows to his fat face.

He then turns his attention to his fourth and final adversary, as he delivers a bullet fast snap kick to his unprotected crotch, dropping him to his knees in groan.

In a masterful display of martial arts and unbridled ferocity, Slater handily picks off his unwitting opponents. Within a minute or two, maybe three, all four are sucking sand, as Slater calmly brushes off his trousers, collects his shoes and walks off into the night, like an avenging angel.

The crowd bursts into cheer, celebrating Slater's decisive victory.

"Drinks are on me!" Ernie declares, as the Reggae band resumes.

TJ lingers back, relishing his dad's impressive conquest, as the battered bullies quietly disperse in hope of avoiding further humiliation.

The red morning sun peers above the distant horizon, soon penetrating the limits of TJ's beachfront bedroom.

Later, TJ heads outback to join his dad (already positioned on the rear porch), savoring a mug of freshly brewed coffee.

Barely awake, TJ plops down into the rocker next to his dad.

Slater's uncharacteristically quiet, savoring the serenity of the moment as the warm morning sun readies a new day.

"You mad?" TJ timidly asks.

Slater (deliberately avoiding eye contact) takes a long, purposeful sip and replies, "Nope."

"Then why are you being so quiet?" TJ inquires, with a wondering expression.

Slater takes another long sip then changes lanes. "I knew the drinking would catch up to you one day, just didn't know when," he follows with a simper of disappointment in his otherwise tolerant tone, still staring out toward the calm ocean.

After a brief gap in conversation, TJ questions, "You knew

I was drinking?" trailed by a perplexed expression; framed by surprised eyes.

"You've been drinking since last summer, June 6th to be precise. Your pupils were a dead giveaway. Mints were my second clue. You always hated mints," Slater calmly adds. "Don't forget, I was once a teenager too, T," he glibly concludes.

"How come you never said anything?"

"I suppose some lessons are best learned through experience, good or bad." An awkward silence ensues.

"You really kicked butt last night, Dad!" TJ says, beaming with a wide, prideful smile.

Slater's slow to respond. He doesn't share TJ's enthusiasm. "Unfortunately, T, there's never a winner in a fight. No doubt those men were drunken bullies and clearly no one should ever strike a minor. That said, I should not have allowed that to escalate into a physical confrontation. Clearly, I errored... In retrospect, I should have summoned the police," he finishes in a solemn tone, anchored by a finishing sip.

"Well. I'm proud of you, anyway," TJ adds, hesitates, then asks. "Dad... could you give me a refresher course on fighting? I think I still remember most of the basics; but it would be kinda cool to learn more."

"You mean a refresher course on how to *defend* yourself?" Slater clarifies, with a slow twist of his head.

"Yeah, that's what I meant," TJ qualifies, in a hurried, unconvincing reply.

Slater continues to rock, as he ponders TJ's request.

The following morning, Slater rustles TJ from sound slumber. "Hey, landlubber, let's hit the beach. Last one wet washes-dishes tonight," Slater goads.

TJ hops out of bed, tosses on a pair of faded swim trunks

and races (full canter) through the rear porch door, leaping over the short flight of weathered steps, onto the piping hot sand and into the soothing sea.

Slater eclipses TJ's ocean-entry by a stretched stride, as they swim away from shore, stroke for stroke, until reaching a respectable depth determined by a notable drop in surf temperature, confirmed by their inability to touch bottom.

From there, the pair swims south, away from the jetty, parallel to the shoreline, for what seems to be a half mile, maybe more.

TJ's young arms soon tire, as he gradually veers shoreward with Slater hot on his heels.

Beachside, a winded TJ walks homeward, hands rest atop his hips, head tilted upward, thirsting for a sip of oxygen.

"Race you back?" Slater coaxes.

An utterly fatigued, yet equally undeterred TJ, hits the sand in hot pursuit, soon passing his steady paced dad.

Moments later, he hears the disheartening sound of Slater's feet, slapping the thin layer of receding surf, as he gamely passes TJ's struggling stride.

TJ grunts and hastens his tempo, without gain.

After an exhaustive dash, they arrive back at the cottage.

Slater, hardly winded, turns toward TJ. "Okay, son, let's see what you remember?" he nudges.

Breathless, TJ raises his right index finger, motioning for a moment.

Slater affords TJ time to recover, as he assumes a sideward stance, "Come on, son, no *time outs* on the battlefield," Slater challenges.

TJ's heart is racing like an unseasoned thoroughbred in the final furlong as he begrudgingly steps forward, closing the gap between he and his dad.

Slater (utilizing his elongated reach) playfully slaps the top of TJ's head, shadowed by a haunting laugh. "Too slow, T," Slater taunts.

To humor his father, TJ raises his hands and tries (unsuccessfully) to mount a fitting defense; as each counter strike is easily defended by Slater's ever-impressive skillset.

Having been flipped onto his back more times than he cares to count and with a swim trunk full of sticky sand, TJ ultimately succumbs to a renewed respect for his dad's incomparable talents, and more importantly, a renewed interest in advancing his mixed martial arts training.

What started out as a benign square off in the sand, developed into an invaluable father and son bonding experience and (more importantly) a personalized training regime, from which TJ ultimately emerges as a battle-ready warrior.

Aside from the obvious self-defense strategies, TJ's training sessions offered him an indescribable sense of spirituality, something he truly craved. At some deeper level, beyond simply bonding, TJ was convinced that his dad wanted to be certain that he was properly equipped to physically defend himself, in the unlikely event of another life-threatening situation, particularly if Slater wasn't around to intercede.

Toward the end of TJ's junior year of high school, he starts to focus on college. It is about that time, that he detects a subtle change in his dad's otherwise steadfast demeanor. He wonders if his dad is dreading the day that he will head off to college. He's concerned about him being alone, living a life of solitude. He fears his departure might compound his father's sense of loss. Upon further reflection, TJ rationalizes that he's probably underestimating his dad's adaptability. After all, his father was a decorated Navy SEAL Captain. He's seen it all, and then some.

He reminds himself that his dad (unlike most Navy fathers) encouraged him to go to college, as opposed to a stint in the Navy or even the Naval Academy. Ultimately, TJ decides upon a win/win solution, opting not to venture far from home, so he applies for admission to University of Miami (UM) where he's readily accepted. He decides to live on campus and commute home on weekends.

CHAPTER 26

SUNDAY MORNING, THE day TJ's scheduled to leave for college. It's an undeniably momentous occasion, though tempered with regret. TJ would be leaving his comfort zone and his dad. He's about to embark upon his first tangible step toward becoming an independent, self-reliant, adult. Earning a college degree is an integral part of that plan and his future. Understandably conflicted, he lingers in bed. Emotions swarm as he remises about his oceanfront adolescence. He realizes how truly blessed he's been, having lived here in this tropical oasis with a loving father by his side, guiding him every step of the way. His eagerness to head off to college is (suffice it to say), bittersweet. His thoughts soon intercepted by a cool ocean breeze, funneling through his open bedroom window. In the background he hears the soothing sound of ocean waves as they gently lap onto the sandy shore, occasionally interrupted by seabirds squawking. He smiles fondly, savoring these remaining moments, as he reluctantly emerges from his boyhood bed. He meanders over toward his beachfront window. He sits and stares out toward the limitless sea, as the fiery morning sun shimmers atop the distant horizon. He turns to see a set of mismatched suitcases, positioned inside his narrow doorway. He laughs to himself, realizing that his dad must have retrieved them from their shed earlier that morning. Instead of using luggage, TJ opts for a makeshift sailor's duffle, as he clumsily stuffs his pillowcase with fresh clothes before hoisting it over his broad shoulder.

Downstairs, Slater's seated at the kitchen table, his strong hands cradle his bright yellow, (Jacuzzi sized) coffee mug. A mug TJ had crafted for Father's Day, in elementary school.

TJ drops his overstuffed pillowcase onto the aged, yellow-pine floor, then takes the seat across from his dad. He wastes no time devouring the spicy Spanish omelet that Slater had handily prepared.

Slater tries to disguise his sorrowful eyes behind yesterday's newspaper. "You sure you want to go alone today?" he asks, through a shallow tone.

"Dad, stop worrying, it's hardly a two-hour drive. I'll be fine. You know me, I'm a homebody, I'll probably come home every weekend," TJ reassures.

Slater lowers his paper, "Son, this is your time. Enjoy every moment of it and for God's sake don't worry about coming back to visit your old man on weekends. I'm a big boy. Hell, I'm looking forward to having this place to myself," he jests.

They share a soothing chuckle.

Leaving is hard on TJ, harder than he had imagined. He forces a smile, realizing more than ever, how remarkably selfless his dad is.

Later, TJ and Slater stand out front, beneath the canopy of the majestic tropical trees which frame their serpentine drive, as an invigorating sea breeze (laden with a salty scent) bids, TJ *bon voyage.*

TJ hurls his plump pillowcase into the truck bed of his aged turquoise and white, Ford, F-150 pick-up. He pauses, turns back toward his dad and says, "Thank you, Dad. Thank you for being such an amazing role model."

"You made it easy, T... Best job I ever had," Slater replies with wet eyes.

TJ returns a somber smile.

Slater steps forward and embraces his son with a long, heartfelt hug.

TJ opens his squeaky driver side door and climbs up and into the cab of his truck. "See you soon, Dad," he calls out through the open passenger window.

Slater waves as TJ drives off, soon out of sight, eyes glisten with pride.

Hours later, TJ arrives at UM. Campus is bustling with a sense of newness. Fresh faced freshmen swarm the streets, as TJ cautiously maneuvers around double-parked vehicles, as proud parents help their kids unload their belongings. Arriving students seem gleeful, excited, though tempered by a subtle hint of apprehension. TJ regrets his decision to come alone, now wishing his dad had accompanied him. *Too late for that now,* he quickly concludes.

After a couple of lost laps around campus, TJ eventually stumbles upon his designated dorm, grabs his pillowcase and heads inside to claim his room assignment.

Inside the dorm room. TJ's roommate's already there, thumbing through a sports magazine, in the coveted upper bunk.

TJ extends his hand, "Hey, I'm TJ."

His roommate leans toward him. "Enrique," he greets, with a thick Spanish accent. Enrique looks more like a young Latin movie-star, than an incoming freshman. Thick jet-black hair, square jaw, perfect white smile, not to take anything away from TJ's handsomeness.

His silk shirt probably costs more than my truck, TJ thinks to himself. "Where're you from?" TJ asks.

"Peru," Enrique readily replies, as he slides down from the upper bunk, now standing next to TJ.

"How bout you?" Enrique fires back.

"Florida Keys, just south of Miami," TJ responds, while unpacking his limited belongings.

"Oh yeah, never been there, but hear it's a beautiful spot."

The two have an instantaneous connection and quickly become fast friends.

Eventually, Enrique reveals that he hails from an opulent Peruvian family. Enrique explains that his father is a highly respected cattle rancher who owns and operates thousands of acres throughout the Peruvian countryside.

It doesn't take long for TJ to realize that Enrique has an incorrigible wild side, with an insatiable urge to push the limits, with a *Rules are made to be broken* mantra.

Mid-semester. A nondescript weekday. TJ's rides shotgun in Enrique's Porsche 911, top dropped, recklessly racing through the congested streets of downtown Miami, swerving between cars like a slalom course competitor.

"T!" Enrique hollers out, above the finely tuned engine's roar. "Grab that Wendy's bag on the back floor," he instructs, eyes concealed behind black Gucci sunglasses, focused on the road ahead as they clip along, traveling well beyond posted speed limits.

TJ turns, sees, grabs then passes the Wendy's bag over to Enrique, as he maneuvers a hand over hand, left turn across oncoming traffic, soon circling the Wendy's building, callously intercepting cars in queue as he drives up to the pickup window.

Enrique hands the crumpled Wendy's bag to the (cute)

attendant. "I was here about an hour ago, to get food for my grandparents and you guys forgot their burgers," he fabricates, punctuated by a flirtatious glance.

"Oh, my goodness! I'm so sorry," the overtly obliging cashier profusely apologizes. "What was on their burgers?" she politely asks, prepared to enter the corrective order onto her computer screen.

"Both had pickles and mustard no onions," Enrique recites. "They hate onions!" he emphasizes.

"Was that it?" she asks, as if willing to supplement Enrique's phantom order.

"Oh yeah. They also forgot two orders of fries and two milkshakes, chocolate!" Enrique improvises with a devilish smirk.

In no time at all, the pleasant cashier willingly hands the completed order over to Enrique.

"Thank you," Enrique says with a wide smile, as he drives off.

Seconds later, Enrique bursts into laughter, as he merges back onto the road, tossing a concessionary meal to TJ (his unwitting accomplice). "I love this fuckin country… Americans are so fuckin gullible," Enrique slips.

Stunned by Enrique's outlandish remark, TJ quietly ponders the preposterous context of Enrique's disparaging comment.

That weekend, 2 a.m., on their way home from a popular downtown Miami nightclub, TJ and Enrique drive past the Dade County Courthouse.

A tipsy Enrique slows, reverses, then parks across the street, top down. "So that's where they lock up the hombres?" he rhetorically mocks in a somewhat sarcastic, debatably defiant tone.

They sit for a bit. Enrique (seemingly fixated) points. "You see those bushes up there?" he slurs, referring to two potted plants that bookend the courthouse entry.

TJ turns to look. "At the top of the steps?" he asks, in a perplexed tone.

"Yeah, the ones by the front doors."

"I think they're azaleas," TJ informs.

"They'd look awesome in our dorm room," Enrique states as he exits the car, soon ascending the tall stack of marble steps, in route toward the courthouse entry.

TJ leaps out of the car, leaving his passenger side door ajar. "Dude, you can't do this!" he warns, in a failed attempt to dissuade Enrique. "They'll bust yer ass dude!" a distressed TJ calls out.

Ignoring TJ's repeated pleas, Enrique quickly scales the stone steps and hoists one of the potted plants, hands interlocked, firmly positioning the sizable pot against his pelvis, as he slowly navigates his treacherous descent.

Curbside now, an overexerted Enrique whimpers, "Some help would be nice." As TJ reluctantly assists his inebriated roomie.

Back at their dorm, lights off, Enrique sobers up. "What's your father like?" he blurts from the upper bunk.

TJ's caught off guard by the random nature of Enrique's question, nonetheless he replies, "He's a good man." TJ pauses, then adds, "He's achieved a lot in his life. I hope I can be so accomplished."

"I mean, how is he as a parent?" Enrique rephrases.

"Amazing, actually," TJ glowingly answers with unabridged honesty. "He takes the time to explain stuff to me and he always has my back. Why do you ask?"

After a brief pause, Enrique's responds, "No reason, just curious how other guys get along with their dads."

"How's your relationship with your father?" TJ delicately probes.

Enrique laughs. "We don't have a relationship. No matter what, I can never satisfy him. It's totally impossible to live up to his expectations," he reluctantly reveals, followed by a sorrowful sigh. "He and I are so different," he finishes with a touch of resentment in his voice.

"How so?" TJ follows.

Enrique tosses a nervous laugh and bashes, "To start with, he's a greedy psychopath."

TJ lays there, eyes widened with surprise. "What do you mean?"

"It's hard to explain, but trust me, his world is ruled by greed and power."

Weeks later, Enrique's back in action, living up to his well-deserved reputation as the campus playboy. Most every night their dorm room is wall-to-wall women and weed. By default, (okay maybe by choice), TJ is an unwitting (okay, maybe willing), accomplice to Enrique's endless antics.

By any standard, Enrique was an incorrigible chick magnet. Wherever they go, Enrique's suave style, extraordinary good looks and thick wallet attracts hordes of women. Despite TJ's relentless efforts to contribute financially, Enrique always insists on footing the bill, which makes TJ uncomfortable to say the least. No doubt, Enrique's a devoted pal; but his wild side, is simply not conducive to studying.

Christmas break around the corner, the close of this semester is soon to follow. A panicked stricken TJ is forced to confront the harsh reality, that it may be too late to resurrect his languishing grades. Enrique, despite being TJ's closest pal, is the unquestionable root of TJ's lackluster grades. Nonetheless, TJ rightfully bore the brunt of the blame.

Most days TJ would skip his morning classes (a consequence of late-night partying). After all, how could anyone be expected to get a good night's sleep with a room full of people. Needless to say, TJ's GPA had plummeted into an unrecoverable freefall. He needed to step up and pull his GPA out of the gutter and this week was his last opportunity to do so. Consequently, he spent every night during finals week camped out at the library.

Needless to say, Enrique had a financial safety net, a luxury not afforded to TJ. Deep down, he knew he could never keep pace with Enrique's flamboyant lifestyle. Bottom line, they came from different worlds, TJ's had fiscal limitations and academic mandates, while Enrique's was ostensibly boundless.

Enrique preferred chasing tail to studying and he made no bones about it. Unlike TJ, Enrique was accustomed to doing what he wanted, when he wanted. If Enrique were a racehorse, TJ would've been a plow horse. In any event, Enrique wasn't serious about school, let alone making the Dean's list. A frill otherwise not availed to TJ.

Having just finished his last final, an overtired TJ (having pulled back-to-back *all-nighters*) returns to his dorm to grab some shuteye, before pushing off for Christmas Break.

Enrique's long gone, headed home to Peru on his family's private jet.

After a couple of hours of well-needed sleep, TJ awakens, notably rejuvenated and markedly refreshed. He stuffs his laundry into one of his pillowcases, tosses it into his truck and pushes off.

It's dusk by the time he arrives. The front palms glisten with pink and white Christmas lights.

As he exits his truck, he's invigorated by the refreshingly crisp winter air.

The moment he enters the cottage, he's greeted by the unmistakable scent of a freshly cut, Douglas fir, conjuring memories of Little Creek and holidays spent with his brother and stepmom.

Later, TJ and Slater take seaside seats as Mother-Nature unleashes her fury, as winter whitecaps abound and pugnaciously pound the jagged jetty.

TJ turns toward his dad. "I think I may need to find a new roommate," he reveals above the stirring seas.

Slater, wearing a look of surprise interjects, "I thought you and Enrique were thick as thieves."

"Yeah, he's a great guy; but he just doesn't take college seriously. He literally parties every night. To be truthful, I don't think I've ever seen him on campus," TJ has an epiphany.

"Case closed," Slater emphatically blurts. "If you expect to graduate, you need to get good grades, and to achieve that you need to employ discipline, which includes a reasonable amount of sleep, atop solid study habits. Don't get me wrong, I'm all for a good time; but like anything in life you need to find a balance. Sooner the better," Slater convincingly narrates in an unwavering, patriarchal tone.

CHAPTER 27

By the close of freshman year, TJ's grades remain subpar. Despite his best efforts, he barely makes a dent in his GPA. He feels guilty that he hadn't taken school more seriously, particularly since UM is such a costly private college. His GPA was beyond disappointing, borderline academic probation. After all, he was the son of a disciplined Naval Captain, and he couldn't even maintain a minimal GPA. That was his wakeup call. There was only one course of action to pursue. He needs to man-up. No drama, no formal farewells, he simply needs to cut ties with Enrique, posthaste.

The following semester TJ moves into a dumpy, lowbrow shack of a house. He jumped, when presented with the opportunity to snag a recently vacated room, in a four-bedroom house, positioned on the outskirts of campus. His new roommates were UM rugby players.

TJ explained to Enrique that his dad simply refused to pay for the more expensive dorm, because of his languishing grades. At first, Enrique made a diligent effort to stay in touch. Eventually, TJ made the difficult decision to simply ignore his calls. Enrique ultimately got the message. That was especially tough on TJ. After all, Enrique had been a faithful friend.

Weekdays, TJ's literally MIA, studying. Once he committed to his studies, he saw a marked improvement in his grades. He'd proven to himself that the extra effort truly paid dividends. He stepped up to the proverbial plate and made the grade (literally and figuratively). By the end of his sophomore year, his cumulative GPA had skyrocketed to a respectable 3.6.

With his academics finally in tow, TJ decides to pursue some extracurricular activities. He notices a kick boxing flyer on the cafeteria bulletin-board and jots down the number.

Days later, he attends his first class. The instructor's Don (the Juan) Hopkins, a former WKBA (*World Kick Boxing Association*) contender.

After a few clinics, Don (impressed with TJ's skillset) invites TJ to be his sparring partner, in return for free lessons.

Before long, the pair become good friends. During one sparring session, TJ asks, "Are you still competing?"

"Hell no! too old for that shit," Don responds between gasping breaths.

"Then why the intensive sparring sessions?"

"Helps keep me in shape for my clinics, plus it makes me more marketable for side jobs," Don answers between punch and kick combinations.

"Side jobs?" TJ repeats, while deflecting punches.

Don stops to take a break and answers, "Kick boxing clinics don't pay the bills, my friend. So, I supplement my income by offering protective services. You know, security."

"Like a bodyguard?"

"Kinda. For example, this weekend I have a bounce gig."

"Bounce gig?" TJ repeats.

"Bouncer, dude. What fuckin planet are you from?" Don teases. "You need to speak street my brother." Don mocks through an amiable sigh. "Let's take five," he suggests, as they exit the ring.

"Actually, Bear was supposed to go with me this weekend; but he came down with the flu. You should fill in for him. You have some serious skills. Good money too. A grand for one night's work."

"A thousand bucks for one night?" TJ repeats through a surprised expression.

"You heard me. Some rich-as-shit Latin dudes I know, own a fuckin-castle in Cutler Ridge, and they like ta party hardy."

That Saturday, early evening. TJ accompanies Don, as they proceed toward the front door of a mammoth, coral-stone estate. They segue amidst a parade of exotic autos, meticulously crammed inside the crushed gravel driveway.

Don presses the doorbell, soon summoning a small-framed, flashily dressed, excessively tanned, notably high, Latin male carrying a freshly poured martini.

He slowly opens the towering wood doors and bellows, "Don the mother-fuckin, Juan! My main man," in a thick Spanish accent as he and Don hug it out. "Where's the Bear?" the Latin chap asks, tentatively staring at an unfamiliar TJ.

"He's sick. Flu bug or some shit," Don explains. "Anyway, this is my sparring partner TJ. Phillippe, TJ. TJ, Phillippe," he introduces.

Unable to conceal his apprehension, Phillippe simply nods with suspicious eyes. "You know the drill. If you get hungry or thirsty grab what you need, otherwise cover the door. Remember, girls only! We don't need any competition." Phillippe slurs with a lecherous glare, while spilling his Martini.

"Got it!" Don acknowledges with a thumbs up gesture.

Later, Don and TJ man the door as busloads of college co-eds arrive and unload.

"What the fuck?" a confused TJ, mumbles.

"Chill, dude," Don whispers through a forced smile.

"Why would all of these young girls want to hang out with these old fuckin dudes?" TJ naïvely asks.

Don smirks, without reply.

TJ heads inside to grab a couple bottles of water. Once inside, he observes a wild orgy. Most of the girls are either half naked, having sex or snorting coke from the mounds of cocaine atop most every table.

TJ does an abrupt about-face and heads back out front.

"I can't be part of this shit, man," TJ explains with panicked eyes.

"You have ta be kidding me, dude! What the fuck did you think we were doin?"

"Not this! Sorry; but I'm not gonna get kicked outta college for a thousand bucks," TJ blasts as he walks off, leaving Don solo.

CHAPTER 28

EVERMORE COGNIZANT THAT there's no such thing as easy money, TJ takes on a part-time job to help-out financially. He lands a position at a local clothing store (*the Jean Machine*). His unofficial title *jean jock*. He works the night shift (7 p.m. to 10 p.m.) five nights a week, along with a couple other college kids.

To help spur sales, the owner (a flamboyant fellow named Armando) incentivizes his crew with a hundred-dollar bonus, payable to the salesperson with the highest sales quota each month.

Since the blue jeans arrive unhemmed, TJ thought it might be advantageous to learn to hem pants himself. He began by watching the tailor, then afterhours he would sit at the blind stitch machine experimenting with cloth scraps. Within a couple of days, he was able to hem pants himself, considerably quicker than waiting for the tailor.

TJ's approach turned out to be uniquely successful. He promised hemmed pants within three minutes. His precise pitch was, *three or free* and it worked, making him the recipient of the bonus most every month.

One night, TJ was working solo, preparing to closeup when a couple of sorority sisters wandered into the store. After a bit of browsing, the cuter of the two bought a blouse. She handed TJ her credit card and her number.

Her name was Colette. She was pretty, petite and super sweet. Turns out, she had received a full athletic scholarship as a platform diver on the UM swim team and what an impressive diver she was. Colette's scholarship, however, did not include a housing allowance, so she commuted to and from Homestead, Florida (roughly a half hour south).

A month or so later, Saturday evening, close to 5 p.m. TJ drives south to join Colette and her parents for dinner. They're understandably anxious to meet him.

It's a delightful evening by all accounts. Her parents were purely pleasant, though surprisingly much older than TJ had expected. TJ later learned that Colette was the youngest of four by eleven years. Her parents were welcoming, cordial and kind-hearted people (much like their daughter).

It's approaching 10 p.m. as TJ says his goodnights, before pushing off.

With a near empty gas tank, an overtired TJ stops a few miles shy of campus to fuel up and replenish his waning brain. With limited finances, he pumps three bucks of gas, then heads inside the inner city, C-store, to pay for his petrol and a bottle of iced tea.

While standing in the checkout line, he drums up conversation with an older, authentically kind, grey haired black man, impeccably dressed in a suit and tie.

"If I drank iced tea this late, I'd be up for three days," the older fellow jests with a contagious laugh.

"That's the plan," TJ replies with smiling eyes. "Have a big test Monday." he pauses and asks, "Are you coming from a formal event?" referring to the man's suit and tie.

"Actually yes. My granddaughter just got married. Unfortunately, I work Monday, so we need to get back on the road."

"Congratulations, where you headed?"

"Atlanta," the older fellow answers. He pays for his items then turns back toward TJ and adds, "Good luck on your test young man," followed by a big wave.

"Thanks," TJ replies, as he hands the clerk a crumpled five for his fuel and tea.

As TJ heads outside, he removes the twist top from his iced tea and takes a long energizing swig. In route to his vehicle, he overhears the "*N*" word. He pauses, looks over and notices a few redneck types, heckling the older fellow he just met.

Unwilling to just walk away, TJ stumbles into the conversation as a handful of hooligans hold court in the back of a Ford pickup.

Two take-throne in mismatched beach chairs, loosely positioned in the cab of the flat bed, while three (two shirtless, one clueless) linger, drinking beer and heckling C-store patrons, like a pack of menacing wolves.

The fellow TJ just met, politely stands his ground. "Didn't your parents teach you to respect your elders?" he responds in a non-confrontational, fashion.

TJ approaches the older fellow. "You go on. You have a long drive ahead of you. I'll handle this," he compassionately coaxes.

"No, please. I don't want you to get hurt on my account," the older fellow insists, wearing a fretful expression.

"I won't. I promise," TJ responds with a reassuring wink, as he escorts the gentleman back to his automobile.

As the older chap drives off, he proffers a concerned wave.

TJ nods, then redirects his attention back toward the hillbilly hecklers.

"Here comes the white knight!" one of the rednecks; mocks.

TJ bites his tongue. "Seems a bit unfair, five against one, don't ya think?" he taunts, followed by another gulp of his iced tea. "Tell ya what. Let's even the odds. How bout I take you all on, one at a time, right here, right now," an incensed TJ challenges, through a wild-eyed stare.

No takers.

TJ ramps up the rhetoric. "What's wrong? Not feelin so tough anymore?" as he hurls his half-empty bottle of iced tea into the pick-up cab, as it bursts upon impact.

The culprits remain seated, stunned, and reactionless, as they share worrisome expressions.

TJ offers an enraged stare. "Just as I thought, a bunch a big mouth bitches," he berates, as he turns to leave.

Months later. TJ's working at the jean shop.

He heads home for lunch and parks out back of the rental house. He walks along the side of the house, and as he turns the corner, he's blindsided by a lights-out sucker punch, to the left side of his face.

An hour or so later, he awakens to endless ringing in his ears. Turns out, the vengeful C-store rednecks spotted him working in the mall and followed him home. Fortunately, his rough and ready rugby roomies were home to save the day.

CHAPTER 29

ONCE AGAIN, TJ's back in the grade groove, as he maxes out his credit load, to help stretch his tuition dollars further. UM suggests fifteen credit hours per semester; but TJ routinely takes twenty-one or more, in addition to attending summer sessions. In the final analysis, he earned a four-year degree in just three years.

After receiving his undergraduate degree, TJ follows his heart (destiny) and applies to UM Law School. Not only was he promptly accepted; but he also receives a full academic scholarship.

Early Saturday morning. TJ decides to share the good news, so he packs an overnight bag and heads home to tell his dad.

After a relatively uneventful trip, TJ arrives home.

Slater's out front, wielding a shiny machete, hacking unruly palm fronds and a thicket of invasive vines.

TJ parks midway on the palm covered drive.

Slater turns, pleasantly surprised by his son's unexpected visit, as he wipes his beaded brow (free of sweat) with his shirtsleeve.

TJ exits his truck and walks toward his dad, holding his acceptance letter in the air.

"What's that?" Slater asks as he wipes remnant dirt from his left hand, while the steely machete dangles from his right. He quickly reads the letter, looks up at TJ and says, "That's truly amazing, son. I couldn't be more, proud!"

"Thanks, Dad," TJ replies, unable to suppress a prideful smile.

"What type of law are you considering son?"

"I think I'd like to be a prosecuting attorney. That's always been my lifelong dream," TJ reveals.

"So, you'd work for the DA's office?" Slater questions.

"Hopefully!"

"Sounds like a plan," Slater adds. "Well, this certainly calls for a celebration. Let me change out of these dirty clothes and we'll head down to The *Beach Bum* for some conch fritters," as he reaches out to hug his son.

Later, Slater (having showered) hair damp, rejoins TJ out-back as they head off. Slater's arm cups his son close.

Inside the *Beach Bum*, father and son share cold beers, good conversation and mutual respect. TJ had accomplished something to be proud of.

That Sunday morning, TJ awakens early.

Slater's been up for hours. The unmistakable smell of fried eggs and turkey bacon, swarm the limits of their small beachfront bungalow.

After breakfast they head out back toward the faithful jetty, sharing mid-morning mimosas. The weather's impeccable, another cloudless sky.

TJ observes a hint of apprehension in his father's otherwise stoic demeanor. Slater seems to relish these moments they share, more so recently.

Soon, it's time to go. TJ tosses his over-stuffed duffle bag on the passenger seat, before grabbing a farewell hug.

As he drives off, he peers into his rear-view mirror. He sees his dad standing there, waving goodbye. His thoughts internalize. He worries about his father and his solitary life. He wonders why his dad never remarried. He carries that encumbering thought for the remainder of the day.

With the semester coming to a quick close, TJ decides to secure a new place for next year. Moving closer to the campus will be a welcomed change.

TJ befriends another law student named Sal. Sal's real name is Santos, but since he hails from San Salvador everyone calls him Sal. Sal's more TJ's speed. He too, received a full academic scholarship including a comparable housing allowance.

TJ and his new pal Sal, set out to secure (semi) respectable digs. After an exhaustive search, they end up signing a lease on a well-located, debatably dingy, duplex.

Fortunately for TJ, he only needs a place to rest his head. After all, he expects to be living at the Law library. Sleep deprivation became a mode of survival. Law School was certainly no place for the ill-prepared and TJ made it his mission to make every credit count.

To help make ends meet, TJ secures a clerking position at a small law firm close to campus. His job is to do research and prepare legal briefs for trial. Not only did clerking help financially; but it also gave him a distinct advantage in his chosen profession.

Sal and TJ are incorrigible penny pinchers. Together they developed a surprisingly cost-effective meal plan. They eat sardines on toast during the week, go to Howard Johnson's for an *all you can eat* fish fry every Friday and reserve Saturday as date night, when they splurge on the girl of the week.

Law School flew by surprisingly fast. TJ (to his utter amazement) graduates at the top of his class. After graduation, he fulfills his lifelong dream and secures an internship as an Assistant District Attorney (ADA) for Dade County (Miami).

When asked, he readily acknowledges his insatiable quest to apprehend bad guys. He wasn't quite sure if he was looking for atonement, or redemption or whatever you might want to call it. Maybe he just wants to give back or get even, who knows. In any event, he was ready to embark upon a personal crusade against evildoers.

Days later, TJ's returns to the Keys. He and his dad take side by side seats at the jetty, as they dig into a couple of (reminiscent) thick Cuban sandwiches.

"You sure you wanna work for the government?" Slater questions, while wiping mustard residue from his chin. "I can tell you first-hand, it's like living in a bubble. It's not too late to consider private practice. More money and far fewer rules," Slater cautions.

TJ laughs. "I hear you; but I have a good feeling about this. I really believe it's my destiny to catch bad guys."

Slater offers a concessionary nod.

CHAPTER 30

AN OVER-ANXIOUS TJ arrives at the Dade County Courthouse, well in advance of his scheduled appointment. He parks in the visitor's lot then walks around to the front of the courthouse, soon ascending the steep steps leading to the entry lobby.

Before entering, he stops, glances left and smiles to himself when he sees the dwarfed Azalea bush that replaced the mature one Enrique had commandeered years earlier.

His first day as an ADA intern is entirely unforgettable. TJ, along with three other ADA candidates sit on a cold stone bench, in the middle of the acoustically imperfect courthouse lobby, as presiding District Attorney, Thomas P. Quinn III and his blood red bowtie preps them for the career path, they're about to embark upon.

Quinn's the quintessential (at least in image) well-bred lawyer. More like an English barrister than the ambulance chaser. He certainly wasn't the ubiquitous shyster image that Americans normally conjure when one hears the word, *lawyer*. He is, however, remarkably arrogant, as if arrogance were a perquisite.

"Here's the long and short of it, children," Quinn pontificates in a hurried, debatably disinterested, semi-scripted fashion, delivered by rote. "For the next six months, each of you will shadow an experienced ADA. Thereafter, if you're still here," he snickers for his personal pleasure, "you will receive a suitable caseload, based in large part, on the recommendation of your supervising ADA. In other words, your success over the next six months will at some meaningful level, dictate and determine the quality and quantity of the caseloads you will ultimately receive. In the final analysis, even though you play for the same team, you are theoretically competitors. Questions?" he snappily asks.

No takers.

"Ok then," he concludes with a quick glance at his vintage, generational heirloom, pocket watch. "We have four minutes, so let's get through this. When I point to you, state your full, *legal* name (he emphasizes) and I will give you your assignment."

Quinn points to a skinny, freckled fellow.

"Andrew Robert Raskin," the ADA candidate says excitedly, with a raise of his hand.

"Mr. Raskin, you're assigned to Rita Felling. Meet her tomorrow at 8:50 a.m. courtroom 11B."

He then points to a slightly rotund, kind-looking girl (arguably too kind for this job).

"Sandy McCullum," she replies, in a meek voice.

"Full, formal names – *PLEASE!*" Quinn growls, in a persnickety tone.

"Sandra, Lynn, McCullum, sir," she nervously course-corrects.

"You're to meet Clay Duncan, 8:15 a.m., courtroom 16A."

He then points to a pompous looking fellow, wearing a flashy paisley tie and a silk blend, houndstooth suit, accentuated by a pair of designer-tortoiseshell reading specs.

"Tad – Theodore, Prescott, Donahue," he quickly amends.

Quinn halts, lifts his head from his law calendar, slides his reading glasses down along the bony bridge of his narrow nose and peers overtop with a sadistic smirk. "Ned Donahue's kid?" Quinn asks with a predatory smile.

"Yes," a bolstered Tad pridefully responds.

"Hope you're a better lawyer than your old man," a snarky Quinn, torpedoes.

The rest of the group tries, without success, to stifle their laughter.

"Mr. Donahue, you'll be joining Sebastian Wolcott 9:20 a.m. in courtroom 22A. Maybe the two of you can share fashion tips," Quinn snidely quips, then turns and points at TJ.

"Tane, Harlan, Jensen," TJ responds, prepared for a disparaging retort.

Quinn levels his gaze upon TJ. "Polynesian?" Quinn questions, with implied familiarity.

"Half… My mother's side."

Quinn pauses, then inquires. "Other half Scandinavian?"

"Yes. Norwegian." TJ proudly proclaims.

"Perfect! A sensitive warrior. Just what we *DON'T* need in the DA's office," Quinn derides with a roll of his eyes. "You're assigned to Natalie Gerrard, 8:40 a.m., courtroom 8C. Gerrard's the best of the lot. She epitomizes what a good lawyer should be. Unfortunately, I'm going to lose her to the Public Defender's office in June. Watch and learn, young man. Watch and learn," he repeats.

"Yes, sir," TJ respectfully replies.

The following morning, an ever-punctual TJ shows up as instructed (actually, twenty minutes early). He enters his assigned courtroom, through a pair of tall mahogany doors. His first impression is indescribable. He's never been inside a courtroom before. It's pretty much as he had imagined. The hardscape interior creates an echo chamber, virtually every word, every footstep, exaggerated. The appointments are awe-inspiring, stone floors, polished wood benches and demonstratively tall windows, not to mention the imperious judge's bench overlooking the rows of spectator seats. Then there's the jury box, the witness stand, and the immortal pictures of eminent jurists and of course the ever-present American flag.

There's a female counselor at each bench. *Which is the defense attorney, and which is the prosecuting attorney?* TJ ponders. They both have their heads buried in their legal briefs. No different than any red-blooded American male, he approaches the better looking of the two, first.

"Natalie?" he softly utters with hopeful eyes.

She begrudgingly lifts her (breathtakingly beautiful) head and offers an obligatory but nonetheless affirming, nod.

Suffice it to say, TJ's utterly infatuated with her innate beauty. She's truly striking. Thick, dark brown hair, Godiva eyes, silky olive complexion and full luscious lips. He wishes he had a better recollection of the case she tried that day; but unfortunately, he was hopelessly smitten, lost in a love-struck stupor. Her beauty quite literally zapped his every thought. He just sat there in a brain-dead daze for two and a half hours, relishing her every nuance, her every gesture, her every utterance, not to mention her insatiable exquisiteness.

At the conclusion of that first day's trial, Natalie returns to the table, collects her files, closes her briefcase, glances over toward TJ, and says, "Hope you learned something today, green-horn," leaving him sitting alone, like a drooling fool.

Months later. After work, TJ and his ADA posse congregate at *The Tarpon*, a local tavern, that he and his entourage (Sandy, Drew and *yes*, Tad) routinely frequent.

"I've watched Natalie litigate some ten plus trials, over the past few months, without engaging her in one personal conversation," TJ whimpers his laments to Sandy, who's kind enough to lend a sympathetic ear.

Barely veiling a smirk, she intones, "Oh, poor TJ." She pauses to slurp the foamy head from her second or third beer. "Don't whine to me. From all reports, you've tagged nearly every skirt in town. You could be tried and convicted as a serial dater." She giggles. "My opinion, counselor, you're obsessed with what you can't have," she concludes.

"*OUCH!*" he kids, arms symbolically crossed, covering the emotional wound her callus allegations inflicted.

Sandy smiles.

Tad taps TJ on the shoulder. "Speaking of the devil, isn't that your boss over there?" he whispers, then points.

TJ turns to see Natalie across the room, sandwiched between a gaggle of grey suits, all understandably enamored with her beauty. He gulps down his beer, commandeers one of Sandy's sugar free breath mints and heads over to rescue his fair maiden. Propelled by liquid confidence and a smidgen of old-fashioned jealousy, TJ soon reaches the target of his unannounced affection, with unsteadied strides.

"Natalie," TJ says (ok, yelps) loudly, announcing his unexpected arrival.

Natalie turns and with surprised eyes, replies, "TJ!"

TJ just stands there, lost for words, like a motionless mute.

"Would you like to join us?" Natalie politely asks, breaking the awkward silence.

Unable to conjure an apt response, TJ promptly sits, like a treat-trained pup.

Natalie intercepts further awkwardness as she introduces him around the table. "Tane Jensen, I'd like to introduce you to my future colleagues at the Public Defender's Office. This is Greg Kimber (he stands), Joel Stein (he nods), Rodney Klein (he salutes), Steven Ross (he rolls his eyes), Karen Dean (she smiles, flirtatiously), and Troy Evans (he raises his beer mug, in toast)."

2 a.m. TJ's crew is long gone. The tavern and his pitcher of beer, nearly empty. The score, TJ five beers (he thinks) and Natalie three wines (two too many, he hopes).

"How old are you?" TJ randomly blurts. He immediately realizes that was an idiotic question, but it's too late to recant.

"Twenty-four," she replies.

"I'm twenty-four too," TJ notes, as if it's some mathematical phenomenon. "How is it possible that we're the same age and you already have two years as an ADA under your belt?" he inquires, eyebrows furrowed, bewilderment etched about his inebriated face.

"I think skipping two years of college may have had something to do with it," she humbly responds, inadvertently puncturing his fragile ego, while casually noshing on a small bowl of mixed nuts, anchored by a hypnotic smile.

"Wow. Now that's impressive," he adds, followed by a brief gap in conversation. "So, tell me the Natalie Gerrard story!"

"Not much to tell," she quickly deflects, while scavenging for remnant pistachios, hidden amongst a host of mixed nuts. "My parents met at Oxford. My mom was a hot-blooded Barcelona babe, and my dad was a blue-blooded Parisian baby. They married, moved stateside, and had three kids. He cheated, she left," she pauses, feeling a bit vulnerable, having revealed so much, so hastily. "Anyway, my mother was offered a senior editor position, so we relocated to Manhattan, where she raised three girls." She finally locates and pops a coveted pistachio into her mouth, and adds, "I give her a lot of credit for juggling career and kids as a single mom." She pauses to reflect, then embellishes. "My mother was a good woman. From that horrific experience, my mother taught us two invaluable life lessons: *never rely on anyone, and only marry for love.* She concludes with a doubtful expression.

After a couple hours of fluid flirtation, a semi-sloshed TJ boldly and regrettably takes hold of Natalie's delicate hand and asks, "Would it be remotely acceptable, or should I say ethically permissible, for an apprentice ADA to ask a future Public Defender out on a date?"

She blushes and with an unbridled coquettish glance, responds, "I'm certain it wouldn't violate any known conduct codes; but unfortunately, this Public Defender to be, is also a bride to be… I'm engaged," she informs, revealing her modest engagement ring.

Holy shit! TJ thinks to himself. His world just came to a crashing halt! His heart *stopped!* At the very least, it skipped a couple beats. It felt as if his blood just drained to his toes. His raging hormones evaporated, gone, poof, adios! He feels nauseous. Hell, he never felt like this before. Feelings of humiliation and any rational basis for embarrassment, took a back seat to his first broken heart. Absent any viable, remotely respectable alternative, TJ manages to sober up and compose himself enough to muddle through an adlib, concession speech. "Well, I certainly hope he knows how truly lucky he is. Though I don't know you well, nor have I known you very long, my instincts tell me you're a special, lady," TJ calmly unveils, letting his heartstrings *dead drift.*

Natalie savors the indisputable purity of his words. She appears flattered. Her eyes glisten in response to his heartfelt reveal. Her thoughts mirrored by a doubt-filled expression, so it seemed to TJ anyway.

"You ready to roll?" TJ asks.

"Let's do it," Natalie replies, as she collects her purse and stands.

Outside now. TJ escorts Natalie to her car.

"Goodnight," he proffers, shaking her delicate hand, followed by a respectful peck on the cheek. He turns on cue and heads toward his car, like a defeated prizefighter departing ringside, hoping (praying) for a rematch.

It had been a rough couple of weeks by all measures. It was late Friday afternoon, when TJ makes the last-minute decision to head down to the Keys to spend a relaxing weekend with his dad.

He arrives shortly before sunset, their favorite time of day.

He enters the house and knows exactly where to find his dad, perched out toward the bitter tip of the coral jetty with a cold Corona in his grasp with a second on deck (submerged in the cool ocean waters). TJ tosses his overnight bag onto the soft sofa, opens the fidgety fridge, grabs a bottle of brew, and drops his shiny shoes as he heads off to join his old man.

"Hey there!" TJ shouts, a short distance shy of where Slater takes salty seat.

Slater slowly turns toward TJ. "Didn't expect to see you this weekend," he hollers back, through a surprised smile.

Slater stands to greet his son with a welcoming hug.

TJ's quick to claim a coral rock next to his dad.

"Beautiful, isn't it?" Slater rhetorically remarks, staring out toward the red blazed horizon.

"Sure is," TJ acknowledges, followed by a long, refreshing, well-needed swig of Mexico's finest.

"Wish all of life were so easy, son," Slater adds. "Hell, if it were, I'd probably live to be a hundred. Hell, two hundred."

TJ notices his dad's eyes are bloodshot, as if he'd been crying. He'd never seen his dad cry; emotional sure, but never tears of sadness. At first, he thought of letting it go, without mention, but he couldn't help but wonder what was upsetting him so, particularly at such a seemingly happy moment. Unable to squelch his concern, TJ feels compelled to discuss the heretofore unmentionable, as he takes the plunge. "Ever think about Brandon and Mom, Dad?"

Slater takes deliberate pause, separated by a few courage-inspiring chugs, then responds, "Sure, I do." He hesitates a moment or two, before proceeding. "I miss them a lot." After another short pause, "I try to stay focused on the good times, though." He turns toward TJ, misty eyed. "I try not to torment myself with sad memories, T, especially the stuff I can't change. It's the good memories that get me through the day." He finishes with aged wisdom and a reassuring smile. "Son, the best advice this old man can share is this. Live every day to the fullest without regret. When you were a youngster, I used to tell you, *Life is a gift, how we live life is a decision*." Slater concludes.

TJ smiles. He feels his dad's pain. "I'm sorry, Dad," TJ humbly apologizes. "I'm truly sorry for all of the pain my actions and inactions may have caused you."

Slater turns to face his son. "Sorry for what T?" he asks, as the late day sun shimmers across the calm sea, casting a soft amber glow upon Slater's chiseled face. "You did nothing wrong, son." Slater's left hand grasps the top of TJ's shoulder. "You have nothing to apologize for, I promise you that and one day, you will better understand the context of my words. For now, let's promise to move forward with our respective lives and let those sad memories fade. Tonight, we need to focus on this wondrous view," he says assuredly, lifting his half-empty bottle of beer in toast. "Deal?" Slater proposes.

Both smile and clang Coronas, as the setting sun closes the day and their conversation. "Deal!" TJ replies.

CHAPTER 31

It's been nearly two years since TJ first met Natalie. Today, she's a respected Public Defender, and TJ's been promoted to a supervisory ADA position. They remain friends, actually very good friends. They have an ongoing challenge. Whenever they try cases together, they bet a buck on the outcome, unprofessional maybe; but harmless, nonetheless.

It was day one of a projected two-week trial, as a spiffily fashioned TJ tightens his bright pink tie, as he saunters over toward the jury box, to deliver his opening argument (bombshell). He stops, pivots, smiles then theatrically delivers. "Good morning. For the next couple of weeks or so, it will be my job to prove beyond a reasonable doubt that the defendant is guilty of violently raping a young mother, while her newborn infant slept in the adjoining room."

The jurors exchange horrified expressions and a synchronized gasp.

Goalpost in sight, TJ runs with the ball. "The defense will try to assail the facts surrounding this case with an onslaught of propaganda, in a veiled attempt to glorify the defendant's character. The Public Defender's office," he says pointing to Natalie with an open palm, "represented by the lovely and ever-so talented, Natalie Gerrard, will skillfully attempt to portray the defendant as an upstanding citizen and well-respected member of the community."

Loving the histrionics, TJ paces a bit, offering up some good courtroom drama. He walks off then casually meanders back toward the jurors. Both hands grasp the top of the polished partition; he faces the jurors and unleashes, "Ms. Gerrard will undoubtedly present the defendant as a respected loan officer, a loving husband and father to two young daughters." He pauses, then concludes, "And he may well be all of those wonderful things; but that does not vindicate him of this hideous crime. I caution you; *NOT* to allow the defense to sugarcoat these hardened facts and please don't lose sight of the inescapable truths as this trial proceeds. Ms. Gerrard will most certainly argue that the prosecution has no conclusive forensics. I will save her the words and tell you right here and right now that she is absolutely, correct. We do not. My retort, however, is simple and irrefutable. We have an eyewitness account, who will categorically confirm that the defendant is nothing less than a calculated predator, who took painstaking efforts to conceal his identity. Fact is, the defendant masqueraded as a telephone technician, in hope of gaining access to the victim's home. As the trial proceeds, you will hear from the victim herself, as she boldly reveals the horrific details surrounding this heinous crime. Thank you for your indulgence." TJ nods, then returns to his bench, punctuated with a wink, to Natalie.

Natalie shakes her head, followed by an audible sigh. She takes a deep cleansing breath, before springing from her seat, as she walks toward the juror box, clapping her hands in mock applause. "Wow. The DA's opening argument sounds pretty compelling. I don't know about you, but I'm sufficiently convinced…

Let's just cut to the chase and convict the defendant, here and now. Why waste time and precious taxpayer money, let's just sentence him to life or better yet, let's give him the death sentence, after all, it would be cheaper in the long run. Who cares that he may be innocent? Who cares that he has two loving daughters who might sit in horror, as they watch their father wrongfully convicted? Or might you otherwise have some modest interest in hearing the defendant's side?" She closes with a soft smile, as she returns to her seat.

Natalie takes a moment to collect her legal briefs, then approaches the judge's bench. "Your Honor, I respectfully petition the court to have this case dismissed. My client and his family have already suffered enough, having endured incalculable damage to their otherwise impeccable reputation. The furtherance, of this ill-founded allegation, will only serve to compound an already prejudicial situation. The sole and singular premise of the prosecuting attorney's case is mere circumstantial evidence. Truth be known, this case is no more than a *GROSS* mistake in identity." Natalie passionately emphasizes.

The judge swiftly rules against Natalie's motion. "Motion denied."

Day four of the trial. "Counselor your witness," the judge summons in a no-nonsense demeanor.

TJ stands and annunciates. "The prosecution would like to call Constance Virginia Millsap, to the stand." He waits as his client approaches.

A petite, observably attractive woman, in her early to mid-twenties enters the witness stand. She places her tiny hand atop the proffered Bible, right hand raised, as an overweight, observably disheveled, bailiff swears her in. "Do you swear to tell the truth, the whole truth and nothing but the truth, so help you God?" the bailiff recites.

"I do," she meekly answers.

"Please be seated," the burly bailiff instructs.

Virginia takes her seat, fixes her skirt, and looks up toward TJ, for further instruction.

TJ approaches. "Good morning, Mrs. Millsap."

"Mornin, sir," she replies in a soft Southern drawl.

"I know this is terribly difficult for you, but I'm going to have to ask you to please describe your attack in vivid detail for the jury."

She nods timidly, pausing to muster her courage, then proceeds. "It was about lunchtime. I remember that cause I just fed my youngin, then put her down for her nap, when I heard the doorbell. I closed her bedroom door and seen a phone man standin outside on the front stoop."

"What made you think he was a telephone representative?" TJ interjects with a curious expression.

"Cause, he was wearin one-a them orange jumpsuits they all wear," she innocently recounts.

"Thank you, please proceed."

"Anyways, when I answered the door, he told me his name was Preston somethin, with phone repair. He said they were experiencing some kinda phone trouble in the neighborhood and asked if he could check our phone reception," she describes.

"And what did you say?" TJ asks.

"I said *sure,* then opened the door to let him in," she details with regretful eyes.

"What happened next?" TJ nurtures, trying to set the scene...

She pauses to collect her emotions, then proceeds. "When he entered the house, he asked how many phones we had. I had ta think for a minute and told him we only had two. He then asked where the phones were. I told him we had one in the kitchen and the other was in the master bedroom. He wanted to see the kitchen phone first. So, I showed him to the kitchen. He opened his case, hooked up some wires and seemed to be listenin' for a ring tone or somethin. After a few minutes he asked to see the bedroom phone, so I walked down the hall to the bedroom. Before I could even point to the phone, he covered my mouth with his hand and pushed me onto the bed." She starts to weep, covering her tiny mouth with her laced handkerchief, she takes a moment to compose her emotions, then gathers the courage to continue. "He poked a sharp knife at my side and told me if I didn't do exactly what he said, he'd slice my baby into bite-sized pieces."

The jurors gasp in wide-eyed horror.

"Were those his exact words?" TJ emphasizes in a troubled tone, fashioned to highlight the defendant's evil intent.

"Yes sir," she answers, trailed by an affirming nod.

"What happened then?" TJ fuels.

"He tied me up, then he cut off my clothes with his knife." Long emotional pause. "Then he raped me," she blurts, burying her eyes in her cupped hands, facing the floor in disgrace. Head up now. "After he raped me, he started to choke me. I felt like I was gonna black out. When he was done, he warned, if I ever told anyone he would be back for my baby. He left me there, tied up. I laid there for hours, helpless, while my baby girl cried." She starts to tear up, once again wiping her eyes with her handkerchief. "My husband found me when he got home from work. Hearin my youngin scream for hours on end was the hardest part of that ordeal," she sobbingly concludes.

"Mrs. Millsap, is your attacker present in this courtroom today?" TJ asks in an elevated voice.

Her head hung low. Ashamed, she nods, then answers, "Yes sir."

"Louder please, Mrs. Millsap," he asks in a forceful, yet compassionate tone.

"Yes sir."

"Can you please point him out for the jury?"

She summons her inner courage, lifts her head, and confidently points at the defendant, with a vengeful expression.

"For the record, I'd like to stipulate that the plaintiff has just identified the defendant, Josh Healy, as her attacker. Thank you, Mrs. Millsap," TJ says, before returning to his seat.

"Would the defense like to cross-examine the witness?" the judge asks.

"Yes. Thank you, Your Honor," Natalie replies.

Her client, Josh Healy, is a well-groomed, well-dressed, deceptively kind-looking fellow. By outward appearances, Healy looks like a nice guy. He pretends to scribble notes, trying to appear attentive.

Natalie stands, then approaches the witness. "Mrs. Millsap, let me start by saying, as a woman, I am very empathetic and deeply sorry that you had to experience such a horrific ordeal. That said, please understand that it is also my job, as Public Defender, to make certain, that the defendant is given a fair trial, so not to wrongly convict an innocent man. Therefore, I must ask some equally difficult questions and I want to thank you in advance, for your indulgence," Natalie compassionately conveys as she refers to her legal briefs. "Mrs. Millsap, can you without hesitation, unequivocally identify the defendant as your attacker?"

"Yes, ma'am, I can," she decisively responds.

Natalie pauses. "How can you be so certain?" she probes, gently shaking her head with a puzzled expression.

"I'm certain of it," Constance assuredly answers.

Natalie squints, (embellishing her perplexity) as she refers to her casefile, then challenges, "Mrs. Millsap, in your police report, you indicated that your attacker was a small Hispanic male, approximately five-foot-seven. The defendant is clearly Caucasian, nearly six-foot-tall and tips the scales at two hundred plus pounds," she explains, open palm, pointing to Healy. "So how can you sit here today with such renewed clarity? Moreover, how can you explain the gross disparity between your testimony today and your initial police report?" Natalie pauses, holding Constance's police report in her right hand, as she tactfully goes in for the kill. "Mrs. Millsap, is it possible, even remotely possible, that your attacker may have been a small, Hispanic male?"

"No, ma'am," Constance staunchly rebuts.

Natalie stands there lost for words, authentically bewildered. "How can that be?" she questions in a more interrogative tone, both hands curled upward.

"Cause a, his mole."

Silence in the courtroom.

Constance leans closer to the microphone, "I told the policeman that the mole on his neck looked familiar. I knew I seen it before. I didn't remember where, till my husband reminded me that our loan officer had a mole like that. Ya see, me and my husband got a home loan from his bank, and when he was fillin' out the paperwork my husband whispered to me that the mole on his neck was shaped like a foot."

A stifled giggle blankets the juror box.

"A *FOOT*?" Natalie repeats.

"Yes, ma'am... Mr. TJ told me the mole was our silver bullet."

"Is that so? Thank you... that's all for now," Natalie's face burdened by defeat, as she spins in place and marches back toward her client. She grabs hold of Healy's chin and turns his head to reveal the described mole. Her face blanketed with disappointment, as she rifles through her files, pausing to re-read the police report (more carefully this time) as the look of humiliation consumes her already flushed face, having had the proverbial wind sucked out of her sails.

"Judge, may I reapproach?" Natalie requests.

The judge reluctantly nods.

TJ and Natalie approach the bench.

Natalie holds the police report in her hand. She addresses the seated judge in whisper. "The Defense acknowledges, albeit belatedly, that Ms. Millsap had in fact, indicated that her attacker had a mole on his neck, which (in her opinion) resembles a foot. Nevertheless, Defense contends that there still exists a vast discrepancy between Mrs. Millsap's original police report and her testimony here today. As I stipulated in cross, Mrs. Millsap initially identified her attacker as a short Hispanic male and today she categorically identified the Defendant as her assailant, who's obviously a tall, Caucasian male. The Defense, once again, respectfully requests this trial be dismissed without prejudice."

The judge covers the microphone with his right hand, looks directly at Natalie and reprimands, "Ms. Gerrard, you and I both know that there has been a lot of compelling evidence presented here today, deserving of careful consideration. This court cannot and will not, be held hostage by your less than thorough review of the victim's police report. This case will proceed toward conclusion," he sternly rebuts. "Your request is emphatically, denied. However, in the spirit of compromise, I will consider allowing your client to be released on your recognizance without bail, on the unalterable proviso that you accept sole and unconditional responsibility for his prompt appearance in this courtroom, for the duration of this trial," the judge eloquently orates.

"I object Your Honor!" TJ brazenly interjects. "The thought

of releasing the defendant is nothing short of ludicrous. The defendant is not only a probable flight risk, but he's a potential menace to our community, moreover a direct threat to the well-being of my client and her infant child."

"Mr. Jensen, your objection is duly, noted. Again, it is my well-considered decision, to release the defendant without bail. I expect to see both of you Monday, 9 a.m. sharp. Court is adjourned," the judge declares, slamming his aged gavel.

Natalie and TJ return to their respective tables.

Josh Healy loosens his tie, as he lecherously stares Natalie down with suggestive intent.

She walks past him with blatant disdain.

"Lookin good up there, counselor!" a sleazy Healy remarks.

"Keep it in your pants, Healy," Natalie snaps, as she grabs her briefcase. "And for the record, if you're not here by 9 a.m. Monday or I'll come get you myself."

"You promise?" Healy taunts. "You can come get me anytime you want!" he replies, as he swivels in his seat, as Natalie exits the courtroom.

TJ and Natalie meet up in the hallway. They walk together at her hurried pace.

"Well done, counselor. You just helped turn a rapist loose,"

"Don't be so dramatic, creepy doesn't translate to rapist," Natalie gruffly rebuts. Brief pause. "And by the way, thanks for letting me hang myself in there. I looked like a sophomoric fool," she fires back. "Oh, and thanks for the silver bullet metaphor. That will certainly help advance my career."

"That's the downside of being a speed-reader," TJ pokes fun. "I suppose you needed to read fast, in order to skip two grades," he teases.

"Cute," Natalie remarks in frown.

Outside now, they fork off in opposing directions.

"See *YA!*" TJ amiably shouts out, hoping to squelch any residual tension.

Frustrated with the outcome of today's proceedings, Natalie gestures with an overhead (wordless) wave.

Before long, Natalie approaches her ruby red, VW bug. She opens the driver's side door to help ventilate the sauna-like cab. She removes her navy-blue blazer and places it on the front passenger seat. She starts her engine, then turns up the air conditioning to help expel the heat from her sun-soaked interior, as she directs the air condition vent toward her open blouse. Her driver's side door remains ajar, her left heel rests atop the asphalt pavement, as she waits for her car to cool off.

"Hey there, hot pants!!" Healy crudely announces, as he squats down next to her.

A startled Natalie jumps in her seat. "My God, you frightened me," she nervously yelps.

"Sorry. I just wanted to apologize if I was outta line back there. I guess all this trial stuff has taken a toll on my marriage. Anyway, I've been staying at my brother's place, and I guess I've been feelin a little lonely lately," he explains as he positions his left hand on the inside of her exposed thigh. "So, I thought we might…"

Natalie decisively removes his hand. "Forget it, asshole!" she scolds, as she pulls her leg back inside her car.

Healy blocks her from closing her door with his body.

"Kindly remove yourself or I'll summon the police and have your sorry ass tossed in jail," Natalie demands.

Healy stands and scans the near empty parking lot and calls out mockingly, "Help, help, somebody please help!" chuckling in an eerily sadistic tone. "Sorry, sweet legs, no help today," he intones as he quickly slips his groping hand up and under her skirt.

Natalie slaps his face, as she once again tries to close her door, to no avail.

Enraged, Healy grabs Natalie by her hair and forcibly drags her outside of her idling car, shoving her onto the hood of the neighboring vehicle, as he forcibly hikes up her skirt, as he drops his trousers. "I know what you need, you prick teasing bitch!" he degrades.

Suddenly, Healy's face turns beet red, his eyes bulge in fear, as he desperately gasps for air.

TJ (standing behind Healy) tightens his clenched chokehold around Healy's throat, soon rendering him unconscious, as his limp body unfolds onto the asphalt.

Within minutes, Healy's apprehended and whisked off to jail.

Later that evening. Natalie and TJ share burgers and beer. They sit at a large, pub-style booth.

"I'm curious… How did you know I was in trouble?" Natalie asks with inquiring eyes, while noshing on a mound of sweet potato fries.

TJ grins. "I didn't. I actually turned around to apologize for being so overbearing in the courtroom," he concedes with a smile, tempered with humility.

"Never picked you as the chivalrous type," she teases with a flirtatious glance, blushing.

Deep sigh. "There's a lot you don't know about me." He says, pointing at her with a droopy French fry and a wide-eyed smile, that swiftly transitions into a laugh, when the soggy fry goes limp.

"I'm so mad at myself," Natalie proclaims, shaking her pretty head side to side. "I hate feeling vulnerable," she divulges. "I knew being a Public Defender would involve some unsavory characters and today I let my guard down," she reveals in a disappointed tone.

"You're too hard on yourself," TJ consoles. "Hell, Healy's nearly a foot taller and twice your weight."

Natalie reaches into her purse, grabs her snub-nose, Smith and Wesson revolver, then slides it across the wood tabletop.

"*WOO*, cowgirl!" TJ embellishes with a shocked expression, as he quickly covers her pistol with his napkin, while surveying nearby tables, to make sure no one was watching.

"Relax, Lone Ranger, I have a concealed weapons permit," Natalie reassures. "I normally carry this bad boy with me 24/7. Unfortunately, guns aren't permitted in courtrooms."

"Thank God for that, otherwise you would've put a couple slugs in me today," TJ teases.

"Seriously. For the past year and a half, I literally spent every Saturday afternoon at the pistol range practicing. Fact is, I'm a pretty good shot," Natalie boasts. "You own a gun?" she asks.

"Me? Hell *NO*! I'm not a gun guy. Truth is they scare me," TJ divulges.

She appreciates his honesty, as she sets her hypnotic gaze upon him.

"When you told me you wanted to buy me dinner for saving your life, I imagined a well-seasoned filet. Isn't your life worth more than an overcooked burger, swimming in grease?" he mocks.

"Not on a Public Defender's salary," Natalie defends with a modest shrug of her delicate shoulders.

"I often wonder. Why Public Defender? Why not private practice?" he asks, while dowsing his fries with vinegar.

"Well," she says, pausing to wipe messy burger grease from

the table's edge. "Who's going to defend the impoverished inno-cent, who can't afford competent counsel? Not to suggest that my counsel is necessarily competent, after today's lackluster per-formance." She giggles, followed by a dainty bite of her drippy burger. "Which reminds me." She rifles through her purse, locates and places the coveted dollar atop the table. "This clearly belongs to you. After today's mishap, this trial is certainly over and you my friend, are the deserving victor."

TJ holds the dollar bill in his grasp. "That's respectable," he acknowledges.

"For paying the dollar you earned?"

"No." He smiles. "Your compassion for those who can't afford competent counsel," he remarks, with an adoring smile.

"What about you? Is your ADA position but a steppingstone toward a lucrative private practice position?" Natalie asks with interested eyes.

"Nope," TJ responds without hesitation. "I actually love what I do," he reveals. He pauses in ponder then proceeds. "I have an idea. How bout we order another pitcher of beer, quit our respective jobs and elope in Cabo. When we return, we can start our own law practice, exclusively devoted to defending the impoverished innocent," he finishes, on the cusp of seriousness.

Natalie laughs. "You're incorrigible… Where does my fiancé fit into that plan?" she teases.

"You tell me," TJ deflects, hoping for a favorable reply.

Natalie returns a blank stare. Her expression unveils a sense of remorse, a subtle acknowledgement, or at the very least a degree of uncertainty, about her future with Patrick. "We've trav-eled this road before, T. I'm engaged to be married, remember? If I thought for a moment that you were even half serious, I might reconsider what I'm doing with Patrick. That said, we both know that you have a well-deserved reputation as a player. Moreover,

I worry that you may be more intrigued with my unavailability than you are with me."

Undeterred by her repeated attempts to rebut his advances, he tells her, "I think you underestimate my sincerity." Followed by a deliberate pause. "Have you ever asked yourself why you've been engaged for three years?" Followed by a long, awkward silence.

After an uncomfortable gap in conversation, Natalie looks down at her plate, obviously embarrassed.

TJ knows he went too far. He feels bad. "I'm so sorry. That was way out of bounds," he recants, in an attempt, to walk-back his bluntness.

"No, you're right," Natalie concedes. "I suppose we've been pushing it off until we're settled in our respective careers, which reminds me." She takes a long sip of her frosty beer, then looks back at TJ and unveils, "Patrick and I are planning to move to California in a couple weeks."

"California? A couple weeks?" TJ questions, with surprised eyes, entirely taken aback.

"I know it sounds impulsive, but he's launching a new DOT COM company and his financial partner lives in San Diego."

"What about your job?"

"I've already applied for a PD position out there. Worst case I may have to consider private practice in the interim." She explains.

TJ can't conceal his stunned reaction. "Wow! I suppose somewhere deep down, I thought, okay I hoped, you'd come to your senses and dump Patrick for me," he spews with unabridged transparency.

Natalie laughs. "Don't count me out just yet, Patrick can be a handful at times," she jests.

TJ sits there with a look of shock etched across his face.

There's a noticeable delay in his response, his mind races. "Let's make a pact... New Year's Eve, five years from today." He pauses for mind math.

"That would be January 2000, the millennial," Natalie quickly calculates.

"That's right," he confirms.

She chuckles.

"Like your mother, my dad also taught me two profound life lessons; *life is a gift, how we live life is a decision* and to *never show fear.* He looks at her and asks, "How am I doing?"

"What do you mean?" Natalie emotionally responds.

"I'm just wondering, if I'm able to successfully disguise my fear."

She returns a perplexed smile. "I'm confused, what are you afraid of?"

His facial expression somber, his words authentic. "I'm afraid of losing you," he confesses, with unbridled sincerity, cemented with a longing gaze.

"What are you doing to me?" she sobbingly concedes.

They sit in silence. Natalie struggles to contain her desire, as she stares back at him with hopeless eyes.

"Do you have a pen?" TJ randomly asks.

"A pen?? I'm dying over here, and you want a pen?" she says laughingly through her tears. Natalie rifles through her purse, locates a pen and hands it to TJ.

He inscribes; *1-1-2000* along the bottom border of the coveted dollar, then hands the dollar back to her. He points to the inscription and explains, "By *1-1-2000,* assuming we're both unmarried and you want to give *US* a try, send me this engraved dollar and I'll come for you." He narrates, awaiting her reply.

She smirks. "Come for me?" she banters back. "Are you suggesting that I'm a damsel in distress?" She laughs. "After today's episode I may be… Maybe one day, I'll rescue you," she playfully augments.

"I'm okay with that. Whatever works, so long as we end up together one day," he says, wearing his heart on his sleeve.

Regardless of her feelings for TJ, Natalie knows deep down that she must honor her commitment to Patrick. "So why are you giving me the dollar back? Technically, you won the tie-breaker today. Hell, I'm probably your best witness," she jokes.

They both laugh.

"If I ever see this dollar again, *I'LL* be the winner," TJ passionately reiterates, with honest eyes.

She reacts with a soft acquiescing smile. She trusts his words as truth.

Later, outside the restaurant, TJ escorts Natalie to her car.

Natalie turns to tender a long, impromptu hug.

He gently kisses her soft cheek, then heads off toward his car.

He pauses midway in the parking lot, then turns back toward Natalie, his heart pounding.

Natalie stands next to her car door, staring back at him with empty eyes.

Conflicted, he takes a few steps toward her, then instinctively stops, ever respectful of her commitment to Patrick.

She proceeds toward him.

Unable to suppress his feelings, he pulls her close. He takes gentle hold of her delicate face, as he softly kisses her lips. They share a moment, an unspoken longing and a heartfelt connection. They have something most dare to dream of. The stuff love stories are made of, yet sadly they also know, that they, at this ever-defining moment in time, have chosen to leave what they have, or better said, what they might have had, unanswered, unacknowledged, and untested. Suffice it to say, they are leaving the prospect of love, true love, on the shelf.

On the heels of Natalie's departure, TJ's left with an inconsolable void. Needless to say he's down in the proverbial dumps. Even though they never dated, he felt an inexplicable sense of loss. Sure, there were plenty of women in Miami; but Natalie was truly special.

Days later, TJ opens an envelope his paralegal Fiona had placed on his desk...

"Dear TJ,

I write with tempered pen, in hope that my words properly convey my feelings, without disrespecting the integrity of my engagement, and the promise I made to my fiancé. I will miss you, dearly. I will miss our banter, our laughter, our unspoken glances and shared dreams. I hope our respective lives turn out well for all concerned and I will carry thoughts of you, your silliness, your unrivaled chivalry, your winsome smile and yes of course, your inscribed dollar, with me on my journey.

Forever Yours, N"

Through hollow eyes he stares out from his fifteenth-floor perch, down toward the crowded streets below, as people aimlessly scurry about. He reflects upon life, *HIS* life, *HIS* future, wondering if he would end up alone like his dad, or would he settle for something less than true love.

CHAPTER 32

Spirits down, thoughts adrift, an overwhelmed TJ decides to head south to pop in on his dad, for a strong shoulder and a dose of moral support. *I should be ashamed.* He thinks to himself. *Forget my pity party, what about my dad? After all, he's in his golden years and he's alone,* TJ reminds himself with refreshing lucidity, as he quickly abandons his melancholy mood.

TJ tosses his stuffed duffle bag onto the jump seat of his new, Arles Blue, Land Rover Defender 90. He pushes off, ragtop dropped, soon stuck in bumper-to-bumper Turnpike traffic. *Looks like I may miss the sunset,* TJ concludes with a disappointed gaze.

It's dark by the time he pulls into his dad's driveway. He enters through the front screen door.

Slater's preoccupied cooking pasta.

"Didn't expect you this weekend," Slater calls out, above the noisy stovetop exhaust vent.

"Last minute decision," TJ replies, as he pops the top off a cold brew.

Sunday morning. TJ's ready to hit the highway. "Have some prep work before a big trial tomorrow," he explains.

"No worries. Drive safe son."

Over the next few months, TJ embarks upon a dating spree (okay, a dating rampage), in a fruitless attempt to forget Natalie.

He sits solo at a table for two, at his favorite Italian Restaurant "Gianni's." An ever-punctual TJ, repeatedly checks his watch, eyes roll as he impatiently waits for his excessively late date.

Dino (TJ's long-time fav waiter) approaches and asks, "What's goin on partner, you've been here three times this week, with a different chick every time."

TJ looks up with a defeated expression. "Yeah, I guess I'm having a hard time finding the right one."

"Maybe you're tryin too hard, Romeo. Just relax and let it be. You know what they say. Love will find you when you're not looking. It's called fate, my friend," Dino consoles. "If you want, I can help save you some time and money."

"How so?" a perplexed TJ asks.

"If you order wine by the glass, that's my cue to speed things up. By the bottle, I leave you alone."

"That works."

"You got it!" Dino responds, with an affirming *thumbs up* gesture.

His date eventually arrives. "Sorry I'm late."

TJ (having eaten a basket of breadsticks) begrudgingly stands to shake her hand.

They sit.

TJ's assessment: pretty, ditzy, and dull.

Dino approaches, wine list tucked under his arm. Wearing a smirk, he asks, "Can I get you something to drink?"

"Two glasses of Pinot," TJ responds, holding up two fingers.

Over the next several weeks, TJ ends up ordering a vineyard of wine, by the glass, culminating in an uneventful dating disaster. As a diversion, he decides to immerse himself into a heavy caseload, quite literally running from one courtroom to another, while maintaining his impeccable record.

Desperate for some downtime, TJ dials his dad. After several rings, Slater finally answers. "Hello."

"Dad?" TJ anxiously replies.

"Hey, son," Slater answers, in a debatably depressed tone.

"What's wrong? You seem down?" TJ asks with due concern.

"No. I'm fine,"

"You sure?" TJ probes.

"I'm good!" Slater tries to (unconvincingly) reassure.

"I was thinking about coming down this weekend, if you're up for company."

"That would be great, son. Would love to see you," Slater answers in a perkier voice.

That Friday, TJ arrives just before sunset; parks out front then heads inside.

He grabs a cold brew from the fridge, pops the top and heads outback to join his dad, already surfside.

As usual, Slater's positioned toward the tip of the jetty.

TJ navigates his way between the coral formations, rests his right hand atop Slater's slumped shoulder and takes a seat.

"Hey, Dad."

"Hey, son," Slater replies through a halfhearted smile, as he guzzles a bottle of beer in a single swallow.

TJ takes purposeful note of the empty beer bottles loosely piled around Slater's coral seat, with two on deck.

"What's goin on, Pop?" TJ inquires, unable to shed a troubled gaze. He never saw Slater hammered or even tipsy.

Slater offers no reply, as he stares off toward the distant horizon.

TJ leans in, right hand grasping Slater's shoulder. "Dad, talk to me," TJ encourages with a seldom seen sense of insistency, in his otherwise compliant tone.

Slater turns toward his son and says, "I have something to tell you, T." He takes another big swig then proceeds. "Something I should have told you years ago."

TJ remains seated, interest piqued. He carries a perplexed expression, unable to imagine what might be so horrific.

Slater pauses, then continues. "I've lived a lie for far too many years. A lie that's been gnawing at me, like a cancerous tumor. A lie I need to divulge." He takes another gulp of his beer. "All I ask, is that you allow me to tell the entire story before reacting," he conditions, through a troubled gaze.

TJ's face beckons with bewilderment. He nods and verbalizes. "Of course."

Slater fights his overwhelming instinct to look away; but maintains direct eye contact with his son. "When I was initially reassigned to Key West, I was gung-ho. I truly believed our efforts would make a difference." He pauses then continues. "Initially, our intercepts put a real dent in the Cartel's smuggling operations. We confiscated millions upon millions in cash and cargo and simply handed it over to the Feds. Never once did I ever consider taking a taste, always the trusted patriot. But as time went on, I started to resent my comparatively meager salary, particularly given the life-threatening situations associated with my job description. I started to envy the bad guys I'd routinely apprehend. Mindless morons making millions."

TJ interjects, "Dad, please stop. I'm a duly sworn officer of the law and if you plan on revealing some wrongdoing on your part, you'll put me in a very precarious position," he warns with due transparency.

Slater pauses to collect his courage, then turns toward TJ. "I know that son, I do; but I need to tell you the unabridged truth and let the chips fall where they may. I'm fully prepared for that eventuality," Slater apprises, wearing a pain-ridden expression. "I was not the standup man I purported to be. Sadly, quite the opposite. I was no more than a spineless crook. No better than the bastards I'd routinely bust. You need to hear the truth, a truth that would have exonerated your self-imposed guilt years ago. A truth that I cowardly kept from you, my surviving son," he utters on the verge of tears. "You had nothing to do with your brother's murder or your mother's decision to leave."

TJ sits in awe.

Slater proceeds. "The bikers who distributed the Cartel's drugs, approached me early on. Basically, they bribed me to look the other way. Initially, I scoffed at the notion, but as time passed, I grew more comfortable with the concept. They initially paid me a couple hundred-grand to hook me, and it worked. Lunch money for them, retirement for me. Over time there was even more money. All I had to do was turn a blind eye and occasionally redirect operations from one inlet to another, while they unloaded their product. This went on for a couple of years. After a while, the payoffs became smaller, eventually nothing at all. Who could blame them? After all, they owned me. I was in deep, and they knew it. Hell, if I blew the whistle, we'd all fall, hard!" Slater offers a sigh of deep regret, followed by another gulp of beer.

They sit in silence. No words shared. TJ tries to process what he's just learned.

Slater resumes. "I was unexpectedly summoned to D.C. I wasn't sure why. I worried that my misdeeds had been discovered.

Turns out, I was tapped as the main actor in an undercover operation to bust the Drug Lord's eldest son, who was in charge of distribution. Long story short, we busted the little bastard. With him behind bars, I saw a kink in their armor. Not sure if it was good old-fashioned greed or if I was just tired of being their Bitch. I guess deep down I worried that these Bastards would flip on me if they got busted. Who knows, probably a combination," Slater reveals with a shake of his head. "Bottom line, I hated myself; but I hated them even more. I grew tired of sitting back while these lowlife pricks walked away with millions," he recants with vindictive eyes. "I decided to turn the tables. So, I hatched a plan to assemble a team of naval confidants, to help me steal their money and take their drugs, leaving a pile of dead crooks in my wake, to send a message."

TJ sits there speechless, in utter disbelief.

Slater pushes on. "Hard to imagine… but it gets worse. That following morning, about 5 a.m., I received a phone call. The voice on the other end of the line spoke broken English; but his message was crystal clear. *Return the money and drugs, or we kill your boys,* he warned." Slater takes another emotional pause, as his eyes well with remorse, "I chose to ignore his warning. I disregarded it as an idle threat. I figured we were invincible. Worse yet, I never made any effort to protect you and your brother." Slater turns away and stares out toward the endless sea and concedes through an emotional reveal. "The next day, your brother was raped and murdered. I knew I had erred, terribly." Deep cleansing breath, followed by another swig, as Slater pivots toward TJ. "T, you have no burden to shoulder son. Your mother was disgusted with me and my greed. Her abandonment and your brother's murder, were both consequences of my inexcusable actions, and inactions."

TJ turns away, enraged eyes, literally speechless.

After a brief gap in conversation, Slater concludes. "The day of your brother's funeral, the Cartel called again, demanding the money. They told me I had twenty-four hours to drop the cash and product at a designated mile marker, or you would be next."

With a stunned expression, TJ asks, "So what did you do?" thoroughly dumbfounded by what he has just heard.

"I returned every dollar of course," Slater emphatically defends.

TJ's head is spinning. He's utterly perplexed. "What about this place?" he asks, pointing to their beachfront bungalow. "Did you use drug money to buy our home too?"

"I told you before, I paid for this place with my pension," Slater resoundingly replies.

TJ sits there, carrying a stunned look as he tries to process the content of what Slater had just unveiled.

"I had two choices, neither good. I could have told you what I had done and lose your respect or remain quiet and live a lie." He turns toward TJ, with sorrowful eyes. "T, I cannot begin to tell you how sorry I am, and I don't expect you to ever forgive me! I simply wanted to come clean and relive myself of this heavy burden." He finishes, dropping his head in shame.

Slater's confession was startlingly surreal, and in all events too much for TJ to comprehend in one sitting. TJ needs time to digest the magnitude of all that he discovered today, time to fully process and absorb the ramifications of Slater's admission to murder and as a co-conspirator to drug trafficking. TJ's a lawyer, a sanctioned officer of the courts, whose job it is to prosecute those accused of crimes, let alone harbor a confessed criminal. He stands and leaves without retort.

A conflicted TJ walks off, back toward the cottage to collect his belongings. He stops midway and turns back to witness a defeated Slater, head hung low.

He heads inside and retrieves his car keys.

He travels north toward Miami, his thoughts but a blur. Words cannot begin to describe the pain he carries. *I feel like I've been living a lie,* he thinks to himself, *Was the man I called Dad, no more than a common criminal and a mass murder, masquerading as a father and respected naval officer?* TJ torments himself. He soon concludes that he would be an accessory to murder, if he didn't apprehend his father. Decision made.

He exits the highway and turns into a corner service station. He pulls up to the gas pump and fills his near empty tank, growing madder by the minute. He tops off his tank and decides to head home to sleep on it.

That following morning, TJ heads south to arrest his dad.

After an hour plus drive, he pulls up and parks out front. He takes a moment to collect his thoughts, before entering the house. Arresting his dad would be a tough task, to say the least. He stares at the cottage he and his dad had renovated together, the house that fostered so many happy memories. He sits there, wholly heartbroken. He slowly musters the courage to set his emotions aside and perform his occupational duty. As he enters the house, he calls out, "Dad." Without reply. His eyes pan the limits of the cottage. He walks toward the rear screen door and peers out toward the jetty. Slater's not there. He methodically clears the first floor then proceeds upstairs. He approaches, then gently opens Slater's (partially closed) bedroom door and enters. He sees his father in bed. As he approaches, he notices a blood-soaked pillowcase and a telltale entry wound to his right temple. A 38-caliber handgun, lay next to his lifeless hand. Slater left this world the same way he lived his life, no drama, no excuses, no note!

TJ remains surprisingly calm, and at some level relieved. Wasting no time, he dials his father's long-time friend and confidant, FBI agent, Corbin Cole.

"Hello," Corbin answers, before the second ring.

"Corbin. Tane Jensen here, Slater's son."

"How are you?" Corbin responds.

"Well. I've been better. I'm sad to report that my father's taken his life."

"*WHAT*?" Corbin replies in a shocked tone. "I'm stunned. Your father would be the last person on earth I'd ever imagine taking his life. I'm in total disbelief… Your dad was an icon. I'm so sorry," Corbin remorsefully adds. "Do you have any idea what prompted it?" Corbin inquires.

"I do, but that's a conversation I'd prefer to have in person. Professionally speaking, the circumstances surrounding his suicide will likely constitute further investigation."

"Understood. Where's his body?" Corbin asks.

"At his cottage, in Sombrero Key. 16 Coconut Drive."

"Okay. Let me see if I can assemble a CSI team. Assuming I can, we should be there in about three hours, four hours tops. As you know, please don't touch anything."

"Of course." TJ reassures.

"Once again, I'm so sorry for your loss. Your dad was a truly remarkable man," Corbin says solemnly.

He may change his opinion, once he hears what I have to say, TJ tells himself, with a saddened gaze. He kicks off his shoes and heads out back, through the familiar screen porch door. He walks down the rickety steps and out onto the soothing sand. He pauses to take a deep cleansing breath, as he collects his thoughts. The ocean is particularly calm today, as if to mourn his father's passing, as the soft waves gently caress the sandy shore. His eyes veer off toward the ever-faithful jetty. Not only did the jetty protect them from stormy seas; but it also provided an emotional refuge as well. He struggles to make sense of it all. He feels betrayed by the man he saw as his protector, his rock.

Mentally fatigued, he heads back inside, lays down on the sofa and soon falls asleep.

Hours later, he's awakened by a deliberate, knuckled knock upon the front door.

TJ springs up and off the sofa to answer the door.

Corbin and his team enter.

"His body's upstairs, first room to the left," TJ informs, as he points.

Corbin's crew (carrying their forensic gear) head upstairs.

Corbin and TJ walk out back to talk.

"Over the past couple months, my dad seemed down, borderline depressed. So, I thought to pay him a visit. When I got here, he was drunk. I never saw him drunk before. He looked emotional, as if he'd been crying. I never saw him cry either, not even at my brother's funeral. Anyway, he revealed that he'd taken bribes from the Cartel. He also told me that he orchestrated the Cartel massacre at Big Pine and stole their cash and drugs. He went on to tell me that the Cartel warned him that they'd kill my brother and me, if he didn't promptly return the cash and product. At first, he ignored them; but after my brother's death he told me that he returned the money. I'm not sure if that's true. Anyway, I apprised him of his Miranda rights. He said he understood, and willingly continued. I drove home and returned this morning, to take him into custody. I wanted to spare him the humiliation of being cuffed and arrested. When I arrived, I found him dead in his bed."

"Wow. That's certainly a lot to process," Corbin concedes with empathetic eyes.

"I want to be fully transparent. I'd like to see if your office can determine if my dad had any hidden bank accounts. Again, my dad claims he returned the money and bought this place with his pension. I just want to confirm that's the case."

"Understood," Corbin quickly concurs.

CHAPTER 33

ON THE HEELS of his father's disturbing confession and subsequent suicide, TJ decides to take a leave of absence. He needs time off. Time to digest what had happened, time to process his past, and redefine his future. With that, he assigns his caseload to a senior ADA, Hutch Halvorsen, during his sabbatical.

In the interim, Corbin's team ultimately determines that the cottage was in fact acquired with funds from Slater's pension and not dirty (drug) money as TJ had feared. Consequently, TJ (Slater's heir apparent) received rightful ownership to the bungalow. Fortunately, there was also no evidence of any offshore bank accounts or surreptitious stock portfolios to unveil.

Having just finished a plateful of grilled shrimp and risotto, TJ heads off to the jetty to take in the late day sunset, which casts a pinkish hue across the infinite sea. He finds a dry coral seat and sits in ponder. His mind swarming with mixed emotion. It felt odd, being here without his dad. He felt despondent, angered by his father's misdeeds. He wonders how such a good and honorable man went awry. Why did he veer off path? He remembers his father's succinct words of advice; *Life is a gift - how we live life is a decision.* How hypocritical, TJ thinks to himself. After more than a few brews, he hobbles on home, crashes on the couch, and awakens to a new day.

Weeks later, TJ returns to work. He huddles with Hutch to recap ongoing caseloads.

"Nothing out of the ordinary," Hutch relays. "Busted a handful of hookers and a couple bikers, transporting blow."

"Bikers have any priors?"

"Nothing earthshattering." Hutch responds, as he reads from their arrest tickets, "Danny Quinn, aka *Beaver*, had a couple assault charges and the other guy, Archibald Germaine, aka *Germ* did some time for a variety of drug related offenses.

Hutch hands TJ their arrest jackets, containing their arrest photos.

The instant TJ sees Germaine's photo, he immediately recognizes him as the accomplice in his brother's murder. His eyes widen, unable to conceal an emotional gulp.

"Where are we holding these jokers?" TJ nonchalantly inquires.

"Both drying out in County," Hutch proudly replies.

"Let's move em downtown. Like to see if they'll agree to flip on their supplier. Worth a shot," TJ directs.

"On it!" Hutch confirms, as he stands and leaves.

The following morning. TJ phones his old friend, Warden Russel "Rusty" Dupree.

"T-man! What's up my brother?"

"Like to see if I can get some face time with a perp named Archibald Germaine."

"Let me check my log... Yup, he arrived late last night," Rusty confirms. "No problem, tell me when."

"How does now work?" TJ eagerly asks.

Rusty laughs. "You got it! See you in a few."

Within minutes, TJ arrives and undergoes customary security protocols.

He spots Rusty at the far end of the narrow corridor, headed his way.

"Hey, bubba, what's up?" an amiable Rusty greets. "Sorry to hear about your padre," Rusty adds.

"Thanks, pal." Old friends hug.

"Follow me," Rusty directs, as they head off down a series of interconnecting cellblocks, periodically stopping to swipe Rusty's ID card to gain restricted access.

Before long, they approach the open yard.

"I decided to move him outside. More privacy," Rusty apprises with a devilish grin. "How long will you need?"

"Ten minutes, max," TJ replies, as he hands his watch, car keys and suitcoat to Rusty.

"Roger that." Rusty once again swipes his ID card, followed by a distinctive beep, as the yard door pops open.

TJ enters.

"Go get em, Rambo," Rusty jests with a thumbs up gesture.

The yard's virtually empty, except for Germaine, positioned at the far end of the basketball court. He's seated atop the asphalt pavement, boney back pressed against the rigid chain link fence, desperately trying to draw a drag or two from a discarded cigarette butt.

TJ heads toward him.

Germaine guardedly stands, carrying a puzzled expression, "who the fuck, are you?" he barks in a gruff, confrontational tone.

TJ stops a couple meters shy of where Germaine now stands, without reply.

"You my fuckin lawyer?" Germaine yelps.

"Nope," TJ says with a smirk.

"Then what the fuck do you want?" Germaine snaps.

"Revenge."

"WHAT?"

"I'm here to avenge my brother's murder."

"What the fuck you talkin about?" Germaine dismisses, as he scoffs and heads off toward the exit door.

"You have two options, Germ. You can either be a cooperative informant and walk, or you can be a hostile witness and stand trial as accessory to rape and murder."

Germaine halts his exodus and slowly turns back toward TJ. "You the kid from Big Pine?"

"Good guess," TJ says as he closes the gap between them.

"You know that shit wasn't personal... When the fuckin Cartel says jump, the Club asks how high," Germaine deflects.

"Give me the name of the big-bastard who raped and killed my younger brother."

Germaine hesitates. "What do I get?" Germaine negotiates.

"I just told you. You get to enjoy the rest of your pathetic life outside of prison," TJ responds as he steps closer.

Germaine hesitates, then offers him up, "Muller. Joe Muller. Street tag *Ox*. He's a big mother fucker. Probably six seven or bigger. Anyway, he's a sick prick... has a thing for young boys... After that Big Pine screw up, the Club bounced his ass."

"So, he's no longer a biker?"

"Fuck no! They tossed his sick ass out, long ago."

"You know where I can find him?"

"Last I heard, he hooked up with some skank ass dancer. Think she has a trailer in Dania or some shit. That's all I know."

"I'll check it out," TJ says as he walks off.

"What about me?" Germaine reiterates.

"If your information proves out, you walk. If not, welcome home!"

Germaine offers a subtle, albeit concessionary nod.

Fortunately, Muller (aka *Ox*) wasn't hard to find. As a registered sex offender, he's required to routinely report to his parole officer. TJ makes an appointment to meet Muller's P/O, Eddie Castro.

The pair meet inside Castro's crammed office cubicle.

Castro's a grumpy, disheveled sort who reeks of cigarette smoke.

"I'd like to get some Intel on one of your parolees, Joseph, William, Muller, aka *Ox*" TJ respectfully requests.

"Intel?" Castro questions in a dismissive, unobliging tone.

Perturbed by Castro's curtness, TJ rephrases his question. "Let's try this again, Mr. Castro!!" TJ says in a stern tone. "My name is Tane Jensen. I'm with the Dade County DA's office. I have reason to believe that parolee Muller, may have had a direct role in an unsolved rape and murder. As such, I will need to question him. Any further confusion on your end?"

Castro shelves his attitude. "No sir!"

"Wonderful! Now, I'd like to know where he resides and if there's anything relevant, you might be able to share."

Castro (seated) rolls his chair over to his metal file cabinet. He searches for, finds and removes Muller's arrest records. "Joseph William Muller, (aka *Ox*). Well, he's been steadily employed at a local grocery store for the past eight months and he currently resides with Shelly Reynolds, at 1521 Sterling Road, trailer 212B."

"To be clear, our meeting is of the strictest confidence," TJ informs. "We *CLEAR*?" he reiterates.

"Clear!" Castro quickly confirms, with a submissive mien.

Outside now. TJ heads toward his car as he dials long-time pal, Rico Vasquez, with the Broward County Sheriff's Office (BSO). "Rico. TJ here. How are you, my friend?"

"Can't complain. Been a long time," Rico replies, as he steps out of a meeting.

"Too long! I apologize for not staying in touch… I'm sorry to ask, but I could really use your help."

"Of course. What's goin on, homey?"

"Long story short, I may have identified my brother's murderer. I'd like to see if you can help me circumvent some red tape with Dania Beach, PD. I'd like to move on this guy posthaste."

"Understood. Happy to lend a hand," Rico quickly confirms.

"That would be a tremendous help. Thank you!" TJ replies, through a sigh of relief.

The following morning, Rico and TJ meet with Dania Beach Staff Sergeant Brian Osborne. After being thoroughly debriefed, Osborne assigns an undercover team to accompany Rico and TJ, to present Muller with an arrest warrant.

Before pushing off, all exchange transmission frequencies, then travel in tandem.

4:54 p.m., they arrive and park across the street from *Dania Dunes* trailer park.

5:18 p.m., a rusted pickup pulls into the trailer park. The driver's an enormous fellow, resembling Muller's arrest photo.

"Stay on post, we're goin in," Vasquez informs the undercover officers.

They return affirming nods.

Rico and TJ move out, soon trailing Muller's truck, traveling a respectable distance back, to avoid detection.

After a half block or so, Muller pulls up and onto a grassless yard.

An emaciated, bleach blonde woman emerges from the dingy single-wide, dressed in a tawdry cocktail outfit, as a lit cigarette dangles from her crusty lips.

The unidentified woman hops up and into the truck, as Muller heads inside.

To avoid being spotted, TJ and Rico casually drive on by.

Rico radios the officers, posted out front. "A blonde woman is leaving in Muller's truck. Go ahead and detain her."

"Roger that!" they eagerly respond.

TJ and Rico circle the block and eventually park across the street.

TJ's heart is pounding. Emotions run high.

The undercover officers detain Shelly Reynolds. "Suspect in custody," they apprise.

"FYI, her four-year old son is inside the trailer with Muller."

"10-4," Rico replies.

Inside the trailer, Muller stands in front of the dated fridge, door open to cool off. He grabs a tall Bud, then heads over to a tattered pleather sofa.

Shelly's son sits on the floor, in front of the TV, watching cartoons.

Muller plops down onto the sofa, pops open his can of beer and calls out, "Get your little butt over here."

The little boy gulps, eyes widened in fear (he's been here before).

Unable to contain his rage, TJ (ignoring protocol) exits the vehicle and marches toward the trailer, like a steadfast warrior.

An utterly frustrated Vasquez, remains inside the vehicle, shaking his head as he calls for backup.

TJ approaches the front door, tries the door handle. It's locked. He steps back and effortlessly kicks the flimsy door open.

Muller turns toward TJ, who stands inside the broken doorframe.

The little boy (free from Muller's lecherous grasp) sprints out the door.

Muller slowly stands, as his bald head literally skims the trailer ceiling. He carries a befuddled expression, eyes squint from the bright sun that envelopes TJ's silhouette. "Who the fuck are you, and what the *FUCK* are you doin in my home?" Muller grumbles.

"I'm here to arrest you for the rape and murder of my younger brother, Brandon Jensen," TJ authoritatively reveals. "He was only ten when you violated him and ended his life, you, psychotic prick!!" TJ spews.

After a short pause, "I remember him," Muller casually reveals with a perverted (reminiscent) grin. "He had a real tight asshole," Muller goads. "So big brother's here ta beat up the bad guy. Is that what this is about? Let's see what ya got bitch," Muller challenges.

TJ steps inside the trailer, as he cautiously advances toward Muller.

Suddenly, Muller rushes TJ, literally lifting him off the floor and slamming him into the tinny trailer wall. Muller pins TJ against the wall with a forceful armbar to his throat, as his free-hand pounds TJ's ribcage with a series of bone battering blows.

Unable to escape Muller's death grip grasp, TJ slips in and out of consciousness.

After a few exhausting minutes, Muller's stamina starts to

wane. Winded, he halts, to catch his breath, through successive gasps.

TJ seizes the moment and feverishly bombards Muller's head with pulverizing punches.

Unable to endure TJ's relentless assault, a dizzied Muller ultimately relinquishes his clasp, as he wobbles in place.

TJ takes advantage of Muller's brief disorientation, as he delivers a decisive head butt to Muller's forehead, followed by a thrusting (field goal) kick to Muller's groin.

Muller crouches over in agony, as TJ rams his right knee into the underside of Muller's jaw, launching the big man backwards, shattering the glass-top coffee table. Muller lays there moaning, as he slowly rolls onto his stomach, in preparation to stand.

A quick-witted TJ removes his belt, threads it through the buckle, then sleeves it around Muller's massive neck. He plants his foot on the fold of Muller's back, as he tightens the makeshift noose.

The big man's oxygen deprived face turns eggplant purple.

"Listen carefully, you insidious bastard. Today, is your day of atonement. Today you die!" an enraged TJ, scolds.

Vasquez now inside the trailer, gun drawn. He sees TJ choking the life out of Muller. "TJ! Let him go, dude. This is not how you want this to play out. Let's just arrest this mother fucker and throw his fat ass in prison. Trust me buddy, ya gotta back down!!"

An irate TJ reluctantly loosens his grip.

Muller lays there, face down on his big belly, gasping for air.

CHAPTER 34

MONTHS LATER. TJ and his ADA associates attend an obligatory Florida Bar social. A cynical TJ stands alone by design, strategically positioned off to the far corner, of an overcrowded rooftop event. He sips watered down Cabernet, while enjoying the serene cityscape and its Biscayne Bay backdrop.

His colleagues on the other hand, are on a mission, as they mingle amongst the crowd, in pursuit of a coveted, high-paying, private practice position.

TJ glances at his watch and quickly concludes that he has a few more minutes of political protocol before calling it a night, as he loosens his Windsor knot in preparation for launch.

Decision made, as he skillfully segues through the unobliging crowd. Midway through the societal logjam, he catches a brief glimpse of an incomparable pair of legs, neatly tucked beneath a tightly fitted, red skirt. He does a doubletake, tightens his tie and heads over to introduce himself.

It didn't take long for TJ to realize, that this woman didn't fit his standard M/O. She wasn't just another late-night conquest; but a woman of substance, a *Lady* he wanted to get to know better.

Her name, Cynthia Collins, a respected estate attorney and partner with Lavelle, Kessler, and Clay.

After an hour or so of flagrant flirtation, they leave together, exchanging lingering glances and business cards.

"If you ever need a Will drafted, you know who to call." Cynthia teases.

TJ laughs. "Not me, I plan on spending every dime before I die."

"That's the spirit. Probably the best way to raise self-sufficient kids," she jests. "You would be surprised how money can ruin kids and destroy families."

The valet arrives with her car.

She turns toward TJ. "Good night," she says with a parting wave and a coquettish smile.

TJ takes soft hold of her arm and gently draws her back toward him, as he delicately kisses her on the lips. "A very good night," he adds, as they lock eyes.

Later, TJ drives home, windows down, big grin. *I may have found the right woman after all*, he thinks to himself, as the radio plays.

Their first date is equally memorable. TJ made reservations at Le Mansion, touted to be the best French restaurant in Miami. They're seated at a quiet table for two, overlooking Biscayne Bay.

"I haven't eaten here, but hear it's fantastic," TJ confesses.

"It is!" Cynthia replies with suggestive familiarity, anchored with a seductive stare.

"Good evening," the haughty waiter greets, in a fake French accent, as he hands TJ a five-inch-thick wine list. "Our wine list, *Monsieur*" he proffers.

"Thank you," TJ replies.

"Let me bring you some sparkling water, while you peruse our wine selections," the persnickety waiter, flamboyantly adds, in exit.

TJ opens the wine *novel*, and soon realizes, that all the wine selections have French labels, as he ponders his next move.

Cynthia, noshing on a freshly baked croissant, giggles.

He looks up at her, smiles and asks, "What's so funny?"

"I can help you with that, if you'd like," she humbly offers, with a compassionate smile.

"You speak French?" he asks in awe.

"*Oui!*" she replies with playful eyes, followed by a flirtatious twirl of her long hair. "Embarrassingly, I minored in French. An incorrigible romantic I suppose."

TJ happily hands her the menu and his heart.

Cynthia quickly scans the wine list and asks, "Do you prefer red or white?"

"Either works for me, I'm simple," TJ replies, relishing her innate beauty.

"Well, they have a wonderful selection of Sauvignon Blancs and a marvelous Chassagne-Montrachet if you like white; but if you're a red man, they have a top shelf Chateau Lafite Rothchild, as well as a superb Beaulieu Vineyard Private Reserve."

"You decide, truly," TJ reaffirms, with an obliging gaze.

She laughs and locks eyes with him. "Now that's a confident man. We should work well together," she suggestively notes.

Later, TJ walks Cynthia to her car. He gently kisses her on the lips.

She closes her eyes, savoring the magic of the moment.

"Aren't you going to try to get me into bed?" she whispers with hopeful eyes.

"Good things take time and you're far too special to rush."

"Wow, you know all the right things to say," she replies, followed by a smitten stare and another long, meaningful kiss. Enamored, she leaves.

The following morning, when Cynthia arrives at her office, she's greeted by a fresh bouquet of pink peonies, inside a Baccarat crystal vase. She reads the handwritten note.

"It may be too early to reveal my softer side; but I'm a sucker for peonies. They're a bold and beautiful spring bloom, with an effervescent bouquet, much like you!

Fondly, TJ"

Her face flush with emotion. She smiles to herself. She likes this fellow, a bunch.

Before long, they're a committed couple.

Cynthia's not only beautiful and kind; but an equally brilliant, well-respected lawyer. There was one drawback however, philanthropic events are an integral part of her job description and accompanying her would become TJ's job too. It went with the territory of being a high-powered estate attorney, he rationalizes.

They share common values, and an unmentionable disdain for those brash few, with blood of blue. The proverbial bad apples who spoil the well-intended reputations of the larger bunch. Her clients are not merely wealthy, but the mega-wealthy, not just uncommonly affluent, but exceedingly opulent. Those with less than a nine-figure net worth, are considered working class (an inner-office joke of course). As a rule, the wealth creators are generally respectful, understated and humble people. Unfortunately, the same seldom holds true for their generational heirs, who are generally nothing more than audacious ass holes. Their mere presence makes charitable events wholly unbearable and regrettably intolerable.

TJ recalls one such event, hosted by a particularly pompous punk named Elliott Randolph Westport IV. Elliott's heir apparent to the Westport Wineries (and he certainly was a whiner). He had sponsored an event to help raise awareness for Alzheimer's (a disease that plagued his unhealthy, yet wealthy, grandmother). Elliott's roughly TJ's age, Harvard educated and gainfully unemployed. He did have a job of sorts, pushing his cantankerous grandmother around in her gold-plated wheelchair.

TJ's a respectful man, with a soft spot for the elderly; but Mildred Westport was an incorrigible witch of a woman, affectionately referred to as, *the Wicked Witch of Westport*. She'd routinely refer to the blacks as *coloreds* and those of lesser privilege (like TJ), as *commoners*. She was a reprehensible bigot by all accounts. She makes a point of telling anyone who cared enough to give a listen, who she knew and how much she had, and Elliott is keenly interested in the math portion.

TJ stands bar-side, preparing to order a well-needed, long overdue, on-tap brew, as Cynthia slowly sips a Pinot blend by his side.

Elliot, fancying himself as a lady's man, spots Cynthia and saunters over. He slips her a kiss and strategically places his emasculated arm around her bare shoulder. "Glad you could attend," he suggestively says.

"Elliott, I'd like to introduce you to TJ. TJ, this is Elliot."

TJ extends his hand, which Elliott snootily snubs.

TJ smiles and simply brushes it off as an obvious act of insecurity.

Elliott grabs Cynthia by the arm and tugs gently. "Dance

with me," he coaxes with silly boy eyes, in route to the dance floor.

"TJ, do you mind?" Cynthia respectfully asks, while handing him her glass of wine as Elliott whisks her away.

"Not at all, have at it," TJ winsomely responds with a raise of his beer.

The moment Elliott steps onto the dance floor, the band instantly segues into a fast-paced Latin tempo. Elliot assumes center stage, prompting other guests to relinquish the floor, as he proudly unveils his pre-rehearsed rumba routine. No doubt, this evening was the summation of his costly dance lessons and tonight was his opportunity to cash in. The band was choreographically on cue, and Elliott was completely clueless.

Afterwards, Elliott escorts an unsuspecting Cynthia out back, away from the crowd and onto an ill-lit stone terrace.

Cynthia turns toward TJ and motions for him to join them.

Instead, TJ opts for a second beer, thinking Elliot's entitled to have his time to flop.

Before long, a visually unsettled Cynthia makes her way across the room.

Concerned, TJ sets his beer to rest as he hurries to intercept her exit.

"Are you okay?" he asks in a compassionate tone.

"Let's go please!" she exclaims, uncharacteristically unnerved.

"What's wrong?" TJ repeats with due concern.

"Please, TJ, can we just go?" she reiterates, trying to stifle her emotion.

TJ obliges her request, as they exit the premises.

Their car is soon summoned by the parking attendant.

Driving home he again asks, "Cynthia, what happened?" turning toward her, as he gently takes hold of her left hand.

She shakes her head, staring out the window. "That little bastard told me that I would lose his grandmother's account, unless I slept with him."

TJ bites his lip and lets it go (for the moment anyway).

Months later. Cynthia and TJ are out to dinner with friends, at a trendy, South Beach restaurant called *Grass*. The restaurant floor is literally covered in live grass (maintained by off hour cultivation lights and a soft spray irrigation system).

Everyone's having a fabulous time, until Elliott (and his Vodka Tonic buzz), appears behind Cynthia's chair, as he whispers into her ear.

She rebuts his brazen advance and politely pushes him away, followed by an abrupt turn of her head.

Elliot concedes defeat and returns to his table, anchored by a vocal huff.

Cynthia remains seated.

"Is everything okay?" TJ asks in a consoling tone, left arm rests atop her chair.

She nods, "Give me a minute. I'm sorry," she tells the table, as she heads to the *ladies' room* to compose herself.

TJ stands and pulls out her chair, then notices Elliott trailing Cynthia at a harried pace.

TJ watches as Elliott corners her in the restroom corridor.

He politely excuses himself, sets his napkins atop his seat and heads off to render aid.

As he approaches, he overhears Elliott's idle threats. He then observes Elliott groping Cynthia's buttocks.

TJ immediately steps in and grabs Elliott by his bright blue bow tie. "Pardon us," he says, as he forcibly escorts Elliott into the *men's room*.

Once inside the restroom, TJ releases his grip on Elliott's tie.

An older gentleman (washing his hands), sensing a pending confrontation, wisely exits.

Elliott confronts TJ with fabricated ferocity. "Who the fuck do you think you are?" Elliot berates, stepping into TJ's *no-go* zone, poking his stiff index finger into the crest of TJ's broad chest, with enflamed eyes, gritted teeth.

TJ smiles and grabs hold of Elliott's finger, bending it backward as he walks Elliott, and his attitude, into the tiled wall. "First of all, you entitled brat, if you don't start playing nice, you might end up with a bad boo-boo. Secondly, didn't your mommy ever tell you that gentlemen should never bully ladies?" TJ confidently commands, as he slowly bends Elliott's finger further, evoking a pain-induced response.

"Ouch, you're hurting me," Elliott whimpers.

To TJ's astonishment, the little shitter spits in his face.

TJ nonchalantly wipes Elliott's vodka slobber from his face, then *SLAPS* Elliott's chubby cheeks, stingingly *HARD*. "Elliott, here forward, you have two non-negotiable options. You can either continue to act like a little prick, and I *WILL* hurt you; or you can compose yourself like a gentleman and walk away without further ado. The choice is yours."

Elliott offers an alcohol induced, smart-ass smirk.

TJ shakes his head and walks off.

Elliott unleashes an unabridged verbal assault. "Fuck off. You, presumptuous middle-class moron."

TJ halts his departure, smiles to himself, takes a cleansing sigh then turns to face Elliott. "What did you say you little twit?"

Elliot advances toward TJ and rants, "The gall of you to think yourself worthy to court a woman of Cynthia's caliber and lineal privilege, given your bourgeois background is audacious at best. For fuck-sake, her father was the co-founder of Ingham, Collins and Strauss and the standing Commodore at John's Island and what are your lineal loins, I wonder. Oh yes, I did my research, your father was a mediocre Naval officer, who cowardly took his meager life, leaving you, his bastard, Army brat son," he finishes with a pompous smile.

Unable to restrain himself, TJ grabs Elliott by his throat and squeezes hard!

Elliot's oxygen deprived face turns radish red, his eyes water profusely.

"Elliot, if you continue to say nasty things, you leave me no choice but to wash your mouth out," TJ finishes, before releasing his grip.

"Fuck off, asshole!" an emboldened Elliot yelps.

"Don't say I didn't warn you!" TJ threatens as he grabs Elliott by the back of his belt, literally lifting him up and off the floor, as he walks him into an open stall, soon plunging his head into the toilet.

Afterwards, TJ casually walks over to the sink, washes his hands, and combs his hair before returning to his table to rejoin Cynthia and their friends.

Before long, Cynthia and TJ are fundamentally inseparable. They have all but formally moved in together, alternating between their respective places. During the week, TJ would stay at Cynthia's loft apartment in downtown Miami and on weekends, they would venture south to the Keys to unwind. Their lives effortlessly melded as one. They would cook together, exercise together, and laugh together with uncommon synchronicity. They shared parallel hopes and lofty dreams. The only point of contention was the uncertainty surrounding their future together. Cynthia wants more. She wants to take their relationship to the next level; but TJ cannot (not yet anyway). For some inexplicable reason, he feels hostage to his self-imposed deadline with Natalie. He tussles with his inescapable inner conflict, a dilemma he obviously can't share with Cynthia. A personal turmoil he's been wrestling with for a long while. An issue he needs to reconcile soon, or risk losing Cynthia.

It's late December 1999. Cynthia and TJ board an early morning flight to Denver, to meet up with a group of friends for a weeklong ski trip. The skiing conditions are purported to be exceptional.

Later that evening, the group's at dinner. Cynthia nestles close to her man. TJ feels the pressure of his self-imposed, millennial deadline. No doubt, he loves Cynthia with all his heart, and he can certainly imagine their lives together, married with children, yet he remains conflicted. *What if, by some twist of fate Natalie reaches out – what would I do?* He deliberates. Similar thoughts had woken him up in the middle of the night. He decides it's best to wait and see what the New Year holds.

January 3, 2000. TJ, Cynthia, and their entourage are at the Denver Airport.

For TJ, the long-awaited deadline had come and gone, eclipsed like any other day. To be fully certain, he phones the office.

"Fiona... TJ here."

"Hello. How's your trip?" she enthusiastically asks.

Cellular service is a tad sketchy.

"We had a wonderful time, anxious to get back to some warmer weather though. Any messages or overnight deliveries?" he asks, trying to muffle flight announcements with his free hand.

"No. It's been relatively quiet during the holidays. Why,

was there something in-particular that you were expecting?" she inquires.

"No. All good, thank you. See you tomorrow," he awkwardly replies.

"Travel safe," Fiona says in close.

Decision made. After a deep consoling breath, he marches toward the ticket counter and upgrades their seats to First Class.

Hours later, midair. TJ orders a medium-rare filet and a bottle of top-shelf champagne. He heads to the restroom ostensibly to wash his hands before dinner.

The flight attendant makes an impromptu announcement. "While we prepare the cabin for dinner, we would respectfully ask everyone to please return to their seats as we have a special announcement."

Over the intercom, TJ's voice surprises Cynthia and their friends.

"I promise to be brief," he emotionally concedes, as he retrieves, then reads his handwritten note.

Her eyes touched my soul,
Her spirit captured my heart
I am best in her presence
I am less when apart
If angels could speak
They would whisper her name
From the moment we kissed
My world never the same
She gave my life meaning
This love of my life
I ask for her hand
As partner and wife

Cynthia sits in wide-eyed surprise. Flush with emotion, she starts to sob, particularly when her girlfriends swarm her with loving hugs, wet eyes and well wishes.

She stands, wobbly legged as she rushes into the arms of her soon-to-be hubby. They embrace, as the passengers and airline staff, *ROAR* in applause.

After their engagement, TJ debated telling Cynthia about his father's confession; but ultimately concludes that it's best not to worry her unnecessarily.

Three months later. They're married beachside, on the bitter tip of the old faithful jetty (of course). The ceremony was casual, the backdrop breathtaking, the moment unforgettable.

TJ's best friend, a dapper Dillon, nails his *best man* speech. "I've known TJ since high school." Dillon chokes up, as he pushes through his emotion. "TJ's unquestionably the kindest person I have ever known. He's the best friend I ever had, and in my heart, we are truly brothers from different mothers. Please join me in toast, to my brother TJ and his lovely wife Cynthia."

TJ's eyes well with emotion. He's truly touched by his pal's heartfelt words.

All stand, glasses raised, as bride and groom kiss.

The newlyweds ultimately decide to sell Cynthia's condominium and reside beachside, despite the hour-plus commute. Life is grand. They balance well, every day a new adventure.

CHAPTER 35

LESS THAN TWO years into their marriage, they're blessed with the birth of a baby girl. They named her Samantha (Sammy) Lynn. They're happy, very happy and TJ loves his new life with his girls.

Cynthia decides to be a stay-at-home mom until Sammy's school age.

Life's different, better, uncomplicated, and finally complete. TJ has a family, a loving wife, and an adorable daughter. He finally found his purpose, as a protector and a provider. Needless to say, he's an amazing dad. Always prepared to step up, be it a diaper change or a midnight feeding. His little girl redefined him as a dad. He needed this. He needed her.

Years later, Fourth of July. All sit beachside. Sammy (seated on TJ's lap) can't contain her excitement. She stares up at the night sky, startled by each colorful explosion, trailed by little-girl giggles.

"You know she'd love Disney World," Cynthia suggests.

"Good idea," TJ acknowledges.

"What's your summer schedule like?"

"I'll make it work," TJ replies. "Nothing earth-shattering," he adds with a turn of his head, as he steals a quick kiss.

Later that month, they embark upon Sammy's first Disney adventure.

On the way, they stop off to visit Cynthia's parents, who reside in Vero Beach.

Cynthia's dad, Niles, was a highly respected, Harvard educated lawyer. He was exceedingly fond of TJ, the son he never had.

They sit out back, sharing cold beers and war stories of questionable clients and jaded judges.

Dusk. Cynthia follows Sammy (belly laughing) as they try to catch fireflies in a small jelly jar.

"This is what it's all about son," Niles reminisces, emotional reflection, staring lovingly at Cynthia and Sammy as they scurry about in the backyard, riddled with old oaks, bordered by the tranquil Indian River waterway.

"I get it," TJ solemnly replies. "I get it." He repeats.

"Life is funny, T, we live it, then we give it." Niles turns toward TJ to emphasize his point. "And the *give it* part, is what's most rewarding. Savor these days. They don't last long." Niles finishes with a paternal smile. "Having children teaches us to become ever-more selfless," Niles elaborates with wise eyes, followed by another sip of his beer.

The next morning, TJ and Cynthia pack their vehicle for their trip to Disney.

Niles holds Sammy, preoccupied with her grandpa's white beard.

TJ takes the handoff and fastens her into her car seat.

"Have fun, angel," Niles calls out.

"I will, Grandpa," Sammy replies.

Niles and Kathleen wave, as they back out of the driveway.

TJ beeps as they drive off, down the winding, oak lined road.

A couple of hours later, they pass through the gates of the Magic Kingdom.

Before long, they pull up to their hotel. Sammy's fast asleep in her car seat. TJ lifts her up, and gently repositions her into her stroller. They unload their belongings, toss the valet their car keys and head inside to check-in.

As they enter their hotel room, all eyes are instantly drawn to the massive window which reveals Cinderella's Castle.

Sammy leaps out of her stroller, points and squeals, "Cinderella's Castle!" as she dances around in tiny circles.

Later, they're immersed amongst the masses, as they stand in endless lines, amidst the sweltering midday sun.

By day's end, they've experienced most, if not all, age appropriate, rides. TJ and Cynthia hold hands, as TJ pushes Sammy (fast asleep in her stroller).

After three exhausting days at Disney, TJ and Cynthia are physically spent and happily homebound.

Back home early morning, too early for the beach crowd. Sammy splashes in the soothingly warm shallows, trying to grasp the concept of snorkeling.

Cynthia approaches, clutching a fresh cup of herbal green tea. She smiles, eyes upon Sammy, as she kicks her skinny legs, snorkel up, dive mask down, in search of sea life.

TJ, standing in waist high water, calls out, "This kid's an amphibian." He laughs. "I can't believe how quickly she caught on," he pridefully adds.

Cynthia, seated in the sand, just smiles.

Later that evening, TJ fires up the backyard BBQ.

Cynthia steps outback, carrying a tray full of marinated chicken and corn on the cob (tightly wrapped in aluminum foil).

TJ stares at Cynthia with a loving gaze. No words needed. She smiles back blissfully before pirating a kiss.

"She's a little pistol, just like her mama," TJ teases, as he methodically positions the chicken, onto the piping hot grill.

Cynthia wraps her narrow arms around TJ's idle arm, while panning the calm seas. "We couldn't ask for a better life, sweetheart. We're beyond blessed," she whispers.

"We are indeed," he says with a soft smile and loving eyes.

Later. TJ positions a few precut logs around a makeshift fire pit, in preparation for a beachside bonfire.

"T-man, *what up?*" TJ's oldest and dearest friend Dillon greets, with a mile-wide smile and a brotherly embrace.

TJ hugs Dillon's lovely wife Nina (a former schoolmate), then chases their rambunctious twin boys (Luke and Sebastian) around the beach with his BBQ tongs, as Sammy tries to defend her friends (giggling).

After dinner, TJ and Dillon sit fireside, as their wives prepare dessert inside. They share an uncommon kinship and a couple Coronas.

"I think a toast is in order," TJ suggests.

"Toast? For what?" Dillon questions.

"Are you kidding? Your remarkable success, of course," TJ praises. "Dude, everybody on the island is talking about how you turned the family business around, running a new fifty-footer with a full crew and a house under construction on Pelican Point. You should be so damn proud of yourself," TJ elaborates, elated voice, as they touch bottles in toast.

Beachfront BBQs became a Sunday ritual. Somedays, TJ would have to pinch himself. It was almost surreal, how blessed his life had turned out. He was married to a wonderful woman, father to an amazing daughter and long alas reunited with a best pal.

Sammy had a front row seat, to witness her parents' uniquely loving relationship. From the moment they met, TJ and Cynthia never had a single argument. They may not have always seen eye to eye on every issue; but their lawyering backgrounds equipped them with conflict resolution skillsets. In addition, TJ adopted a relatively simple, yet foolproof domestic philosophy. In every household, one person is always right and the other one is the husband.

TJ and Cynthia were hands on parents. They made a conscious effort to expose Sammy to everything. Every day was a new adventure. Their days and nights were action packed, from water sports to beachside badminton, to long lazy walks along the beach. Bedtime was particularly special for TJ. He loved to read Sammy the same childhood fables his dad would read to him.

It is a nondescript Wednesday afternoon at the office.

Fiona plops a late day, letter-sized UPS delivery, atop TJ's (semi-cluttered) desk.

TJ glances down at the UPS package and does a double take. The sender's *Natalie Gerrard*. His mind races. His first impulse is to simply trash it; but curiosity gets the better of him. He decides to open it (slowly). He sits, heart racing, as he reads Natalie's handwritten note with her business card attached…

"Hello TJ,

It's been a long time. I hope this letter finds you in good health, and spirits. The other day I was pulled over by California's finest. I was doing 48 in a 35. When

I dug into my wallet to retrieve my driver's license, I inadvertently dropped your inscribed dollar onto the ground. I had it crisply folded, behind my license. The officer laughed. He said, "Normally bribes start with a fifty." He let me go with a stern warning. I sat there long after he drove off. I had a lot to think about...

My relationship with Patrick ended years earlier. I broke off the engagement shortly after we arrived in California. It just felt wrong. Our engagement seemed to be more about keeping my promise to Patrick, while ignoring the promise I made to myself, to only marry for love.

I presumed that you were likely in a new relationship and decided not to reach out. I guess at some level, I was equally afraid of being rejected.

Anyway, here goes. I think about you often. I think about how you always made me laugh, how you made me feel safe, how you defended me and how the mere sight of you, and your soft smile made me flush with emotion. I know it's been many years, probably too many years; but if you have any interest in meeting again, someday, any day, please don't hesitate.

Yours, N"

TJ sits behind his desk, in sobering thought. He stares out his expansive window, toward the bustling cityscape below. He ponders his life, his decisions, both good and bad. He rereads Natalie's letter over and over; but ultimately comes to the same inescapable conclusion. He opts not to reply. His life has taken a different and wonderfully unexpected turn. He's finally happy. Married to a wonderful woman who he loves dearly, and he would never do anything to jeopardize that. Not to mention their beautiful little girl, the undisputed joy of his life. That doesn't discount how he once felt about Natalie; but circumstances have changed. Unable to disregard her heartfelt letter, he places it, back into to the UPS envelope, tucked away, inside his file labeled, *'past due.'*

TJ's world is finally complete. For the first time in his life, he found balance, purpose, a reason to wake up. Every day, literally every moment, was rich in newness. He saw life differently, through Sammy's eyes, the eyes of an angel.

Days later. TJ stands shore side, watching Cynthia and Sammy splash about in the shallows.

A jogger passes, then slows to a stop, just beyond where TJ stands. He removes his earphones (music continues to play, loud enough for TJ to hear). "How cute," the stranger engages, with a kind smile.

"Thanks!" TJ replies, then adds, "They grow up fast."

"That they do," the jogger responds. "How old is Sammy? Four?" the stranger asks, as he reinserts his earphones and jogs off.

TJ stands there, with a befuddled expression. "Hey!" he calls out, to no avail, as the unknown jogger is soon out of earshot.

Friday morning. TJ's at work. His cell phone rings. Caller ID displays *an unknown number*. TJ silences his phone. He then receives a text, *Answer your phone!!* It rings again.

"Hello," TJ answers, in a firm, yet curious tone.

"Was nice seeing Sammy the other day. She's getting big."

"Who is this?" TJ demands.

"Not important who I am. What is important however, is that you return the money your thieving father stole or that lovely little daughter of yours, may disappear." Click.

Saturday morning. TJ remains understandably unnerved by the disturbing threat. He chooses not to tell Cynthia. He doesn't want to alarm her. *Best for them to stay away for a while*, he thinks to himself.

Like every Saturday, Dillon hangs out in the kitchen, while TJ prepares Sammy's favorite breakfast; a marshmallow omelet, (sounds inedible but she loves it).

A groggy-eyed Cynthia enters the kitchen.

"Morning," she greets, as she pours herself a cup of java.

Dillon, seated at the kitchen table sipping coffee, yelps, "Here for my caffeine fix." Followed by a kind smile and a celebratory lift of his coffee mug.

Cynthia ambles over behind TJ, as he commandeers the stove. She rests her hand on the small of his back.

"Next couple weeks are going to be super hectic at work. Might be a good time for you and Sammy to visit your parents," TJ suggests.

"You sure?" Cynthia confirms. "Hate to leave you alone."

"Don't worry I'll watch him," Dillon interjects.

"Actually. If you and Sammy head to Vero, I may stay at Roland's place for a few nights. That way I can get an early start at work." TJ encourages.

"Make sure to take US-27. You don't want to get entangled in Miami traffic," Dillon suggests, between sips.

"Good point," TJ echoes, as he flips Sammy's omelet into the air, as she squeals excitedly.

10 a.m. Cynthia and Sammy pack up and push off for Vero (a four plus, hour drive north).

Shortly after they leave, TJ phones Corbin.

"Hey there, TJ," Corbin gleefully greets.

"Sorry to bother you on a weekend,"

"Don't be silly. Never a problem. What's up my friend?"

"I received an odd call yesterday. The caller threatened to abduct my daughter, unless I returned the money my father allegedly stole from the Cartel. I know you confirmed that our house was paid for with his pension; but I wanted to reconfirm that your search never revealed any hidden bank accounts or offshore investments."

"Nothing. We even searched under your mom's name. Nada. If he hid any money, he was certainly clever about it. I'll email you our search results in the morning. Want me to dispatch security to your place?" Corbin asks in a concerned tone.

"No. My wife and daughter are going to stay with my in-laws for a while. Thank you though."

CHAPTER 36

I T'S FAST APPROACHING 4 p.m. and Cynthia has yet to arrive. Neither TJ, nor Cynthia's mom Kathleen have heard from her, which is highly unusual.

TJ repeatedly redials her cell phone, which immediately goes to voicemail. They've been on the road for nearly six hours now. TJ's understandably concerned. He phones the Florida Highway Patrol (FHP) and asks them to check their accident log.

After a few agonizing minutes, Sergeant Dan Nichols from FHP phones back. "Mr. Jensen, Dan Nichols, from FHP. I wanted to let you know that our accident log doesn't show anything, except for an abandoned work bus. That said, I just ordered a thorough patrol of the area."

"Thank you," TJ replies.

6:03 p.m. The phone rings again.

"Hello!" TJ promptly replies, with worried eyes.

"Mr. Jensen? Sergeant Nichols here." There's a long pause. "I'm sorry to report, that we found your wife's car in a roadside canal. Worse yet, it looks like your wife and daughter may have been murdered."

TJ's face wilts. "Murdered?" TJ repeats. He stands there, frozen in place.

"Yes sir. Their bodies are in route to Belle Glade Hospital," Nichols adds.

TJ's face is shrouded in disbelief. He's incapable of comprehending what he's just heard. He's entirely inconsolable. He drops the phone and collapses onto the floor, sobbing uncontrollably.

Later, a heartbroken TJ travels north toward Belle Glade Hospital, to identify his wife and daughter's bodies. In route, he calls Corbin to apprise him of the situation. His drive seemingly endless, the road dark, his future bleak.

It's nearly 9 p.m. by the time TJ arrives. He approaches the entry to Belle Glade Hospital.

Inside, he walks toward the reception desk.

The receptionist's face is buried in a fashion magazine.

He summons his inner strength and asks. "Can you please direct me to the morgue?"

She points to the elevator and says, "Fourth floor," in a compassionate tone.

"TJ," Corbin calls out form the waiting area, as he and his associate, Doug Reese approach a bewildered TJ.

Corbin embraces TJ with a well needed hug.

TJ breaks down.

"Wait here. I'm going to accompany TJ upstairs," Corbin advises his associate.

Inside the morgue, TJ follows the quirky coroner, toward Cynthia's cooling chamber.

TJ can't shed his defeated expression, still unable to absorb the harsh reality that awaits.

Corbin walks alongside his pal's son.

Together they watch, as the coroner slowly unzips the black body bag. The bullet entry in Cynthia's forehead, is readily apparent.

TJ's sorrowful expression escalates to anger. In an enraged tone, he rhetorically asks. "Why on earth would anyone do this to such a kind soul?"

The sympathetic coroner shakes his head. "Is this your wife, Mr. Jensen?" he gently asks.

"Yes," he says, followed by a confirming nod.

They then proceed to an interconnecting room. The coroner pulls out a much smaller tray. Once again, he unzips the body bag, revealing Sammy's innocent face.

TJ, once stoic, cannot control his emotion, as a stream of tears wash over his face. His baby girl lay dead. No more nighttime stories. No more kisses. No more hugs. No more silly omelets. His angel is forever gone.

"How did she die?" TJ reluctantly asks, establishing eye contact with the coroner.

The coroner pauses, then replies, "I'm afraid she drowned, sir. Our autopsy revealed that her lungs were full of water. She was strapped inside her car seat when we found her... I'm so sorry."

"What a torturous death!" TJ mumbles. "She was a child. An innocent, loving little girl," he yells aloud.

Later that evening, an emotionally spent TJ arrives in Vero. Kathleen and Niles greet him out front. All carry empty stares of disbelief. They hug, cry and head back inside.

Inside now, all take seats around their small kitchen table. Everyone's understandably distraught, conversation's limited. TJ chooses not to reveal the horrific details. No need to upset them anymore than they already are.

The days to follow are equally challenging, as TJ musters the strength to make funeral arrangements.

Kathleen requests they be laid to rest in their family plot, atop a soft hill at Lone Oak Cemetery.

Of course, TJ agrees.

The ceremony is simple. The gathering is small and informal.

The priest's a close family friend. He performs a brief, albeit profound service.

"We ask not why, but instead rest upon our faith," he says to the small, hilltop gathering. "Our Lord's purpose is not always apparent. We can only trust that it is part of a divine plan... a plan which often challenges even the most faithful. Today we lay to rest two of His angels. I knew Cynthia as a child. She was a selfless, loving soul. Always volunteering to help those less fortunate. Her compassionate ways were contagious. She leaves this world having been a loving daughter, devoted wife, and proud mother. Today she is set to rest beside her beloved daughter Samantha Lynn." He bows his head in prayer, eyes well with emotion. "Amen."

For TJ, the ceremony was but a blur. Despite the priest's reassuring words, TJ remains inconsolable. His girls are gone. He was hard pressed to come to terms with that harsh reality.

After the service, TJ walks with Kathleen and Niles over to their gravesites. Niles tosses a red rose atop each casket. He's beyond grief-stricken.

The ride home is quiet. All mourn in silence. Niles sits in the back, blindly staring out the window. Kathleen rides up front trying to be brave, clutching her Rosary Beads.

Back in Vero, TJ helps a frail Niles to bed.

He and Kathleen sit at the kitchen table, sipping tea. She seems stoic; but inside she's an emotional wreck.

TJ spends the next few days with them, making sure that they're okay. His visit was surprisingly cathartic. He sleeps in Cynthia's childhood bed.

Days later. TJ's back in the Keys. Unable to work, he has no choice but to request a leave of absence.

TJ phones Corbin, to check in.

Corbin answers "How are you holding up?"

"Having a hard time processing it all. It's a struggle to say the least. I wanted to reach out to see if you had any luck finding the Bastards that did this?"

"This is my number one priority, I assure you! That said, I don't want to give you false hope. Unfortunately, chasing the Cartel is a slippery slope."

"I understand," TJ acknowledges, in a defeated tone.

TJ's days are empty. His mind hampered with sadness, as he walks the empty hallways of his lifeless home. He's chosen to keep Sammy's bedroom door closed. Too many visual memories.

He spends most every day out back, in his teak rocker. Some days he rocks for hours on end, until the pesky mosquitos compel his retreat.

Early evening. Dillon and Nina pop over, to bring supper. They've been a constant in his otherwise tumultuous life.

TJ tries to stay busy. He makes a point of staying in touch with Kathleen and Niles. Fortunately, Kathleen's younger sister Trish, moves in with them. She proves to be a big help.

Months eclipse like hours. A brokenhearted, zombie-like TJ, takes post, at the bitter tip of the familiar jetty. His face unshaven, his dreams shattered, his future pointless. He stares out toward the distant horizon with hopeless eyes and a near empty bottle of Bourbon, as the turbulent seas march in battalion-like formation, toward a defenseless shoreline. He finds it impossible to concentrate on anything. He's lost his zest for life, including his passion for the Law.

He routinely rebuts well-intended visitors, except for a relentless Dillon, who refuses to take *no* for an answer. Even Dillon (TJ's closest friend) is unable to soothe his pain.

Monday, approaching 4 p.m., TJ phones Fiona. "Hello, Fi," TJ greets, in a monotone voice.

"TJ, is that you?" Fiona (who hasn't spoken to TJ since the tragedy) asks, ever so happy to hear from her boss and beloved friend. She pauses to collect her emotion. "I'm so, terribly sorry," she solemnly expresses with unbridled emotion. She's been TJ's devoted paralegal for nearly a decade.

"Every day's a little better, I suppose," he unconvincingly replies, then adds, "I've decided to take early retirement. I'm afraid I simply don't have any more fight left in me."

Unable to find a fitting response, tears stream down her face, leaving a trail of mascara in its wake.

"Anyway, I would like to stop by one day next week, to gather my belongings, collect some of my personal items and say good-bye to you and the rest of the team."

"I understand... It will be wonderful to see you," she replies through her emotion, nodding her head, hand covering her tiny mouth.

Despite TJ's preference for a lowkey, under the radar exodus, Fiona and TJ's legal team insist upon throwing him a farewell party. The guest list was endless. Everyone wanted to be included. After all, TJ was highly respected and infinitely loved by all. He was not only a brilliant and talented lawyer, but a kindhearted and compassionate soul. Suffice it to say, TJ was an integral part of Dade County's legal system. Over the years, he had forged limitless friendships, and everyone wanted to bid a final farewell, to their beloved colleague and friend.

The moment TJ enters the lobby, Natasha (the new receptionist) notifies Fiona.

Fiona soon appears in the lobby. She rushes to hug her boss, as she sobs uncontrollably.

TJ's emotional too. He'll sorely miss her.

Together they head back toward his office, soon entering the open cubicle area, where a hundred plus well-wishers stand in applause, wet eyes all around.

TJ stands there, overwhelmed with emotion, swarmed by friends and colleagues.

Later that day, the crowd has thinned, as most head home.

TJ and Fiona are in TJ's office, boxing up his belongings.

"Hey. It's after five, you have a hubby and three kids to feed. Get outa here," TJ teases with a compassionate smile as he hands her his office keys. "Here are my keys, the cleaning crew can lock up after me," he informs.

She turns toward TJ with sorrowful eyes. "I want you to know, working for you was a privilege." She fights back her tears, then continues. "You have more integrity than anyone I have ever known. You were so much more than a boss. You were a mentor and a beloved friend. I will miss you dearly… My heart breaks for you," she reveals through a cascade of tears. "I know how much you loved Cynthia and Sammy and I cannot begin to imagine how hard this has been for you." She loses it and starts to sob.

TJ reaches out and hugs his longtime confidant. It's an emotional moment to say the least.

Fiona turns and leaves.

TJ remains alone, seated behind his desk. He pauses to look out toward the city lights below. A city he had come to know well. A city full of friends and business acquaintances. A city he will truly miss. Too tired to ferret through his personal belongings, he simply dumps his drawers into a large packing box, tapes it closed, scribbles '*office stuff*' in black marker and heads home.

The following morning, he places the box atop a dust-covered shelf, in a detached storage shed, then heads back inside to make lunch.

Later, he walks the lonely limits of his empty home. He emboldens himself to step inside Sammy's room, strewn with stuffed animals and childhood photos. He collects his courage, as he flops atop her tiny bed, clutching her favorite stuffed monkey and eventually falls asleep.

Months slip by, as TJ becomes evermore reclusive. He's been a stranger to sleep and a slave to starvation. Eating's optional. He keeps to himself, captive inside his home, seldom venturing out and if so, only to the jetty. He even avoids television. No extraneous communication whatsoever, total self-imposed imprisonment, isolationism, deprivation, as if to punish himself.

He torments himself with blame. *I should have told Cynthia about my dad's misdeeds, and I should have warned her about the threat I received. At the very least, I should have driven them to Vero,* he laments.

Days later. Dillon and TJ are on the rear porch, rocking side by side. TJ's dangerously emaciated. He just stares out toward the sea, in a bug-eyed gaze.

Dillon places a sympathetic hand atop his friend's forearm.

An emotionally wounded TJ turns toward his pal, forcing a smile. They share a long history, but no words today, as they rock in silence.

Dusk draws near. "How about we head over to the *Beach Bum* for something to eat?" Dillon encourages, in a compassionate tone.

TJ shakes his head and mutters, "Thanks; but I'm okay." through an empty stare.

"T, you need to eat something, buddy. You're literally wasting away," Dillon insists.

No reply.

Dillon heads off and returns with food.

TJ's already transitioned inside.

Dillon knocks softly, then enters "T" he calls out. No answer. Dillon proceeds inside the unlit house. TJ's whereabouts unknown. Dillon speculates he must be upstairs, hopefully asleep, so he places the food inside the near empty fridge and leaves.

More than a year later. A boney, bearded and virtually unrecognizable TJ, stools up at the *Beach Bum* bar.

Ernie does a double take, then approaches his old pal. "T?" he asks, unsure.

A skunk drunk TJ, turns toward Ernie, then literally falls off the stool and onto the hardwood floor.

Ernie phones Dillon.

Dillon soon arrives.

The pair help TJ home.

Inside TJ's cottage, they steer a limp legged TJ toward the sofa. He lands face down, out cold.

Dillon pauses, staring sympathetically at his old friend. He props TJ's head onto a decorative pillow, covers him with a thin blanket, turns off the lights, shuts the door and heads off.

The next morning, Dillon returns to check in on TJ. He knocks softly, then enters.

TJ's still passed out on the sofa.

Dillon tries to wake his pal. "T." He shakes him more forcibly now.

TJ slowly opens his tired eyes and with Dillon's help, sits up, notably disoriented and undoubtedly hung over.

Dillon hands him a cup of freshly brewed coffee.

Wearing a blank stare, TJ takes small, repeated sips.

"T, you can't keep doing this to yourself, buddy. You're slowly self-destructing. And I love you way too much to sit back and watch. You need professional help," Dillon insists.

An unresponsive TJ continues to sip his coffee.

"You remember Cynthia's friend Dana? The psychologist? You need to see her dude," Dillon finishes in an unflinching tone.

TJ offers a slow, concessionary nod.

That following week, Dillon drives TJ to his first appointment with Dana.

A disheveled TJ sits in the waiting room of Dana's quaint, cottage-styled office.

She opens her office door.

TJ stands.

Dana, unable to shed her stunned expression, steps forward to greet her old friend.

They enter her perfectly appointed office. The décor is tropical bohemian. "Can I get you something to drink?" she proffers.

"I'm fine, thank you," he replies, sitting stiffly in a deep, cushy club chair, facing Dana, positioned behind her Scandinavian styled desk.

"Dillon tells me you're having an understandably tough time," she conveys with sympathetic eyes.

He nods and redirects his gaze toward her embroidered rug, hoping to avert direct eye contact. "It's been a rough road," he concedes in an uncharacteristically meek tone.

She sees this otherwise confident man broken, crumbling before her eyes. She takes a pause to catch her breath and reconcile her emotions, ever mindful that TJ (though a friend) is now a patient, deserving of her professional expertise. "How long has it been since you visited their gravesites?" Dana cautiously treads.

"Not since their funeral. I can't even imagine it. Too painful," he purges, in a distressed tone.

Dana pauses, takes a sip of her cranberry infused water, then proceeds. "It's normal to avoid things that make us sad because it's a vivid reminder. That said, it can be an equally therapeutic, first step toward closure. At the expense of short-term pain of course." She sits, hopeful eyes, awaiting his response.

TJ ponders her advice and to her surprise, he softly blurts, "Okay."

"Good," Dana confirms, with an empathetic smile. "Do you think that is something you might consider doing sooner, than later?"

"I'll make plans to head up soon," TJ promises, with a hint of equivocation in his tone.

"You sure?" she reiterates, trying to flush out any hesitancy.

"Yes… I'm sure," he insists, punctuated by a reassuring smile.

"Wonderful. After that, we'll meet again to discuss how it went. How does that sound?"

He stands, "Sounds good."

Dana walks toward him, reaches out and hugs a boney TJ.

TJ's first session with Dana proved promising.

The next morning. TJ wastes no time. He's clean-shaven, keen eyed and duly determined to execute her suggestion.

He travels north to Vero, to pick up Kathleen, Niles and Trish. He needs moral support this first trip.

Later, all stand atop the soft hillside, next to their gravesites.

After an hour or so, Kathleen and Niles tire. An ever-more, feeble Niles, is reliant upon a walking cane.

Trish accompanies Kathleen, while TJ helps Niles manage the hillside descent.

Afterwards, TJ drives them home. Kathleen and Trish ride in the back, Niles up front, staring out the window. Conversation limited, not much to say, it's been an emotionally draining day for all.

"How are you holding up, Niles?" TJ asks with a quick twist of his head.

Niles turns toward TJ, then replies, "One day at a time my son, one day at a time." In a shallow voice.

After a short, uneventful drive, they arrive home.

TJ helps Niles out of the car and inside their home.

"Please spend the night TJ, it's simply too much for you to drive home so late, please," Kathleen coaxes.

"Thank you, but I'll be fine. I'd like to stop at the cemetery again, on my way back."

Kathleen's eyes well with emotion. "You're a wonderful man, TJ," Kathleen lovingly conveys, followed by a supportive, heartfelt hug.

TJ smiles and waves as he backs down their driveway, in route to the cemetery.

Later. TJ parks and (once again) proceeds uphill, toward their gravesites. A cool, late day breeze greets his return. A pair of frisky squirrels scurry up and down a nearby oak, as a lone crow announces TJ's presence. He rests on his knees and reaches out, tracing the engravings on their tombstones, with his finger, tips. "I'm so lost without the both of you," he whispers, as tears wash over his saddened face. "What do I do now? You were my life," he softly concedes, as he lays down next to their gravesites.

Darkness soon falls. The evening air grows uncomfortably cool. TJ presses his palms flush against their tombstones. He leans in and kisses each. "Goodnight, my angels." He stands and heads off, down the soft slope, toward his car.

Thereafter, TJ commits to regularly visiting his girls, as a weekly ritual. On occasion, he would stop off to collect Kathleen and Niles. After a while, they were simply incapable of making the journey to the cemetery. Niles had suffered a small stroke, shortly after the tragedy and Kathleen's health had drastically declined as well. Trish's presence turned out to be a true blessing. With each visit, TJ would place a fresh floral arrangement aside their tombstones. He would spend hours talking to his girls, eating lunch there and at times napping next to their gravesites. Each visit proved surprisingly cathartic.

CHAPTER 37

AFTER SEVERAL MONTHS, the eight-hour round-trip started to take a toll on TJ, emotionally and physically. By default, he chose to make fewer trips, which was hard. It was tough not to see his girls as frequently as he once did. He was happiest when visiting them. It wasn't uncommon to be woken up in the middle of the night, thinking it was all a bad nightmare, soon awakened to his bleak reality that they were gone.

It was a bright sunny morning. TJ decides to take a walk along the beach, to unwind and decompress. Plagued with thoughts of hopelessness, he's concerned that he might be sinking into a deep depression. He makes the well-considered decision to schedule another session with Dana.

Days later, a pensive TJ sits inside Dana's office.

Dana reviews her notes. "Wow, it's been a long time since I last saw you. My notes indicate that you were going to visit their gravesites," Dana recaps.

"I did and that proved very helpful," TJ replies.

"So how are you doing?" Dana asks.

"Well. When I visit their gravesites, I feel better, still sad of course; but certainly better. As you can imagine, the eight-hour round trip is taxing to say the least. Consequently, I visit them less frequently," he notes. "Unfortunately, when I'm not with them, I feel lonely and anxious," a more articulate TJ reveals, as he looks up at Dana with beseeching eyes, for advice.

Dana pauses. "Have you ever tried meditation?"

TJ chuckles.

"I'll take that as a *no*... Meditation is a great way to set your troubled thoughts adrift. It's certainly worth a try," Dana informs, unable to shed her lingering concern. "Maybe you start out with something less formal. After all, the beach is the perfect backdrop for meditation. Maybe find a spot to sit late day, after the beach crowd disperses. It might afford you a well needed opportunity to free your thoughts and allow your mind to seek restful pause. Again, there's no more cathartic place on earth than the ocean," she reiterates, as she hands him a small leaflet on meditation. "This is a great reference guide by the way. No pressure, give it a read and let me know what you think. Just something to consider," she closes, with a warm smile.

"Thank you," he says, with a grateful nod, as he stands and exits her office.

The following day, TJ reads the leaflet front to cover, a couple of times and decides to give it a go.

He heads toward the faithful jetty and takes a familiar seat on a flat-top, coral rock. It takes a while (more than an hour) but he soon settles in, finding refuge in quasi meditation.

He repeats the ritual for several weeks, eventually finding his Chi.

A month or so later, Dana and her husband Kyle, are taking a walk along the beach with their dog *Karma*. They decide to extend their normal walk to check in on TJ.

As they approach his cottage, Dana notices TJ in a respectable Lotus position, perched out on the jetty. She smiles to herself then places her business card securely between his screen door and the door frame. On the back of her card, she writes, "*Glad you decided to give meditation a try. Call me when you're ready for the next step! Dana.*"

The following week, TJ and Dana meet again.

"So how are things progressing?"

"Better than I expected. I think I'm actually getting the hang of meditation," a surprisingly reinvigorated TJ, replies.

"Are you ready to take the next step?" she asks, as a loose finch flutters about her small office.

"I think so," TJ replies, with a hint of enthusiasm in his heretofore, somber tone.

"I worry that you've placed your life on hold. As you can imagine, that's not very healthy," she notes, awaiting TJ's response.

He just nods, no words.

"In other words, it's unhealthy to live in the past. Obviously, you cannot bring Cynthia and Sammy back, though it's entirely normal to mourn their passing. That said, it's not your destiny to punish yourself, by living a life of self-imposed, grief-stricken, solitude either." She takes a big leap, pausing to assess his reaction thus far, none. *Good,* she thinks to herself, as she leans in, "TJ, I would like to see you move forward with your life, in hope of resuming a sense of normalcy. That said, I also think it's important to periodically visit their gravesites, but less frequently, maybe special occasions, like their birthdays, Mother's Day, or Christmas," she articulates, emotionally vested.

TJ looks uncharacteristically frightened. "Not sure I can go that long without seeing them," he softly rebuts.

"That's my point. You're not seeing them, because they're not here. Their gravesites merely memorialize their passing. Their souls have moved on and I truly believe that they want to see you move on too."

TJ fidgets in his seat, desperately trying to remain stoic.

Dana believes she's making progress. She presses. "I believe with all of my heart, that they both want you to be happy again… It pains them to see you so sad and so inconsolably lost," Dana says. Her eyes tear up. "I know how much you loved them. We all did." She pauses to regain her composure. "But it's time to let them go, so that you can move on with what's left of your life. That doesn't mean that you won't miss them or love them any less." She pauses for him to process her words. "It's time that you think about the rest of *YOUR* time on this earth, TJ," she finishes, trailed by an emotional sigh.

TJ stares up at Dana, as tears fall from his eyes. "I know," he mutters, followed by an acknowledging nod. "What should I do?" he asks, through a hollow tone.

"This may be a tall task… But if you can muster the strength, it will be profoundly helpful." She takes a deep breath, then unveils her plan. "I would like you to start by sprucing up the house, jazz it up with a fresh coat of paint, a new beginning as it were," she animates, with a sense of enthusiasm in her voice. "The second, albeit more difficult step, will be to box up their belongings, clothes, toys, trinkets and so on. I'm not suggesting that you discard anything, simply box up their personal items for storage and safekeeping."

He processes her words. He knows what he needs to do.

After a couple of soul-searching days, TJ finds the courage to implement Dana's succinct plan. Unable to tackle it alone, he dials Dillon, for moral support.

"Hey. Sorry to bother you on the weekend but wanted to see if you might help me out. Dana suggested I spruce up the old place and box up some of the girls' belongings. Just not sure I have the strength to do it solo," he finishes with an emotional pause.

"Say no more, I'm on my way!" Dillon readily obliges.

Before long, Dillon and TJ take to task, repainting the old place, its original *happy yellow*, which turned out to be, a week plus project.

Afterwards, they tackle the more grueling mission of boxing up Cynthia and Sammy's items. Dillon knows this will be a much tougher chore for TJ. He places a comforting arm around his friend's shoulder. "You got this, pal," Dillon reassures.

After a couple arduous hours and a lot of reminiscing, the duo has packed and labeled some fourteen plus boxes, which they carry to the storage shed, for safe keeping.

Inside the shed, they temporarily stack the boxes on the floor, while TJ makes room on the shelves. In the process, he notices a dust ridden, box labeled *office stuff*. He carefully removes the box from the shelf and repositions it atop his workbench. As he stares down at the box, his thoughts travel back in time.

Dillon, alerted to TJ's sudden mood change, bluntly inquires. "What's in that box bro?"

TJ doesn't respond but proceeds to open it. The *past due* file, containing Natalie's UPS, is fatefully positioned on top.

"What is it?" a curious Dillon repeats.

"You remember Natalie?

"Of course." Dillon responds.

TJ hands the UPS envelope over to Dillon.
Dillon opens the envelope and reads her letter...

"Hello TJ,

*It's been a long time. I hope this letter finds you in good
health, and spirits. The other day I was pulled over
by California's finest. I was doing 48 in a 35. When
I dug into my wallet to retrieve my driver's license, I
inadvertently dropped your inscribed dollar onto the
ground. I had it crisply folded, behind my license. The
officer laughed, and said, "Normally bribes start with a
fifty." He let me go with a stern warning. I sat there long
after he drove off. I had a lot to think about...*

*My relationship with Patrick ended years earlier. I broke
off the engagement shortly after we arrived in California.
It just felt wrong. Our engagement seemed to be more
about keeping my promise to Patrick, while ignoring the
promise I made to myself, to only marry for love.*

*I presumed that you were likely in a new relationship
and decided not to reach out. I guess at some level, I was
equally afraid of being rejected.*

*Anyway, here goes. I think about you often. I think about
how you always made me laugh, how you made me feel
safe, how you defended me, and how the mere sight of you,
and your soft smile, made me flush with emotion. I know
it's been many years, probably too many years; but if you
have any interest in meeting again, someday, any day,
please don't hesitate.*

Yours, N"

Dillon turns toward TJ and asks, "Did you ever respond?"

"Of course not. I was married with a child!" TJ explains.

"Why don't you call her now?" Dillon encourages.

"No. It's been too long. She's probably married with kids. I'd feel like a stalker."

"You should at least call to see if she's still with the same law firm. If she hasn't changed her last name, she's fair game," Dillon presses.

Later. Dillon places the UPS envelope on the kitchen counter. "I'm leaving it here in case you change your mind." Dillon defends in an encouraging tone. "Don't forget the buck she owes you."

The next day, TJ looks over and sees the UPS envelope on the kitchen island. He ambles over, removes Natalie's business card and robotically dials her office number.

A soft voice answers, "Barton, Walker and Reid."

"I'd like to speak with Natalie Gerrard, please," TJ nervously requests.

After a brief pause, "I'm sorry, but Ms. Gerrard is no longer with the firm," the pleasant receptionist informs.

He pauses, then asks, "Did she leave a forwarding number or address?"

"Let me pass you to the office manager. Maybe she can help you."

After a brief hold. "Joyce Cohen, may I help you please?"

"Yes, my name is Tane Jensen. I'm an old friend of Natalie Gerrard. We worked together at the Dade County Courthouse several years ago."

"Yes, I remember her mentioning you," Joyce acknowledges.

"In any event, I'm trying to contact her, and I understand she's no longer with the firm," TJ informs.

"That's correct, if I recall, she moved back to Rhode Island, to be closer to her family. Unfortunately, that's all I know," Joyce apprises.

"Thank you for your help," TJ replies.

Later, that day. Dillon knocks as he enters, "What's up?" he asks, in a gleeful tone.

"Nothin much." TJ responds.

Dillon's eyes scan the kitchen countertop, "Where'd you put the UPS package? Dillon questions.

"I put it back in the shed... I did, however, call. Seems she's no longer with the firm. Sounds like she moved back to Rhode Island to be near to her family. Case closed," a deflated TJ, apprises.

"Okay... Where in Rhode Island?" Dillon persists.

"I love you like a brother, but some things in life are best left alone. Like I said, she's probably married and frankly I don't want to go down that road again. Fate put me here and it's my destiny to start anew and I can't do that, if I'm constantly looking in the rearview mirror."

"Fair enough," Dillon concedes.

CHAPTER 38

MONTHS LATER, TJ's mood, modestly optimistic. The temperature a bit chilly for his liking. He tosses on an old cream-colored sweatshirt (which highlights his bronzed skin and piercing emerald-green eyes) as he steps out back, onto his rear porch.

Off in the distance, threatening black skies advance, fractured by periodic lightning bolts. He stands there as beachgoers abound, frolicking about, seemingly oblivious to the looming storm. He hears a group of young girls giggling, reminding him of Sammy's contagious laugh.

He steps down, onto the warm, soothing sands, in route toward the familiar jetty.

Once at the jetty, he instinctively navigates his way out toward the bitter tip, effortlessly balancing between the exposed rocks, as the inflowing tide quickly fills the crevasses, between the coral formations. He finds a dry seat and sits, unable to ignore the ill-tempered seas that surround his unfettered post.

His quest for calm is soon interrupted by beachside commotion.

He turns to watch as frenzied beachgoers scurry to gather

their wares, in a futile attempt to evacuate the sandy white shores, as dark clouds swallow remnant blue skies.

TJ too, opts to abort, as he relinquishes his post and hustles on home, albeit too late, soon doused by the pelting rain.

Home now. He stands in his kitchen with a warm wool blanket draping his broad shoulders. Hunger prevails, as he opens his near empty, oval-shaped fridge, searching for the makings of a meal. He stares at a bottle of ketchup, a half stick of margarine and three cold Coronas.

The phone rings. TJ answers. "Hey, pouty boy. Ready to take a break from the pity party," Dillon jests. "I'm headed to the *Beach Bum* for a late lunch. Join me!" Dillon demands.

"I don't think so, maybe another time," TJ gently replies.

"I wasn't asking, big guy! See you there in ten," Dillon insists, then hangs up.

TJ shakes his head, smiles then begrudgingly grabs a taxi-yellow raincoat, before heading off toward the *Beach Bum* for some conch fritters (one of the few constants in his otherwise unpredictable world).

Beachside, TJ tackles gusting winds and frigid rain, in route to the *Beach Bum*.

Inside the *Beach Bum*, TJ claims a bar-side stool. Thirty minutes later, Dillon's a no show. TJ orders up a cold draft, in a frosted mug and a plate of Ernie's famous conch fritters, with a side of slaw.

"T!" Ernie (pushing sixty)shouts from the far end of the bar, with a toothy smile.

TJ (mouth full of food) proffers a concessionary wave.

Ernie (while drying a shot glass) heads his way. "How've you been, partner?" Ernie asks, with compassionate eyes.

"Better. Was supposed to meet Dillon here a half hour ago. You know him, he's as reliable as the weather."

Both men chuckle.

"Ain't that the truth," Ernie adds.

TJ devours his meal and plops a stale twenty onto the weathered bar-top, as Ernie heads off to tender change, while TJ savors a finishing swig.

Ernie returns with TJ's change.

TJ does a double take when he notices the *inscribed dollar* setting on top. "Where'd you find this?" he anxiously asks, with stunned expression plastered upon his face.

Ernie draws nearer. Wearing a devilish smirk, he points with a tilt of his head. "I think it belongs to the lovely lady over there," he says through an emotional gulp.

TJ spins in place and sees Natalie, his ever-so lovely Natalie, standing in the entryway, like a heaven-sent angel.

Her eyes glisten longingly. Her emotion infectious.

TJ rushes toward her.

They meet midway.

He stares at her with hopeful eyes and a longing heart, as they share a heartfelt embrace.

Dillon (responsible for orchestrating their reunion) emerges from the kitchen, as he and Ernie clap, spurring a bar-wide applause.

Their reunion was comfortingly cathartic. After so many lost years, they were finally together at last.

Their lives melded and meshed with familiar fluidity. They shared many memorable moments, the same last name and a small downtown office. Their work, Natalie's passion, pro bono legal assistance, to help the impoverished innocent.

CHAPTER 39

Inside their new offices, TJ's cell phone rings. He notices an unfamiliar number. "Hello?" he answers, curiously.

"TJ?" the caller excitedly asks, with a slight Spanish accent.

"Speaking?" TJ replies, still uncertain as to the caller's identity.

"It's Enrique, from the UM!" the caller responds, followed by an authentic belly laugh.

"Enrique! How are you?" TJ excitedly replies.

"Doing well. I finally wised up and decided to work for the family business… I also married a great lady and have two wonderful kids, seven and nine."

"Holy shit, the infamous skirt chaser, settled down. Never thought I'd see the day," TJ teases.

"So, how are you, old friend?" Enrique inquires.

"Good. It's been a bumpy road; but better now."

"Listen, I'm in Miami on business, headed back Thursday. I wanted to see if you might be available tomorrow for an early lunch," Enrique inquires. "Would love to catch up."

TJ flips through his calendar. "I have a 10:30, which shouldn't take long. How about stopping by the office around 11:30. I'd like to introduce you to my wife, then we can go grab a bite from there," TJ suggests, excited to see his old friend.

"Fabulous. What's your office address?"

"1200 Biscayne Boulevard, Suite 1441."

"See you then," Enrique confirms.

"Looking forward to it."

That following day, a suited, still remarkably handsome, Enrique enters their small law office lobby.

"Good morning, can I help you?" Anita, their shared receptionist, asks.

"Yes. Here to see TJ. I mean Mr. Jensen," Enrique quickly corrects, through a pearly smile.

"Sure. Please have a seat and I'll let him know you're here."

"Thank you," as he takes a seat on an old sofa, as he thumbs through a stale magazine.

Before long TJ appears.

Enrique stands.

Both men share a hug.

"Look at you. You look amazing," Enrique remarks, genuinely happy to see his college pal.

"Come on back to my office, we can catch up while Natalie finishes her meeting."

TJ leads the way, down a short, narrow hallway.

Enrique trails, as they pass the glass-walled conference room, where Natalie hosts her meeting. Natalie smiles and offers a discrete wave.

Inside TJ's office, Enrique takes one of two mismatched chairs, positioned at the front of TJ's unassuming desk.

"So how long has it been? Twenty something years?" TJ approximates.

"At least," Enrique replies, unable to shed his Spanish accent.

"So, what brings you stateside?" TJ curiously asks, casually leaning back in his swivel seat.

"Here on business. Regrettably, I now handle the family's collections," he says, anchored by a quirky smirk.

"That's a long way to travel, must be a ton a money," TJ teases.

"Oh yes, quite a handsome sum indeed," a shifty-eyed Enrique replies, "In excess of six million dollars, to be precise."

Enrique's words instantly resonate with TJ. His face grows wary.

"Obviously, that money is long gone," Enrique coolly footnotes. "Not bad, for one night's work. Seems your father invested wisely, place in the Keys and let's not forget your wonderful education... Money, well spent, no doubt. Hell, look at you, he says," pointing at TJ with an open palm. "A former DA. Wow!... Don't fret, old pal. I have no expectation of collecting a dime of that money. My trip here today is simply to fulfill a promise made."

"And what promise might that be?" TJ fires back in an unflappable tone, unwilling to be threatened.

"The promise my father made to yours of course. When he told your father, that he'd take the lives of both his sons, if the money and drugs were not promptly returned. A warning your father foolishly chose to disregard."

"My father paid back every penny after my brother's funeral," TJ insists.

"Is that what your double-dealing daddy told you?" Enrique rebuts, unwilling to believe a word of it. "Not so, old friend. Your father was supposed to deliver the product and cash, to an agreed drop site, but as expected, he was a no show and that, is an unfortunate fact." Enrique casually sits back and continues. "Bottom line, your father was a murderous thief, blinded by greed. Not only did he slaughter three of our men and a handful of bikers, but he absconded millions in the process. He's also responsible for my stepbrother's incarceration, which by the way, took a tremendous toll on my father, as one might imagine. My father gave your dad a simple and reasonable ultimatum. Return the money and the drugs, and your sons will be spared. Sadly, your money hungry father chose bounty over his boys." Enrique's attention is briefly averted, as he callously studies his fingernails.

TJ remains surprisingly calm, unwilling to be intimidated.

Enrique stands now, revealing a large, steely, high-caliber pistol, with a gaudy gold-plated grip, from beneath his (tacky) white sports coat. His eyes shark dead, as he boldly brandishes the wide barrel chamber, now aimed at TJ's unflinching face.

TJ remains seated, defiant and unyielding.

"Our college meeting my friend, was not a happen-chance. I was supposed to kill you some twenty plus years ago. Unfortunately, I was too weak. I didn't have the gonads back then. For fuck sake, we were buds!" Enrique exuberantly declares. "And believe me, I paid a price for that weakness." He pauses in somber recollection. Angered expression. "Anyway, by the time I grew some balls you were a DA. My father wasn't comfortable killing a DA. He said it would be bad for business, too much political pushback, so we waited. After you retired, we agreed that nobody would care about a former DA, so we revisited the idea, which brings me here today. I hope you know amigo, this isn't personal, just business. A debt is a debt, and a promise is a promise. If we failed to follow through on a promise, we would look weak and looking weak is equally bad for business." Enrique finishes. He cocks his pistol hammer, steps closer and presses the wide-barrel revolver into the bridge of TJ's forehand.

TJ, ever the warrior, closes his eyes, prepared to die.

BOOM, a deafening blast echoes throughout the confines of the small office, lagged by the distinctive *THUD* of a lifeless corpse, collapsing upon the hard floor.

CHAPTER 40

VERO BEACH. A parade of cars, stack in queue, as they slowly traverse the serpentine roadways of Loan Oak Cemetery.

Dillon ascends the soft hillside to pay his respects in advance of the service. He stands alone, reddened eyes. He takes a deep breath, as he sets his blurred gaze upon his best friend's closed casket, draped in a soft purple cloth, positioned beside his freshly dug grave. His thoughts muddled with emotion. He reminisces about the good times he shared with his beloved pal, as tears stream down his freshly shaven face.

He sighs and turns, looking downhill, as a sea of mourners, funnel in queue. Hundreds upon hundreds of sad souls, respectfully dressed in black, have assembled to pay their final farewells to a very special man. A man loved and admired by so many.

He retrieves his hand-written speech, from his tight trouser pocket and hurriedly tries to memorize his penciled words, but soon concludes it's simply too much to digest in one sitting.

Feeling lightheaded, he returns to his front row seat, between his wife and twin boys.

No church service, not for TJ. He wasn't the church going

kind, a casual, closed casket, gravesite gathering was more his style.

FBI Special Agent Corbin Cole was there too, to offer his respects, while supervising an undercover team covertly dispersed amongst the crowd, on the lookout for incongruous characters, aka suspected Cartel members.

At the direction of the FBI, Natalie will not be attending. She'd already been placed in protective custody.

All seats are quickly filled, as last-minute stragglers willingly stand.

Dillon sits (knees knocking) as he nervously pans the somber crowd. He summons his courage, stands and proceeds toward the podium. He bridals his emotion, turns toward the mourners and delivers. "It is my honor to eulogize this wonderful man." He pauses to corral his emotion "TJ was a son, brother, husband, father and friend. More importantly he was the person we all aspire to be. Truly the measure of a man. I met TJ in high school. He was the only kid in my school who didn't grow up in the Keys. Ironically, I knew him better than any of my lifelong friends. TJ was easy to know and easier to love. He was an open book, a kind soul, no pretense, and no charades." He discards his scripted speech and speaks from his heart. "TJ was pure, honest, compassionate and kind." Dillon's eyes well, unable to control his tears, as they flow down his face, spurring his wife to sob in her seat. He pushes through the emotion and proceeds. "TJ's life was a bumpy road at times, but he always persevered. He never complained or sought pity, instead he refocused his energies toward others, always ready to lend a helping hand, forever a selfless soul. Today, his body will be set to rest, next to his girls, his late wife Cynthia and loving daughter Sammy. I love you, my friend." He drops his head. "Goodbye, my brother!" he closes in whisper.

CHAPTER 41

A YEAR PLUS passes. Special Agent Corbin Cole joins friends Donna and Oliver Peterson for supper, at their modest home in Wilmington, North Carolina.

The evening temperature's a bit nippy, as a coatless Corbin knocks on the Peterson's Royal Blue door, clutching flowers in his idle hand.

Donna opens the door, as Corbin presents her with the perky pink orchid.

"How thoughtful!" she exclaims. "Come in, out of the chill."

"A belated housewarming gift," Corbin concedes, as he hustles inside, escaping the cold evening air.

"Would you like something to drink, before dinner?" Oliver calls out from the kitchen.

"Would love a warm Brandy if you have it," Corbin replies, rubbing his frostbitten hands in front of their stone-hearth fireplace.

Later, all gather around their small dining table. It's been a long day's travel, as a voracious Corbin digs into some Southern home cooking.

"Try the peaches," a prideful Donna encourages. "They're

truly the most delicious peaches you'll ever eat. Grew them out back," she boasts, fork poking her garden salad, searching for another maple glazed walnut.

"From gunner to gardener," Oliver teases, as he lifts his wine glass, with an adoring gape.

All chuckle aloud.

"I actually think Wilmington was an excellent choice, and your location's amazing. You can actually hear the ocean from your front yard," Corbin exclaims, sharing eye contact between them.

"I look forward to the day I can hear anything again. If the ringing in my ears ever stops," Oliver (*aka TJ*) jests.

"You should be thankful," Donna (*aka Natalie*) lovingly defends.

"I am my darling, very thankful… Annie Oakley," TJ jokes, with admiring eyes.

All unify in laughter.

Corbin pauses and redirects his attention toward Natalie. "I never got a chance to ask, how did you know TJ was in trouble?" he inquires, temporarily resting his otherwise active knife and fork aside his plate, anticipating Natalie's belated reply.

Natalie swallows, then answers, "Well, my meeting wrapped up earlier than expected, so I headed back to TJ's office to introduce myself to Enrique. From the hallway, I overheard him threatening TJ, so I hustled back to get my revolver from my purse. When I returned, I saw Enrique's pistol pressed into TJ's forehead. I had no choice but to take aim and fire," she humbly explains.

"*WOW*!! That's harrowing. What an incredible story. Sorry the both of you had to endure that," Corbin empathetically replies.

TJ interjects, "I honestly thought I was dead," taking a

moment to reflect upon that dreadful day. "Once I heard the ringing in my ears, I knew I had to be alive. When I opened my eyes, I was shocked to see my lovely bride... all ninety-five pounds of her... "

"Ninety-two," Natalie quickly interjects with a smile.

"Ninety-two pounds of her," TJ quickly corrects, "standing in my doorway, with a trail of smoke emanating from the barrel of her snub-nosed, Smith and Wesson revolver," TJ recollects, as he lovingly sets his gaze upon his faithful wife, his left hand gently caressing her narrow arm.

"I told you that I might rescue you one day," Natalie emotionally declares, returning a soft smile.

"And that you did, my love. You did indeed," TJ acknowledges before retiring the conversation.

Corbin pauses, again sharing eye contact between them. "Before I forget, on behalf of the DEA task force, the FBI and the President himself, I would like to extend our sincerest appreciation to the both of you for your bravery. No doubt your testimonies clearly helped clinch Don Marco's long overdue conviction. Of course, your office surveillance footage was very compelling; but as you well know, having two eyewitness testimonies allowed the prosecution to seamlessly knit their case together."

"It was our pleasure," TJ replies for the pair, followed by a savoring sip of wine. "Speaking of Don Marco, where did you ultimately find him?"

Corbin swallows a forkful of food. "By the way, remarkable pork, perfectly seasoned," he praises. Eyes swing back to TJ. "Fortunately, we found him stateside. We apprehended him in Vegas. As you can imagine, extradition would have been a nightmare," Corbin concedes, with a subtle simper, followed by another sip of wine.

"Vegas?" TJ repeats with surprised eyes.

"Yeah," Corbin answers, utensils in his clutch. "He's been on our radar for years. Great place for drug dealers to launder cash, even after a calculated loss. Don Marco would routinely lose up to twenty million a year, gambling." While cutting his pork, he continues. "Once we were able to identify Enrique as his son, we were finally able to connect the dots. Don Marco's conviction yielded a slew of bad actors. He employed a pay to play philosophy and his sphere of influence stretched from stateside boat operators, all the way up to members of congress," Corbin exclaims, with a raise of his steak knife.

"That's wild!" TJ notes, still processing Corbin's words.

"Did you see the look of shock on Don Marco's face when you testified? He obviously thought Enrique had taken you out." Corbin reminisces, through a prideful grin.

"Did his conviction impact the Cartel?"

"Unfortunately, no. Not even a dent. Enrique's widow Isabella succeeded him at Don Marco's behest. And no one would dare challenge Don Marco's decision. From what I'm told, she's one mean mama... I felt bad for Dillon though. He looked like he saw a ghost when you entered the courtroom," Corbin conveys, solemn expression, once again setting his utensils to rest. "His eulogy at your mock funeral, was remarkably heartfelt. Not a dry eye in attendance. Hell, I knew you were alive, and I even cried,"

"I know," TJ concurs. "I feel bad."

"Who knows, maybe one day the two of you can be reunited," Corbin loosely suggests.

"Is that even possible?" TJ asks through a surprised expression. "I thought the concept of protective custody forbids any past reunions," TJ responds, in a questioning tone.

"Generally, that is the case; but I don't think Dillon would pose any risk, particularly since the trial is over," Corbin rationalizes.

Spirits and wine glass lift. Glasses clang in toast.

Later, half past eleven, Corbin bids farewell. "As you know, part of my job is to assure your continued safety, since you have no direct connection to the outside world. If this is a good time of year for the two of you, I'll plan to circle back each fall, with plenty of advanced notice of course."

"Works for us," TJ answers.

"Thank you for everything, Corbin. You've been a true beacon of light, throughout this otherwise tumultuous process," Natalie adds.

"That's my job and the two of you make it easy," Corbin replies with compassionate eyes.

"I feel bad. I know you have more important things to do than babysit us." TJ reiterates.

"Don't be ridiculous. I volunteered for this assignment. It's truly my honor, your father meant the world to me." He pauses to collect his emotion. "At some level, it allows me to stay connected to your dad." Corbin reveals.

CHAPTER 42

OCTOBER 14ᵀᴴ, THE following year. Natalie and TJ have settled into a simple life in Wilmington. Corbin's annual visit is scheduled for this evening.

6:44 p.m. Corbin pulls up and parks out front.

TJ heads outside to greet his old pal. They share a hug and exchange welcoming words.

"Always a delight to return here," Corbin opens, eyes pan the tree lined street. "How have you been?" Corbin asks, right arm gently rests against TJ's back, as the two ascend the modest driveway incline, toward the front door.

Inside, Natalie greets Corbin with a hug. "Hope you like Italian food, because we have reservations at a fabulous place called Vito's," Natalie enthusiastically apprises.

"Like it? I love it. My ex-wife was an amazing Italian cook. Frankly, her cooking probably added five years to our otherwise rocky marriage."

All laugh, as they head outside toward TJ's tan Taurus.

Later. Inside the restaurant, they share fluid conversation, red wine and fabulous food.

Plates empty, bellies full.

"You have to try their homemade tiramisu, it's absolutely decadent," Natalie suggests, with a devilish smirk.

"You twisted my arm," Corbin surrenders with a conceding smile.

"Last trip you mentioned the possibility of reconnecting with Dillion. Is that still something we might consider?" TJ asks, while fiddling with his fork.

Corbin pauses, eyes in his plate as he contemplates TJ's request. He lifts his head and explains, "Again, the primary objective of the witness protection program is to keep Federal witnesses safe, so they can testify during trial. Now that the trial has long passed, that decision, largely rests with the two of you," Corbin states, eyes locking onto TJ's. "As I said last time, I don't see Dillon posing any threat to your safety. Nevertheless, if we were to even consider such a reunion, there are certain protocols we'd need to observe," Corbin apprises.

"Such as... ?" TJ inquires, swirling a half glass of wine.

Corbin again rests his fork aside his dessert plate. "Well. We would need to employ a series of precautionary, measures of course. Probably best to avoid air travel, too many records. Thinking a bus to Jacksonville. From there, I'd have a couple of agents pick him up in an unmarked vehicle and drive him via some circuitous route to say Charleston, changing cars a time or two along the way, to make certain they aren't being followed. And I'd probably drive him the final leg myself," he notes before finishing his dessert. "Talk it over and let me know," Corbin suggests.

"Unless Natalie shares a different viewpoint, I would appreciate it if you could look into it," TJ replies, turning toward Natalie to weigh in.

"Perfectly fine by me. I'd love to see Dillon," Natalie affirms.

CHAPTER 43

MONTHS LATER. TJ's out back, vacuuming the pool, while Natalie tends to her herb garden. A droopy sunhat shields her flawless face, from the sun's damaging rays.

TJ's cell phone rings. He recognizes the familiar ringtone as Corbin. "Hello Corbin. How are you?" He answers with a grin.

"Doing well my friend... sorry for popping in unexpectedly, but I'm out front of your place. Would you be kind enough to open your garage door for me?"

"Sure thing," TJ replies, as he hustles inside to open his overhead door.

Corbin's metallic grey Ford Focus slowly advances up and into the garage.

TJ's beyond surprised when he sees Dillon in the front passenger seat.

Corbin exits the vehicle, then escorts Dillon (still wearing blackout glasses) into the house.

Old friends embrace, in a heartfelt hug.

"My apologies for not providing advanced notice, I thought it might be safer to deliver Dillon unannounced." Corbin rationalizes.

"No worries," a surprised TJ replies.

"Anyway, I'm off," Corbin interjects, bidding an abrupt farewell, as he turns toward Dillon, points to his watch and reminds, "Pick you up, tomorrow, 7 a.m. sharp. We have a long ride and the last bus back to the Keys leaves at noon."

"Got it!" Dillon affirms with a *thumbs up* gesture.

A beyond ecstatic TJ, relieves his old pal of his bulky backpack, and sets it on a nearby sofa.

Later, all reminisce about better times. They share a home-cooked meal, fond memories and impromptu laughter, relishing their belated reunion.

Shortly before midnight, Natalie excuses herself and retires to bed, hoping to afford the boys some private time to catch up.

Having polished off their first bottle of wine, the gents grab a fresh vintage and transition out back to avoid waking Natalie.

Outside now, Dillon's quick to claim a poolside seat.

"So, tell me, how are Nina and the boys doing?" TJ asks, as he drops into a cushy chaise lounge, angled toward Dillon.

"Good… Everyone's doing surprisingly well. Nina has her hands full with the boys, as you can imagine. Luke's our Olympian and Sebastian's our Einstein," Dillon boasts.

"Funny how twins can turn out so different. They must be getting big. Not sure I'd even recognize them," TJ notes, with a somber expression, reminiscing about Sammy.

"By the way, kudos again… Who would have guessed that *Chillin Dillion* had a burning fire in his belly?" TJ flatters with a fulsome smile. "You should be very proud of yourself, my friend." TJ closes in toast.

Dillon offers a lift of his glass, flanked by a halfhearted, almost undeserving smile

1.:47 a.m. "Think I'm gonna turn in, old pal," an overtired TJ announces, through a long yawn. "I'll set my alarm for 5:30, so we can have breakfast before you push off."

"Sounds like a plan," an ever-amiable Dillon, replies.

Both men stand to share another brotherly embrace.

"It was wonderful to see you, old friend," an emotional TJ speaks from the heart, as he turns and heads to bed.

"Mind if I hang back to smoke a cigar?" Dillon calls out, intercepting TJ's departure.

"Since when did you start smoking cigars?" TJ teases.

"I know, it's a horrible habit; but it relaxes me," Dillon sheepishly replies.

"Of course not. Please be sure to lock up when you're done, this sliding door can be tricky."

Preoccupied with lighting his cigar, Dillon responds with an affirming *thumbs-up* gesture.

Later. Dillon sits solo. He takes long, studied puffs from his thick Cuban cigar. His thoughts elsewhere. His expression, observably pensive.

3:19 a.m. The evening air grows uncomfortably cool, drawing a thin-skinned Dillon, back inside. He clutches the parch bottle in retreat, as he enters through the open slider. In route toward the kitchen, he grabs his backpack from the sofa and sets it up atop the kitchen counter then quickly rummages through it. He retrieves his cell phone and fires off a quick text.

3:28 a.m. At the end of the long narrow hallway, the master bedroom door remains ajar.

Inside the master bedroom, the indirect kitchen light reveals the silhouettes of Natalie and TJ, asleep in bed.

At the foot of their bed stands a conflicted Dillon. He carries a burdensome expression and a high caliber pistol (elongated by a chrome silencer) in his gloved grasp. He hesitates, squints, then begrudgingly discharges two silenced rounds into each body. Remorseful mien, he tosses the handgun onto the bed, before exiting the bedroom.

As he enters the family room, he's surprised to see Corbin. "You're early!" he yelps, in a threatened tone.

"*WELL?*" Corbin authoritatively questions.

"Done!" Dillon nervously relays.

"Where's the gun?" Corbin grills.

"I threw it on the bed like you told me!" Dillon belligerently replies. "I'm fuckin-finished! No more runs and no more fuckin guns. I'm done, dude," Dillon emphatically blurts, shaking his head in self-deprecating disgust.

"Like I told you. This was your last assignment and I'm a man of my word," Corbin reassures, as he casually removes his holstered pistol, nonchalantly firing a fatal shot into the center of Dillon's forehead, as Dillon's body collapses onto the floor.

Without missing a beat, a remorseless Corbin holsters his firearm then proceeds toward the master bedroom.

Inside the bedroom. Corbin's quick to grab Dillon's pistol from the bed with his gloved hand and slips it inside the front of his trousers. He pauses, puzzled expression, wondering why the entry wounds haven't bled through the bed linens. Suspicious, he strips back the bedsheets, revealing strategically positioned pillows, intended to simulate human body contours, as wise eyes widen with concern.

"Don't move a muscle you pathetic, prick!" TJ commands, with unfiltered disdain, from the darkened corner of the room.

Corbin sensibly complies, as he slowly raises his hands. He faces the wall, back toward TJ. "Relax!" Corbin nervously cautions, hoping to diffuse the situation before things escalate.

"I have to hand it to you Corbin. You had me fooled. Never pegged you as a Cartel crony," TJ concedes, through a disappointed tone.

Corbin smirks to himself. "That's because I play in the shadows my friend, never on stage. Always the faceless, puppet-master," a cocky Corbin boasts, hands remain raised. "So, what tipped you off?" a curious Corbin inquires.

After a brief pause, TJ replies, "You pushed the reunion with Dillon too hard. It seemed forced, disingenuous. Then it clicked. Dillon's a great guy; but he's certainly no business mogul. Then it registered. He obviously used his boat for more than fishing," TJ finishes in a disappointed tone, then asks, "By the way, how'd you turn harmless Dillon, into a drug running, murderer?"

"Am I on fuckin trial here?" Corbin brazenly barks.

"Answer the question... *ASSHOLE!!*" TJ demands, in an elevated, no-nonsense tone.

"The drug runner part was easy. Never underestimate the insatiable lure of easy money, the American aphrodisiac as they say... Dillon's a nice kid, but dumb as mud. Totally malleable." Corbin chuckles. "Timing is everything. When his family fishing business was in trouble, we advanced him fifty-grand. After that he was hooked, no pun intended. Bigger boat, bigger house, faster cars, you know the drill. The murderer role, not as easy. I gave him an ultimatum. Either he killed you or we torture and kill his wife and kids. Looks like you lost." Corbin boldly blurts.

"Did my father know about your affiliation with the Cartel?" TJ probes.

"*HELL NO!* In your dad's eyes I was his humble protégé. The loyal FBI agent. Unfortunately, the Cartel bought my loyalty years before. Your dad thoroughly trusted me. In fact, right after he confessed his misdeeds to you, he phoned me. He told me that he wanted to turn himself in and testify against the Cartel."

TJ hesitates, then clarifies "I'm confused, if he wanted to turn himself in, then why did he commit suicide?"

Corbin rambles past TJ's inquiry. "I loved your dad, I truly did," he solemnly avows. "He was like a big brother to me. After the Big Pine fiasco, I assured the Cartel that I'd put your old man on a short leash though. In the final analysis, I couldn't stand by and let him topple the Cartel and me along with it. Unfortunately, self-preservation trumps friendship," Corbin reveals. Sadly, your money hungry father chose bounty over his boys."

FLASHBACK...

Slater phones Corbin. "Corbin, I'm going to turn myself into the authorities. I'm embarrassed to tell you, that I've been a bad actor. I took Cartel kickbacks for many years and far worse," a sloshed Slater emotionally reveals.

"Slater, where are you?" Corbin asks, in a concerned tone.

"I'm at home," Slater mumbles.

"Stay there, and DON'T speak with anyone. I'm on my way," Corbin insists.

Hours later. Corbin knocks at Slater's front door. No answer. Door's unlocked, Corbin enters.

Inside. Slater's passed out on the sofa, in a drunken stupor.

Corbin approaches, and shakes his pal, "Slater. Wake up. Let's get you to bed, old buddy, so you can sleep it off," as he helps an inebriated Slater upstairs, and into his bed.

Corbin exits the bedroom, and soon returns, holding one of Slater's pistols in his gloved hand. He stands over a sleeping Slater. He carefully folds Slater's right hand around the gun

grip, then (with a stone-cold stare) presses the barrel against
Slater's right temple and pulls the trigger.

"I'm guessing you also played a role in our abductions. TJ orates in a distressed voice.

"Okay. I am now officially done with your interrogation Bullshit!!" Corbin resists.

"You're done, when I say you're done!" TJ firmly qualifies.

Corbin hesitates, then reluctantly answers, "That was supposed to be a simple grab and go. Kids for cash, no more!" Corbin emphatically defends. "Nobody knew that psycho biker would veer off script. Unfortunately, we can't rewrite history. What's done is done!" Corbin callously concludes.

TJ's utterly astounded by Corbin's lack of remorse. "This is beyond fuckin-crazy! Tell me, please God tell me, you didn't have a hand in my wife and daughter's murders,"

"You can thank your dead buddy Dillon for that one. He couldn't wait to share their departure route and timeline."

"That wasn't my question Corbin!" TJ scolds "Did *YOU* sanction their murders?" TJ repeats in a vengeful tone.

Corbin dodges the question. "Enough of your fuckin-bedroom interrogation. There are only two paths forward my friend. We either walk away or you're gonna have ta fuckin-shoot me my friend, cause I'm done answering yer fuckin-questions."

"Shoot you?" TJ scoffs. "Shooting you would be too easy! I want you to feel the pain of your actions." TJ defends.

Corbin pauses, "That's right... I forgot" Corbin says with a smirk, "You're a law-biding pacifist!" He scoffs as he drops his hands, grabs Dillon's gun and spins in place, blindly discharging several (silenced) shots into the darkened corner of the room.

Corbin stands there, as gun smoke emanates from the barrel of Dillon's pistol. He carries a befuddled expression, waiting for the sound of TJ's body to hit the floor. His eyes squint, as he tries to peer into the darkened depths of the room.

SUDDENLY, a bullet-fast foot, *SMASHES* into Corbin's nose, launching him backwards, slamming his head into the bed-frame, as his handgun slides across the floor. Corbin lays there, observably disoriented, as blood spurts from his nose. After a brief recovery, he notes, "Okay, maybe you're not such a fuckin pacifist after all." Corbin chuckles, hand pressed against his battered nose. "Or maybe I'm just gettin too old for this shit," as he reaches for his handgun.

This time, Corbin's assault is swiftly thwarted, as TJ effort-lessly severs Corbin's gun-toting hand, with a single slash of his razor-sharp sword.

"FUCK!!!" Corbin *SCREAMS*, in excruciating pain. "You son of a fuckin bitch, *YOU MOTHER FUCKER!!!"* Corbin blasts.

Panicked, Corbin stands, strips, then wraps a nearby pillow-case around his forearm, feverishly trying to control his blood loss. Enraged, he *YELLS*, "Know this, asshole… I told my crew to fuck your slut wife before they shot her ass. That's right! They told me she came twice," he yells, followed by a sadistic chuckle. *"FUCK YOU!!!"*

TJ steps into the light, carrying his ancestral sword and a wild-eyed expression. He pauses, then decisively decapitates his nemesis, with a two-handed, life-ending, thrust.

Corbin's detached head, momentarily wobbles before flop-ping onto the floor with a resounding thud, trailed by the collapse of his headless corpse.

TJ stands there, wearing a warrior's glare, face speckled in blood spatter, as he casually sheaths his blood laden sword. Lightheaded, he rests upon one knee, right hand pressed against his chest as warm blood spews from multiple bullet-wounds, that speckle his torso. Growing dizzier, he lowers himself onto the floor, soon slipping in and out of consciousness, ultimately awakened by bright blue lights which illuminate the room. *Natalie must have summoned the police,* he concludes, in a brief, moment of lucidity.

Within minutes police swarm the residence, guns drawn. Once they've contained the crime scene, paramedics are ushered inside, as they swiftly attend to TJ.

Strapped onto a gurney (draped with a warm blanket) they whisk him outside and into the waiting ambulance.

Off they race to the ER, siren blaring.

Natalie kneels by his side, clutching his blood-soaked hand, as tears stream down her fretful face. Heartbroken, she whispers, "I love you my darling" gazing hopelessly into his loving eyes. "I love you so much!" she proclaims, as her free hand gently strokes his hair. "You're the most loving soul I have ever known, a great husband and protector of many," she sobbingly conveys.

"I hear Sammy… She's calling me," TJ incoherently mumbles, with a quick lift of his head.

"Your girls are waiting for you, sweetheart," Natalie selflessly utters, in a compassionate, tone.

Embracing her words, he smiles. He gently squeezes her delicate hand and stares into her loving eyes. "I love you with all of my heart! I will love you forever!" TJ avows through a shallow breath. Calmer now, he gasps one last breath, before closing his eyes in rest.

THE END

www.ingramcontent.com/pod-product-compliance
Lightning Source LLC
Chambersburg PA
CBHW031659170626
46808CB00005B/1527